A Note to Readers

To my readers, please be aware, this book deals with major infertility issues and the loss of a first trimester pregnancy due to complex medical conditions. It also deals with the emotional damage living with and through the constant losses and failures, which can and do occur, when a woman is trying to conceive.

If this is your experience, this book may be a trigger for you, and I would urge you to consider not reading it.

But…if you do decide to read, I hope the heroine's journey through her wreckage of past and current loss, and then finally healing her wounds, may somehow help to heal yours too.

Books by Dorothy F. Shaw

Arizona K9
Avoiding the Badge
Redeeming the Badge

Published by Kensington Publishing Corporation

Redeeming the Badge

Arizona K9

Dorothy F. Shaw

LYRICAL PRESS
Kensington Publishing Corp.
www.kensingtonbooks.com

To all the women who struggled with infertility and were never able to conceive, I hope and pray your hearts find peace.
And to you. May your heart and mind find peace too.

Chapter 1

"License and registration, please." Officer Robert Caldwell stood just behind the driver's side window of the out-of-state bright red Mercedes he'd pulled over.

The blond woman behind the wheel glanced up at him, squinting from the bright sunlight. "Yes. Of course, Officer."

You have got *to be kidding me.*

Rob almost swallowed his tongue to keep himself from saying that out loud. Never in his life would he have expected to run into the one and only Heather Winters. Stepping fully in front of her open window, he took the requested documents from her petite hand and somehow managed to not betray any bit of WTF running through him.

Rob cleared his throat. "The reason I pulled you over is due to that wide right turn you took back there."

"Oh, I don't think I realized I did that." She frowned, looking a bit dismayed.

Well, that was fine. Rob was feeling pretty damn dismayed too. "Stay in your vehicle, please. I'll be back in a moment."

"Yes, sir."

Absolutely gobsmacked, Rob walked backward—out of precautionary habit—away from her vehicle toward his patrol SUV. For fuck's sake, Heather Winters? Seriously? Goddamn… Of all the people in the world, he never expected to run into *her.* Then again, why wouldn't he?

As a cop, crossing paths with people from his past was always possible, considering this particular person grew up here. They both did, albeit not even close to where he'd pulled her over. But still.

Except, hadn't she moved away?

Duh, based on her Maryland license plate, that was a big affirmative. Long time ago, if memory served. With his mind racing like a hamster on a wheel, Rob settled in the front seat of his patrol truck. His canine partner in the back, Tricks, was calm and quiet, staring out the side window at the passing traffic.

Heather—aka prom queen, high school "mean girl" clique president, captain of the cheerleading squad—Winters. Rob glanced at the Maryland driver's license in his hand. Correction, Heather Stratton now.

She'd gotten married. No reason to think she wouldn't have. Rob blew out a breath and stared at her picture. Of course, she looked fucking amazing in the photo. No one on God's green earth *ever* looked amazing in their DL picture, but she was the exception to the rule.

Heather was the exception to a lot of rules.

Glancing at her registration, he noted the car was registered to Charles Stratton and Heather Stratton. Yep, definitely married. Letting out a sigh, Rob typed her information into the mounted laptop inside his cruiser.

Jesus, she likely didn't even recognize him. He'd changed more than a little since his insecure, lanky, and pimply-faced high school days.

Rob had certainly grown up, and he definitely lived in a different world now. Then again, that should be the case for everyone fifteen years post–high school.

Rob glanced at the dog in the rearview mirror. "Tricks, you see that Mercedes I pulled over?"

The dog let out a little whine and shifted in the back.

"In that car is a woman that's all heaven and hell mixed in one smoldering package." He shook his head and stared at her picture. How was it possible that she'd gotten hotter? "Now I gotta go pretend I don't think she's gorgeous. Wish me luck."

Tricks gave Rob a half yawn, half whine.

Rob rolled his eyes. "Lotta help you are. Stay here. I'll be back." Angling out of the truck, he approached her vehicle…this time with more caution.

Not because he was concerned she might try something aggressive or be difficult. It was himself he was worried about. Seeing her had him feeling like an awkward teenager again. Sweaty palms and all. But, really, screw that. This was not high school, and he was a grown man.

Pushing down the unwanted insecurity, Rob squared his shoulders and faced his greatest fantasy. "Here you go, Mrs. Stratton."

"It's just Ms. But thank you." She took her ID and registration back.

Hmm, trouble in paradise? As he pulled his hand away, her fingers brushed his, and a bolt of heat filled Rob's veins. His physical reaction wasn't a surprise, but in an effort to keep his shit under wraps, he took a small step back.

She glanced over at him. "Sorry about the wide turn. Guess I wasn't thinking."

Rob drew in a deep breath and rested his right hand on the butt of his service weapon. Just as captivating as they'd always been, her light green eyes sparkled in the sunlight. She wore jeans and a plain, faded black T-shirt, definitely way more casual than her wardrobe had been fifteen-plus years ago.

From what he could see, she still had the same figure she carried in high school though—which was un-fucking-believably sexy. Fucking hell, this woman. Perfection knew no bounds with her, and as was typical, even after all these years, he was still attracted to her. It didn't seem to matter that she wasn't a nice person; it never had.

In high school, he'd crushed on her hard. Really hard. Just about every guy he knew did. She was one of those girls, the kind that was filled out in all the right places before the end of freshman year. She was the kind of girl who had an audacious air about her, one so sexy it caused him to wake up in the middle of the night, rock-hard dick in hand with Heather center stage in his brain.

Unfortunately, she was mean.

She was stuck-up.

She was a snob.

Simply put, Heather Winters was a bitch.

Rob had also despised her. Talk about a dichotomy of emotions. "No problem. I'm going to let you off on a warning, considering you're not from here." Unable to stop himself, he cracked a small smile.

She gave him a small smile back and— Jesus, what was he doing? Trying to stir up more conversation? Trying to flirt? Really? Because *that's* professional and appropriate.

Why was she being so polite to him? Heather Winters was not polite. Ever. It sure as hell wasn't because he was a cop, though maybe she dug the uniform? That thought sent another wave of arousal through him.

She raised her brows and tipped her head to the side. "Well, technically, I *am* from here. I just—"

Yeah, no. He needed to stop this now. "All right then. Enjoy the rest of your evening, ma'am." Rob gave her a curt nod.

No stirring. No conversation. No nada.

"Thanks. You too."

More with the polite? Talk about a mind fuck. As he turned and walked away, he barely spared her a glance. Judging by the arousal pulsing through his system, he needed to get away from her immediately. Not unlike recoiling from a hot flame. Heather was hotter than any blaze he'd ever witnessed. She was pure five-alarm-fire temptation.

Sliding behind the wheel, he checked in with dispatch and closed the log on the laptop. He started his patrol truck and stared at the back of her car. Damn. Truth be told, if given the opportunity now, and she was single, he'd spank her ass until it shone bright pink for always being so sassy in school.

Instead of fucking her, he'd drag it out, make her wait while he teased and touched her body until she was mindless and begged him to have sex with her. With a scowl, Rob adjusted his stiff cock in his pants and then pulled out into traffic.

Heather Winters, or Stratton—whatever the hell her name was now— was a fantasy. She was married, hopefully happily. Living in another state and, judging by her E-Class Mercedes coupe, probably in a big-ass house. The fact that she looked really, *really* good still didn't mean a damn thing.

She was part of his past, whether she knew it or not, and that's exactly where she needed to stay.

* * * *

"How strange." Heather Stratton looked through her rearview mirror at the police officer who'd pulled her over.

She'd never been let off with a warning in her life. Not that she made a habit of getting pulled over, but still. The few times she had been over the years, she'd always gotten a ticket.

Miracles never ceased…

With a shrug, Heather leaned over and slid the registration into the booklet in the glove box. After she straightened, she shoved her license back in her wallet. She really needed to trade in her Maryland license for an Arizona one. She should've transferred the registration for the car by now too.

If the officer had known she was a resident here, he likely *would've* given her a ticket. She'd nearly gone and told him, confessed everything, except he'd cut her off. Which was also strange.

Either way, both tasks were on her to-do list—which was getting rather long. Over the past year, she'd been meaning to take care of the registration, her license, and a great many other things. It was just...she hadn't had the time.

Hadn't *made* the time was more accurate, but no one was keeping score, so it didn't matter.

Except it kind of did.

The revving engine of the officer's patrol SUV yanked Heather from her self-deprecating, excuse-making reflection as he zoomed past her open window. She glanced at the vehicle and caught a glimpse of the large lettering on the back window: *K9 UNIT.*

Interesting *and* cool. Maybe that's why he cut her off and walked away, so he could get back to the dog. Made sense. She'd never been pulled over by a K9 officer before, but she would've thought he'd have gotten the dog out too.

Although, she probably didn't look like much of a threat. A Mercedes, even with out-of-state plates, plus blond hair didn't exactly spell dangerous criminal.

Then again, maybe she did. Lots of people could be— Okay, stop. Shaking her head, Heather moved her purse back to the passenger seat, started the car, and navigated back into traffic. She had a list to get to.

With her divorce finally done, Heather had purchased a small house in the Southeast Valley. And thank God for that because staying at her parents' home in Glendale any longer than she already had would be the death of her. Or maybe just make her crazier than she already was.

The endless look of pity in her mother's eyes and the disappointment in her father's could be enough to make anyone want to off themselves. Not that Heather had ever entertained *that* particular idea.

No, she was far too chickenshit for that route. Besides, wrapping herself up in a self-pity/self-loathing blanket, night after night, while watching reruns of anything remotely interesting on Netflix, was her regular routine... much more entertaining too.

At least she'd stopped drinking herself into oblivion in the bathtub. Progress, right?

Right.

Just another day in paradise, for sure. But not today. Today, she was shopping, while indulging in much smaller but still consistent doses of self-pity.

A few traffic lights later, Heather pulled into the shopping plaza parking lot and found a space. Home Goods was her aim for the day; after that, Target. With the exception of three suitcases full of clothes and some other precious mementos, when Heather left Baltimore she took nothing with her.

Saying she had a shit ton of things to buy was an understatement. Today she was starting with linens for the bathroom, sheets and blankets for the new bed she'd gotten at IKEA, and silverware. Maybe table linens. Oh, and pots and pans too. Not that she felt anything like cooking, but still.

After shutting off the engine, she checked her face in the mirror and then stepped out into the bright Arizona day. Five years ago, life was so very different than now. And in every way possible. Heather had her nursing career and was doing quite well. Charles was in the middle of his fellowship in cardiology.

They'd bought a beautiful home in a gorgeous and prestigious neighborhood...and they'd filled it with beautiful things. So many things. Too bad in the end, "things" meant nothing.

Heather sighed at the memory. Every room was precisely the way Charles wanted it. The man had great taste, and if he was happy, Heather was happy. But the one room they hadn't decorated? The nursery.

Heather had been 100 percent ready to take that next step. She was so sure that having a baby would make everything perfect. More so than any fairytale ever written in the history of ever. After all, why would she have thought any differently?

Boy, was she wrong.

Swallowing down the deluge of memories, Heather dug into her purse, located her sunglasses, and walked toward the entrance of the store. Towels. Bedding sets. Silverware. Linens. Pots and pans. And finally...home to her small couch, and self-pity binge-watching could commence.

Chapter 2

Fuuuuck!

Rob stopped dead in his tracks when he spotted her. He'd just come out of the cereal aisle, about to head down canned goods. He tightened his loose grip into a stranglehold on the handle of the grocery cart.

Rob stood transfixed, watching as she turned into the frozen food section two aisles away from him. All of ten, maybe fifteen seconds she was in his sights, but it was long enough that he saw *allll* of her from head to toe....

On her petite, perfect body she wore light gray workout leggings and a black workout tank. Both fit her like a second skin, highlighting all her amazing curves. Black Nike runners on her small feet. Hair pulled up in a high ponytail. No makeup from what he could tell, but then again, he *was* two aisles away and a cop, not Superman.

What the hell was she doing in his Fry's? Better yet, why was she still in town? It'd been two weeks since he'd pulled her over. Maybe things weren't as perfect as he figured they would be for her and she was taking a break from her perfect life and perfect husband. She did correct him when he addressed her as Mrs... Though, she could be on vacation.

Not that he planned on asking her any of that. Or maybe he would. Hell, why not? Yeah, she looked *really* good and was superhot, but that didn't mean he didn't have game too. He needed to dial back this giddy-schoolboy-with-a-crush persona he was channeling and get back to the man he'd grown up to be. They weren't in high school anymore, Toto.

With his head on straight, Rob plugged an AirPod into one ear, turned on his workout playlist, and continued on with his shopping. Focused on his music, he grabbed items he needed and put them in the cart.

Just as Ed Sheeran's "Shape of You" came on, Rob swung the to the right, heading to the next aisle to—

BAM!

Rob jerked his cart back. "Shit. I'm—"

"Oh my God! I'm so—"

"Sorry." He sighed and couldn't help but focus on her pretty face.

"No, no. It's okay. Really." Heather took a step back, taking her cart with her.

Rob shifted his as well. "You sure you're good?"

She smiled and gestured down her front with a hand. "I think so, yes. Nothing broken. Not even the cart."

Rob nodded and pulled his lips between his teeth. Fucking hell, she was cute.

"Well, take care." She shrugged a shoulder and started to walk past him.

"Yeah, you too." The need to say something more, to talk to her a little longer, hit him like a sledgehammer to the side of the head. He reached for her arm but stopped himself from touching her. "Hey, do you—"

"This is going to sound funny, but are you a police officer?"

She'd stopped just past him, an inquisitive and almost hesitant look on her face. Like she wasn't sure if she should ask or not but went for it anyway.

He was glad she had. Rob smiled and jerked his chin up. "Yeah. I'm the one that pulled you over a couple weeks ago."

"I thought that was you." With a smile, she turned to face him, one hand resting on the cart handle. "I had to ask. And, wow, you have an incredible memory."

"Part of the job." Even if he hadn't already known her, he would never have forgotten her. Every time he saw her, she took his breath away.

"I guess so." She laughed, the sound of it hitting every nerve in Rob's body.

He smiled. "Doesn't say much for my cart-driving skills though."

She dipped her chin and raised one brow. "It really wasn't your fault. I wasn't paying attention."

"Oh, I see. Should I issue you a ticket this time? Reckless carting?"

She laughed again. "Do you have jurisdiction in all the Fry's or just this one?"

"Definitely all of them."

"Guess I better be more careful." She smiled, her eyes dancing with laughter. A beat passed between them before she shrugged and let out a breath. "Well, time to get my shopping done. Take care."

"You too." Knowing it was time to let her go, Rob smirked and dipped his hands in his front pockets.

She gave him another smile before turning away and moving on. He stood, watching her as she rounded to the corner to the next aisle. Funny, he hadn't expected she would remember him from pulling her over. It wasn't like he was in uniform, which meant it was possible he'd made an impression on her.

She still didn't recognize him from high school, which was a good thing...right?

Chapter 3

From the back of the gym, where the treadmills, ellipticals, stationary, and recumbent bikes were positioned, Heather scanned the various people scattered about.

The good part about going to work out after midnight meant there weren't many people in the gym. If she was right, she'd counted five so far, including two competitively built men who were taking turns bench-pressing what looked like far too much weight.

She'd never been attracted to big, muscly guys, yet they always seemed to be attracted to her. Some of them, at first glance, seemed like pretty strong guys as far as personality went, but sadly, most weren't. At least to say, their personalities weren't stronger *than hers*.

None of that meant anything except that she was definitely staying away from the free weight area. Not that she'd head that way anyway. She was running her five miles and going home.

After wiping her forehead with the courtesy towel she'd grabbed on her way in, she flung it over the top of the machine. The strum of the acoustic guitar in "Chrome Plated Heart" by Melissa Etheridge flowed through her earbuds. An old but awesome song.

Heather was all of three years old when it came out. She loved it though. Loved all of Melissa Etheridge's music. Her lyrics told a story, always. And Heather identified with most all of them. This song was no exception. Heather turned up the volume, and as she ran, staring almost blindly across the gym, she got lost in the lyrics and the steady rhythm of her Nikes hitting the treadmill.

A minute or so later, the song ended. Right as it did, a tall, very fit, *very* handsome man she hadn't noticed before wandered over to a treadmill three rows in front of her. Without looking at her, the guy dropped his bag on the ground, popped in a pair of AirPods, and mounted the platform.

Wait... As she caught a glimpse of his profile, Heather tilted her head to the side. *Hmm.* Was that? He kind of looked like the cop who had pulled her over a few weeks ago. The same cop she'd run into last week in the grocery store. Of course, he'd hit her cart with his. And then teased her a bit afterward.

The whole interaction with him had been a shock, especially because she'd become accustomed to keeping to herself, but also, the short time they'd talked, it almost seemed like he was flirting.

The possibility of seeing him again had curiosity tickling the back of her neck. Heather drew in a deep breath and blew it out. That *had* to be him. A better look to be sure would help. Maybe when she walked by on her way out? Heather rolled her eyes at the ridiculous idea.

Looking would be too obvious and might invite more attention from him. And attention was something Heather for sure did not want. Wait...did she? No, now was not the time for a man. Keeping to herself was a better idea. Safer for all parties involved. Plus, what would she even say to him?

The music played and Heather ran.

And she watched him run.

More like studied him. Nice calves. Nice ass too.

Truthfully, even from their brief and curt interaction the day he pulled her over and later their teasing, flirty banter in the grocery store, he seemed like a he had a pretty strong personality—though most cops did.

Either way, she'd always found that to be a huge turn on and something she was always attracted to. And aside from his personality, she *had* found him very good-looking. However, when he'd pulled her over, with all the body armor, belts and such that he wore, she couldn't tell what his body type or build was. When she ran into him at the grocery, she'd been too caught off guard to really notice.

Now she had a front-row seat to the back of his body. From what she could make out through his T-shirt and shorts, he had muscle but wasn't bulky. Definitely lean...almost like a swimmer's build with just a little bit more definition. Nice. Very nice.

Heather shook her head, laughing at how silly she was being. But, really, why not look at the goods? After all, she was still a living, breathing woman with functioning eyes; it wasn't like she was going to order off his menu or anything.

Regardless of whether or not she felt dead inside, her heart still beat. Her blood still flowed. Speaking of blood flowing, Heather's was pulsing hot in her veins. She wiped her forehead with the towel. The man had sexy calves.

Dammit to hell, her hormones and reproductive system might be completely fucking defective, but her sex drive was definitely alive and kicking.

Yeah, nice calves. Nice ass too. Nice...everything.

Her treadmill shifted into cool-down mode, and that was probably a very good thing. She wasn't doing herself any favors getting lost in a stranger's perfect butt and calves. Never mind his very defined back, traps, and lats...all visible through his clingy, damp white T-shirt. He might have the most perfect body she'd seen in a long time.

Her ex, Charles, used to have a body like that. "Used to" being the operative words. Just like magic, the thought of her ex doused the flames that had been burning nicely. Probably for the best.

Heather took a swig of her water and wiped her forehead and chest with the towel. Despite the possibilities of what she could get from a guy like him, it was past time to cool down.

The machine beeped again, giving her final warning, before coming to a slow stop. Heather stepped off, grabbed her water bottle and keys off the floor, and headed through the four rows of machines toward the exit.

Yes, she walked past him.

Yes, she glanced over her shoulder as she walked by.

Yes, it was for sure the cop that'd pulled her over and a couple weeks later ran into her at the grocery.

Their gazes locked for a nanosecond, the air popping between them. For a heartbeat in time, everything froze. And then started again.

No, she didn't stop.

But she felt his eyes, all over her body...until she rounded the corner to the exit.

* * * *

A petite blonde caught Rob's gaze as she walked past him.

No, not just any petite blonde. *The* one and only petite blonde.

What. The. Fuck.

Rob's heart raced, pounding in his ears, and not because he was running on a treadmill.

Heather Winters was haunting him. How the hell was this happening? *Why* was this happening?

The expression on her face, it was almost…primal. Like she was checking him out and liked what she saw. Was she checking him out? Christ, *how* was *that* even possible?

With her hair pulled up, she wore another pair of those skintight workout leggings. Pink this time. Tank top was gray. Same Nikes as last time.

God help him, her ass. Rob grabbed his water bottle and took a long swig. Why was she in his gym at—he looked at his watch—almost one a.m.? For fuck's sake, she was walking out to her car in the dark. Alone? Not happening.

The urge to hop off the machine and go after her rose like a tidal wave inside him. Rob gritted his teeth, gripped the handrails on the treadmill and held himself there, but it took every ounce of self-control he could muster.

She was grown woman; the parking lot was lighted. He didn't need to be anyone's savior. The woman wasn't asking for his help, and she sure as hell was no damsel in distress.

Still. He should go, though. Just in case. Make sure she was okay, right? Right. Sure. He was a cop after all. It was his duty to serve and protect…. That, and to maybe see what that look in her eyes was all about too.

Before he could talk himself out of it, Rob hit the stop button on the treadmill and hopped off before the thing stopped moving. Halfway to the exit, somewhere in a far corner of his mind, he reminded himself that no matter what, he was not the kind of man who chased women. Ever.

He sure as hell wasn't going to chase Heather Winters. No matter what she did, how she looked, or what she said.

Not that she'd said anything. She'd just looked at him. Fuck… Heather looked at him like she wanted him. Talk about a wet dream come true.

So, hell no, Rob didn't stop. He hit the exit door handle and pushed the door open like he was a bat out of hell. Meatloaf had nothing on him. Channeling his inner caveman, Rob scanned the few cars in the parking lot and—bingo. Red Mercedes.

As he jogged over to her car, the engine started, the lights came on… then the backup lights. Heather reversed out of her parking spot, the ass end of the car *coming right toward him.*

Just as the car was about to connect with his knees, Rob skidded to a halt and slammed both hands down on the trunk lid.

She hit the brakes, the car coming to an abrupt stop.

With his hands planted on the trunk lid of her car, Rob stared at her through her back window.

Heather stared at him through the rearview mirror, eyes wide as flying saucers.

Rob took a step back and crossed his arms over his chest, waiting.

She got out but remained standing right beside the car. "Holy shit, are you going to arrest me?"

He stifled a chuckle. "Aren't you going to ask if I'm okay first?"

She frowned. "Of course, yes, but—" She raised a hand, motioning toward him. "I can see you're okay. I mean, shit…" She placed her palm on her forehead. "I'm sorry but I'm totally freaked out. Are you okay? Wait, why are you behind my car? Didn't you see me?"

"Didn't *you* see me?"

"No! You were inside when I walked out!" She shook her head. "Oh my God, I'm so sorry. You're right. This is completely my fault."

Rob took a step toward her. "We really do need to stop crashing into each other like this."

Heather blurted a laugh and after a few moments, once her laughing subsided, she spoke. "Of course, now all I can hear is 'Crash into Me' by Dave Matthews Band. Sorry." She laughed again. "Let me say, it's just my luck that you hit me with a grocery cart, and I go full bore and hit you with my car."

Rob watched her in fascination. She was all flustered, her nervousness making her laugh at her own jokes and also talk too much. He loved it. It was cute, sexy, and once again, Rob was completely smitten with her. "You saying this was intentional, Heather?"

"Wow, you remembered my name too?" Her eyes went wide again, and she raised both hands in front of her. "And, oh my God no! Of course, it wasn't intentional."

"You saying that because you're afraid I'm going to press charges?" Now it was Rob's turn to laugh. He shook his head, knowing he should probably pump the brakes a little. "Relax, I'm just pulling your pigtails."

She frowned. "Oh." She smoothed her palm over the top of her head and down her ponytail. "Why are you out here, again?"

He shrugged. "Just wanted to make sure you got to your car safely."

"Oh."

"No biggie."

"Well, okay. I guess." After shifting her weight to her other foot, she shrugged. "So, is this your gym?"

Rob let his gaze roam down to the curve of her hip before returning to her eyes. "As in, do I own it? No."

She laughed. "No, sorry. What I meant was, is this where you always come to work out?"

"Pretty much, yeah." He scratched an itch on his arm. "What about you?" The idea that he might get to see her again sent tidal waves of excitement flowing through him.

She swallowed. "Well, yeah, for now. I think."

"You think?"

She blew out a breath and smiled, twisting her hands in front of herself. "Yes, for now it's where I'm working out."

Rob nodded and couldn't help but let a small grin curl his lips. "Good to know. Guess I'll see you around then? At least until you find someplace better."

She smiled. "Guess so."

"Cool. I'm going to get back inside." He motioned over his shoulder toward the building. "Try not to hit anyone else and"—he turned and started jogging away from her—"watch those wide right turns." He laughed.

"I'm never going to live this down, am I?" She shook her head, smiling.

He turned, facing her as he jogged backward, raised his arms, and shrugged.

"Fair enough." She nodded and got into her car.

Rob turned back around before he fell on his ass. What an odd encounter. Not that he wasn't grateful, more the way all this was going down between him and Heather was bizarre. He should've asked her what nights she was at the gym. Though, he didn't want to come on too strong, but he definitely wanted to see her again.

It was Heather Winters, for fuck's sake. How could he *not* want to see her again?

Chapter 4

In a bar she'd never been to before, Heather sat at a four-person high-top table. She'd found one in the corner directly across from the entrance so she could keep an eye out for her new friend, Kim Duke.

The woman was Heather's neighbor across the street, and Heather had just met her last week. A single mom with two kids, two dogs, and as she'd told Heather over coffee and cigarettes (Kim's not Heather's) on Heather's back porch the other night, an ex-husband who had a habit of overstaying his visits. But at least the alimony and child support from the guy was current. Win-win.

They'd talked for what felt like hours that night, though Kim did most of the talking. Heather asked a lot of questions, which meant she didn't have to talk. By the end of the night, Kim had made Heather promise to meet her Thursday night at this little country bar called the Whiskey Barrel in downtown Chandler for Ladies Night.

So here she was, but Kim had yet to show.

Heather hadn't really gone anywhere in what felt like forever. Definitely hadn't been back to the gym, that was for sure. Two weeks had passed since she'd run into the hot and sexy cop there, and she was on a mission to not run into him again. She was way too attracted to him for her own good. Her solution had been to hibernate, but frankly, she'd started to go stir crazy. Kim's invite was definitely perfect timing.

Heather scanned the wall of liquor bottles behind the bar and understood immediately why the place was named what it was. There had to be at least a hundred and fifty different whiskeys up there, maybe more. Unsure of what she wanted to drink, a whiskey or a beer—she'd had enough wine to last her a lifetime—she scanned the menu. They had a bunch of different kinds on tap. Hmm…choices, choices.

"*Hiiii!*"

She looked up to see Kim rushing toward her. Heather smiled and waved. "Hey! Glad you made it."

Clad in a white tank top, skintight dark jeans with white stitching, and cowgirl boots, Kim slid onto the seat across from Heather and plopped her rhinestone-studded purse on the table. "No way I was going to miss this. Just had to get the kids and dogs settled." She brushed her long hair off one shoulder. "Did you order yet?"

Damn, she should've worn something a little less casual. "Nope, I was just looking over the menu." She slid it toward Kim. "Take a look. You look great, by the way. I feel underdressed."

Kim waved her hand at Heather. "Ah, one, I don't need the menu. I've seen it a million times. Two, you look adorable, and with this mix of a crowd, not at all underdressed. Guys are gonna be drooling over you for sure." She pulled her cigarettes and lighter from her purse and set them on the table. "Wonder if Bethany's working."

"I'm definitely not looking to inspire any drooling." Heather laughed, scanning the small crowd. "Bartender or waitress?"

"Waitress." Kim turned in her seat to face the rest of the bar room. She glanced back at Heather, talking half over her shoulder. "Adorable little thing. Total girl next door. Ah, there she is." Kim raised her arm in the air and waved. "Hey, Bethany!"

The waitress Heather presumed was Bethany came over and hugged Kim. "Hey you! Haven't seen you in so long. You look wonderful!"

"It's been way too long. Feels like I've been locked up in my house *foreverrrrr.*" Kim laughed. "Aw, you're so sweet. You look awesome too. What's new?"

"Well, my boyfriend and I are moving in together." Bethany smiled, her eyes lighting up with excitement.

Resting her chin on her fist, Heather couldn't help but smile at the young waitress and the bliss in her expression. She did in fact look like the textbook girl next door, and her smile was contagious.

"Boyfriend! How did I miss this? And now you're moving in? Holy cow! Sounds serious."

"Told you it's been forever. About six months now, I guess?" Bethany shrugged and grinned, batting her eyelashes. "We're in *loooove.*"

How sweet for this young girl. Heather hoped things worked out for her and her boyfriend. She knew all too well how life could turn out completely different than what was planned for. God knew Heather's life didn't turn out anything like it was supposed to.

"This is my new friend Heather. She just moved into my neighborhood, so I figured I needed to dust off the boots and get her out on the town." Kim looked back at Heather, smiling.

Heather shook Bethany's hand. "Nice to meet you, Bethany. Congratulations on your big step with your boyfriend. You seem very happy; it's making your face glow."

"Is it?" She touched her reddened cheeks. "I'm beyond happy. Anyway, enough gushing for me. What can I get you two gorgeous ladies to drink?"

"I saw a coffee beer on there?" Heather scanned the menu, searching for the item.

"Oh yes, the Koffee Kölsch. You got it. It's in a can. Do you want a glass for it?"

Heather nodded. "Yes, please."

"For you, Miss Kim?"

"Definitely the usual. I've got a couple new flavor packets in my purse I've been dying to try." Kim unzipped her bag once more and started digging inside.

"Ooh! I bet. Coming right up." Smile still in place, Bethany pivoted and was gone.

Heather tipped her head to the side. "Flavor packets?"

"Hell yes. My usual is just vodka and water, plus this." Kim pulled a long, narrow packet of a store-brand equivalent of what appeared to be Crystal Light powder flavoring from the bowels of her purse and held it up. "All the flavor, none of the sugar!" She grinned. "I got watermelon last night when I was grocery shopping."

"Huh, never thought of doing that. Great idea."

Kim winked. "Stick with me, lady. I got all the tricks."

"Deal." Heather laughed and scanned the crowd again.

She wasn't sure if she'd be able to stick with anyone really, but she'd definitely hang out. Kim seemed a little crazy, but also a little fun too. Maybe even a lot fun. If memory served, those two things together usually spelled excitement. And truth be told, Heather probably needed a little excitement. Hell, maybe a lot of excitement.

She'd been in the dark for so long, it was hard to see anything in color. For tonight, she planned to check that baggage at the door and *try* for fun. Easier said than done, but she was going to give it hell anyway.

The bar was filling up, the band was setting up, and Bethany was on her way back to their table with a drink in each hand. Yes, fun would be a nice change.

Dare she say a welcome one too.

* * * *

Rob saw Heather the minute she walked into the bar. To his detriment, he hadn't gone over to her, but he hadn't taken his eyes off her either. Perched at his table near the dance floor, he tried to reconcile the times he'd run into her in the last several weeks.

Was this a punishment, or some sort of fucked-up gift from the universe? Was Heather Winters supposed to be part of his life? Or was he just being tempted like Eve with the apple, except instead of taking a bite, like the weak-willed Adam did, Rob needed to run in the other direction.

There was only one way to find out.

There were complications though. Her marital status was still a question. Also, when around her, his normal confidence was non-existent and suddenly he could understand why Adam ate the damn apple.

Ready to face her head-on, he swallowed the last of his beer, shifted to get to his feet, but then reversed direction, settling back down. Sighing through his nose, he shook his head and crossed his arms on top of the table.

Uncertainty weighed heavy around his neck and shoulders like a chainmail shawl and filled his gut like a twenty-pound boulder. He glanced over at her again. Well, damn, Kim Duke had joined her at her table, and he probably shouldn't go crash their party.

Small world that they had a mutual friend. Though Kim was more of an acquaintance. Just someone he knew from around the pub and country bar scene.

Weird thing was, Kim was nothing like the type of friends Heather had kept company with in school. In fact, she was more like the kind of people Heather regularly made fun of.

Fab. Another fun fact Rob couldn't reconcile.

Who was Heather Winters now? Tonight she wore a pair of short-but-not-too-short shorts, a loose-fitting, flowy-type top with thin straps, and a dark-colored pair of Converse on her petite feet.

Once again, an outfit far too down-to-earth for what he'd ever seen Heather wear when they were kids. Not that any single outfit defined a person, but in a lot of ways, an entire wardrobe did. Still, high school was long gone; what kind of person was she currently? Maybe she'd changed? Or maybe she hadn't—

"You want another?"

Yanked from his thoughts, Rob turned his attention to Bethany. "Yeah. Grab me a shot of American Honey, too, please?"

"You got it." Bethany grabbed his empty glass. "Where's everyone else?"

"They'll be here. Derek and Rayna were out to dinner with Derek's daughter but when they're done, heading our way. Not sure why Jeff isn't here yet though." Rob shrugged.

"Eh, I'm sure he'll be here any minute now. Be right back." Bethany smiled and stepped away.

Rob's buddy Jeff Pearl, another K9 officer, was definitely running late. If the dude didn't hurry his ass up and get here, Rob was going to go crash Heather's party of two and simply ask the woman why she was here—not in the bar, but more specifically, in town.

Basically, why the hell was she in the East Valley? Or, better yet, ask her if she remembered Rob, and not as the cop who pulled her over. Did he look even *vaguely* familiar to her?

However, doing any of that was an asinine idea. One, it wasn't really his business why or how long she was in town. Two, why did it even matter if she recognized him from when they were kids? It had no bearing on the now, and clearly, the two times he'd run into her in the last few weeks, she hadn't remembered him from high school. The more important thing was that she seemed interested in him. At least he thought she had.

"Here you go." Bethany placed his beer as well as the rocks glass filled with two fingers of whiskey in front of him.

"Thanks, Little Bit." He nodded and cradled the short glass of deep gold liquid in his palm.

The urge to turn around and check out Heather again rode Rob like the devil himself was chasing him. His heart raced, pounding in his ears. His hands were damp, and he couldn't think past the fact that the woman was no more than twenty-five feet away from him.

Fucking hell, this was stupid. He was being stupid. Enough was enough, he was going to go confront her.

Rob tossed back the double shot of American Honey, licked his lips, and before the warmth of it hit his stomach, he got to his feet. Turning, he ran smack into—

"What up, Rhonda? Sorry I'm late." Jeff grinned and slid onto one of the empty seats at Rob's table.

Dumbfounded, Rob stood there, staring at his buddy.

"Off to the head?" Jeff placed an elbow on the table and rested his chin on the heel of his hand. "Go on, I'll wait."

Rob placed his hands on his hips and let his head fall forward. Of course, Jeff showed right when Rob was about to go do something stupid. Like try to talk to Heather. After shaking his head, Rob glanced up at his friend. "Yeah, the head. Back in a minute."

"Gotcha. I'll order."

"Yeah, do that." Rob stepped away and walked across the empty dance floor, down the back hall, and into the men's room. It was a sign (sent in the form of Jeff Pearl?) that Rob needed to leave well enough alone with Heather Winters. Except that was just stupid.

After taking care of business in the bathroom, he washed his hands and splashed cool water on his face. He needed to get a grip and let this mess in his head go, or go over to her and see what the deal was. That was it. Two choices. Neither difficult.

As he emerged from the bathroom, Rob looked up and—

Heather...

Chapter 5

Oh. My. God.

It was him!

The cop…

Heather stopped short, so fast she almost stumbled. The cop was here. And not just *here*—but right in front of her in the narrow hallway with barely a couple of feet separating them—*here*.

Their gazes were locked, and Heather didn't dare blink. Wow, his eyes were really blue…beautifully blue. Had they been that blue when they talked at the grocery store?

Heather's face, and pretty much every inch of her skin, heated, remembering how much she'd focused on him that night at the gym. Especially how her body had reacted to his physique. She swallowed through a parched throat.

With his eyes still on her, he leaned a hip against the wall and slid his hands in his pockets but said nothing. Instead, he looked into her soul—or right through it. She couldn't be sure which.

To steady herself, because her knees were suddenly made of rubber, she raised her hand and pressed her fingertips to the wall next to her. She should move, keep walking, say something, do something. Anything… But she couldn't find the words or her voice.

Awkward or not, Heather was entranced by him. Which made her desire to stay right where she was greater than her instinct to flee. And still, he stayed silent, taking her in—fueling the gallons of uncomfortable vulnerability racing through her veins.

His eyes moved from hers, made their way down her body, before returning to catch her gaze once more. "Do you remember me?"

What a strange question. Of course she remembered him. And, God, his voice. Not that she hadn't noticed how smooth the tone of it was in their prior encounters; she had. But now…now she could actually *feel it*, like he was touching her. Everywhere. Cool silk wrapping around her.

With her heart racing out of control, she forced herself to inhale slowly. Christ, this close, he was *really* freaking good-looking. Could she handle this encounter and not look like some sort of desperate lunatic in heat? Either way, she needed to answer him.

Clearing her throat, Heather hoped for the best. "Yes."

Okay, not too bad. Her answer came out pretty clear. Only one word but sti—

"All right. Who am I then?" He glanced away, lips pursed before swiping his tongue along his bottom lip and shifting his eyes back on hers.

Sweet baby Jesus and all the saints. A bolt of lust at the sight of his lips and tongue shot through Heather, and her stomach tightened. Did he know how sexy he was? "Um, pretty sure you're the cop I keep running into."

"Only pretty sure?"

The deep rumble of his voice vibrated along her skin, and she had to suppress a groan. "No, no. I'm sure. It was you…right?"

The corner of his mouth twitched as if he wanted to smile but was determined not to, yet his sky-blue eyes softened, betraying his control. He took a step closer. "If you're sure, then why are you asking if you're right?"

Tall. So, so tall. He was over six feet for sure. No more than a foot separated them now, and Heather had to look up, tipping her head back to keep her eyes locked on his. "Because there's always a chance I could be wrong."

Once again, a quick purse of his lips, then a nod. "I've noticed doubting yourself is a thing for you. Do you always doubt yourself?"

"A thing?" She almost laughed but managed to hold it back in favor of a smile. If he only knew… She had a lot of "things"; some would call it baggage. Heather shrugged one shoulder. "I prefer to think of it as being cautiously realistic."

"Fair enough." He laughed, his straight white teeth visible, before his lips settled into a sexy smirk. But the laugh—nothing more than a soft chuckle, with a rasp to it that made Heather want to rub herself against him like some sort of cat in heat.

God help her, her libido was alive and kicking, like it'd just been electrified by a set of defibrillator paddles. Or a set of gorgeous blue eyes and an unbelievably sexy body.

God, who was this beautiful man? And aside from the fact that she seemed to be running into him—literally—everywhere, why would he ever want anything to do with her?

What was she supposed to do now? Should she walk away, politely excuse herself and head to the ladies' room? Or...close what was left of the distance between their bodies and see if he felt as good as he looked? Honestly, she *had* planned on having fun tonight. Maybe he was the fun she was supposed to have. Heather licked her bottom lip.

"Yes, I'm the cop you keep running into, but we both know you knew that already."

She smiled. "Glad to know I'm not losing it, and was right."

"You were." He nodded. "But I guess the next question is, *why* do I keep running into you everywhere?"

"You've seen me other places besides the grocery store and gym?" Had he seen her more than the two times she saw him? Heather let her gaze roam over his face. He had the start of laugh lines around his eyes and the corners of his mouth. But he had a baby face, too, which meant the lines didn't make him look older, they made him doubly attractive.

"Sadly, no, that's all." He rubbed the back of his neck before letting his arm fall to his side. "I still feel bad for crashing into your cart."

Sadly? Did he mean he wanted to run into her more? Oh, wow. Wow! Wait, she should not be as excited about that as she was. Heather waved her hand at him. "Well, I guess we're even, right? I did back into you with my car."

He laughed. "This is true. Though, technically that was also my fault." He raised his arm, as if reaching for her hand, but before he made contact he dropped it.

Heather's stomach jumped at the idea of him touching her, and she nearly leaned closer to him. She for sure wanted to touch him, be touched by him. Christ, it was crazy how attracted to him she was.

She'd done her best to ignore the attraction before, but there was no point in denying those feelings now. Not sure she could if she tried. Heather swallowed past a dry throat. "Wait, are you saying you ran into the back of my car, rather than the other way around?"

He shoved his hands in his front pockets and shrugged. "If I told you yes, would you believe me?"

"Nope." She half grinned, half frowned, and then slid her hands into the back pockets of her shorts. "Do you have some sort of a death wish or something?"

He looked past her, then back to her eyes. "Do you dance?"

Dance? "I, um…"

He held his hand out, palm up. "Yeah, come on. Let's dance."

A thrill at the ease of which he just took control and decided what they were doing blasted through her, and her stomach dipped. More was the realization that denying him wasn't a thought in her mind.

She didn't know his name, and it didn't even matter. In fact, other than knowing he was a cop, shopped at her Fry's, and belonged to the same gym and worked out late at night like she did, she knew nothing about him.

But now she knew those three things plus one more. He knew how to dance.

At least Heather hoped he did.

* * * *

Rob stepped a little closer, placed his hand on her waist, and bent to her ear. "C'mon, Heather. Do me the honor?"

Fuck's sake, she smelled sweet. This close to her, he felt and heard her slow inhale, and after what felt like forever—which he really didn't mind because, hello, her body was pressed against his and her nose kept grazing the skin of his neck—she finally answered. "Okay, but you promise to lead the way?"

Hell, he'd promise her anything.

There were many ways to take that. Many ways to answer. Plus, he needed to remember she was married, at least according to her vehicle registration. Maybe her husband was dead? *Wow, nice guy I am.* Truth be told, he couldn't help but hope she was available, which made him feel like an asshole.

After a mental beatdown for his fucked-up thinking, Rob pulled back enough to see her face. "We still talking about dancing?"

She smiled and rolled her eyes. "I think so, yes."

"Still doubting yourself?" With a chuckle, he slid his palm from her waist and found her hand and led her to the dance floor. After getting them to the center, he turned and placed his right hand on her upper back, just under her left arm, and held her right hand in his left, out to the side.

She gazed up at him, her pretty lips arched in a small smile. "Cautiously realistic."

"If you say so." He winked. "All right. Let's two-step." Rob started moving. He shouldn't be doing this, tempting fate, testing his resolve, but he was. He abso-fucking-lutely was.

She let out a little giggle-squeal but followed him. "I should warn you, I know how to dance, but I never learned the formal steps of country or ballroom style."

"Since *I'm* leading, as discussed, I'm going to remind you that you're supposed to trust me. But I'll challenge you to trust yourself, too." He nodded and spun her.

Best part was the big smile on her face and then the sight of her throwing her head back with a laugh as he quickly tucked her close to him once again.

"All right, sir. You are in charge." That big smile stayed in place as he steered them around to the edge of the floor. She blinked, her pretty eyes shining. "This is a great song. What's it called?"

Rob pushed her out to spin her again, crossed her back in front of him and spun her again, then pulled her close. "'Baggage Claim.' Miranda Lambert sings it."

"Baggage..." Her eyes went wide, and she blurted a laugh, faltering in her steps a little, but got herself back in time with him. Her smile was gone, her face serious. "Whoops. Sorry." Heather looked away, sucking her lips between her teeth.

Really? Did she just apologize? He frowned. Where the hell was the arrogant, good-at-everything girl he remembered from school?

Baffled, Rob dipped her, pulled her back up, and spun her once more. When he had her against him again and her beautiful smile was back in place, he said, "There's no 'sorry' in dance, doll. We just keep moving."

"'Kay. I can do that, I think."

"You think?"

She smiled. "Cautiously rea—"

Rob pushed her out for another turn. This time she rotated twice and came back around to pick up the step. "What was that you were saying? Let me remind you, I'm an officer of the law; don't make me haul you in for defiance."

"Defiance?" She laughed and dropped her forehead to the front of his shoulder. "Sir, yes sir." With a big smile, she nodded, keeping in time with him and following his cues. "I can do that. I can keep moving."

"Good girl."

As the song came to an end, Rob dipped her one last time, then pulled her up tight against his body. With her arms around his neck, she was laughing, breathing heavy. Heather tipped her head back, and Rob stared into her heavenly green eyes, before focusing on her lips, which were arched in a smile.

Jesus, he could kiss her. He *needed* to kiss her.

Chapter 6

Oh, shit!

He was going to kiss her.

Did she want him to kiss her? With her body pressed tight to his, Heather stared up at this unbelievably attractive man. She'd wrapped her arms around his neck and had no idea what to do next. Maybe *she* should kiss him. Wait…did she want to kiss him? Well, yeah, of course, but she was waiting for him to—

Something must've changed in her expression, because a crease formed between his brows and he loosened his hold around her waist. "Thanks for the dance." He nodded and moved to pass her.

Without another thought, Heather caught his arm in her palm. "Wait. That's it?"

He shrugged a shoulder. "Yeah. That's it."

What on earth… Why? "At least tell me your name, please?"

"Wow, shit. I can't believe I… Yea—"

A guy she didn't know came up behind her mysterious dance partner and clapped him on his shoulder. "Hey, Rhonda, just heard from Shirley and his girl. They're on their way." The guy glanced over at Heather, and his eyes went wide as if he'd just realized she was standing there—or wanted it to look that way anyway—then a big smile arched his very nice lips, and he stepped around her cop and held his hand out to her.

"Well, hello there, beautiful stranger, I'm Jeff."

Her cop? Heather blinked. "Um…"

"Jesus, Jeff. Do you always have to be an ass?" *The* cop elbowed his way around Jeff so he was in front of her again. "Sorry. He needs home training. Ignore him. What I was going to say before he interrupted me

Dorothy F. Shaw

was that I can't believe I hadn't told you my name. My apologies. Rob. My name is Rob."

Heather smiled; she couldn't help it. He was all flustered and annoyed, and compared to only the composed, in-control expression she'd seen on him up until three seconds ago, this additional side was an intriguing surprise. She held out her hand. "Officer Rob. I'm Heather Stratton. I'll pretend you didn't already know my name." She rolled her eyes but smiled bigger. "Nice to formally meet you."

"See? It worked. Catch you back at the table, Rhonda." Jeff clapped Rob on the shoulder and walked away.

Rob shook his head before closing his warm palm around hers and with a crooked smile, shook her hand. "Officer Rob works. Nice to formally meet you too, Mrs. Stratton."

"Oh, not Mrs. Just Ms."

Rob dropped her right hand and immediately picked up her left. He ran the pad of his thumb over her ring finger. "Yeah, you said that before, and I did notice you don't wear a ring, but your car is registered to you *and* Mr. Stratton, so I assumed."

The light stroke of his skin against hers sent tingles up Heather's arm. Shit, he was barely touching her and she could feel him all over her body. She glanced down at her hand in his, before focusing on his soft sky-blue eyes. "*Ex*-husband. I just haven't taken him off the registration yet."

The corner of his lips quirked in a grin. "Hmm, what's the timeframe in Maryland for handling that?"

With a mock snore, Heather rolled her eyes. "I don't know. I don't live there anymore."

He raised both brows and placed his free hand on her waist. "Is that so? Then where exactly do you live, *Ms.* Stratton?"

The heat of his palm was like a brand she felt clear through her shirt to her skin. Well now, this just got interesting. "Am I going to be in trouble with the law if I say I live here? As in Arizona, just a few miles away?"

"Careful now, anything you do or say can and will be held against you."

Oh, yes. Lust filled Heather's veins, thrumming in time with her pulse. Another laugh bubbled out of her. "Are you going to take me in for questioning?"

"Considering you're breaking the law—" Rob stepped closer and pulled her tight against his tall, lean frame. "I may just have to do that. Cuffs and all."

Cuffs? Yes, please? Now they were getting somewhere.

He swayed his hips, moving her with him, to the song that the cover band was playing. She listened a little closer. The Eagles, "Try and Love Again." Jeez, was the universe sending her hints? Although, she was definitely *not* looking for love. Fun, for sure. And sex...yep. That too.

When Heather had met her husband, he'd been really adventurous in bed. Such as spanking. Spanking her, to be specific. Especially because of the smart, sarcastic mouth she had.

Every time Heather made a snotty comment or complaint, that same night in bed, before they had sex, Charles spent at least fifteen minutes spanking her for being naughty.

Heather liked it. Hadn't known she would, but during that first time, she got off on the stinging, the pain that immediately radiated into pleasure. Yep, she'd gotten off big-time. And every time afterward too.

Over the first couple of years of their marriage, they'd experimented a lot, trying several different types of sexual play. Bondage, blindfolds, always the spanking. Orgasm withholding was something she didn't care for. However, every time they played that game, when she finally orgasmed, it was cataclysmic.

Ultimately, and as the pregnancy—or lack of—became an issue, being bound and then spanked, flogged, whipped, paddled, any of these things, became a form of release for her in many more ways than just sexually.

In the beginning, Charles had helped her purge all emotional consequences that came along with each failed in vitro attempt. Eventually, as failures turned into the norm, their play didn't work anymore. Soon after, their marriage didn't work anymore either.

The last two years of her marriage, and for sure after her husband left her, Heather was empty inside, a hollow shell of the person she once was. Since what felt like forever, and because the bathtub and wine trick was no longer an option, she was full to the brim with pain and rage and self-hatred.

But maybe, just maybe, Officer Rob with his strong personality, strong everything it seemed, was dominant enough to be her lifeline. Even if only to give her some relief, and possibly a little emotional purging too. At least for one night.

So, yes, staring up into Rob's soft eyes, Heather decided she for sure wanted him to kiss her.

And then, she wanted him to do a whole lot more than that.

* * * *

"Not married, and a resident of Arizona." Rob turned them slowly on the dance floor. "Gotta say, I didn't see that coming, but I guess it explains why I've been seeing you all over the East Valley."

"I promise, I wasn't stalking you."

"Bummer." He winked.

She rolled her eyes, shaking her head. "I grew up here. Well, in Glendale actually."

"I see." Rob looked away from her sparkling eyes. This was his opportunity to remind her of who he was, that he already knew her. But he just…couldn't get the words out. "Family brought you back here?"

"No reason to stay in Maryland. And my parents are still here. So, here I am."

"Fair enough. How long have you been back?" Rob pivoted and started them into a smooth two-step as the band played "Strawberry Wine" by Deana Carter. *God, just tell her.*

"About a year, I guess?"

"You guess? There you go doubting yourself again."

"No—" She laughed. "I'm not. For certain, it's been a year."

"That means you're about twelve months late to get the car registered here." He grinned and pushed her out for a spin, before bringing her in close to his body.

"Uh-oh. Officer Rob, am I in trouble?"

"Yes. I'm definitely going to have to detain you."

"For how long?" Her eyes were wide, as if she were shocked. But the excitement bouncing inside them betrayed her, along with the big grin splitting her sweet lips.

Were her lips sweet? Rob glanced at them. "For as long as necessary."

She sighed and licked her lips. "Well, you know what they say."

"What's that?" Rob splayed his palm on her lower back, pulling her tighter against him, and swayed his hips.

"If you can't do the time, don't do the crime."

He chuckled. "You're accepting of your punishment then?"

After a slow blink, she gazed up at him. "Yes, sir."

Oh, man, the things he wanted to do to her. Hell, by the way this convo was going, it was more like the things he was *definitely going* to do to her. As soon as he fucking could. Never in his life would Rob have thought Heather would be a submissive woman. Hard to believe, but more so, that she'd actually submit *to him, and* be punished?

Not in a million years and a million more fantasies would he have guessed that. Fucking hell, he'd died and gone to heaven.

There was no other explanation for this scenario playing out. He was dead, probably in an alley somewhere, with a rock-hard dick, and this was his version of heaven. Had to be.

He'd take it, because even though fifteen years had passed, this was Heather Winters, for fuck's sake. She wasn't a woman *any* man should turn down.

She said something he didn't catch, and Rob focused on her mouth. "I'm sorry?" Her voice was so low, he bent so his ear was closer to her lips. "Tell me again?"

"Would you like that? To punish me?"

He straightened and managed to stifle the growl that nearly shot out of him. Fuck, if she only knew. Rob cleared his throat. "Heather, punishing you, in a way that apparently we'd both like, would be a gift I haven't earned yet."

Her expression went gravely serious, and she tipped her head to the side. "Okay, then do you *want* to earn it?"

"Is that a trick question?" He smirked and shook his head. "Uh, let's see...hell yes, I want to earn it."

"Okay, good." She let out her breath like she'd been holding it in for years. "Thank you."

What the hell? How could she be this relieved? Did she not realize how incredibly desirable she was? Could she not see all the guys, and many of the women, throughout the bar were practically drooling on themselves staring at her, and yet she doubted herself, her appeal? Wow...

Her husband must've done one hell of a number on her. What the fuck had happened in her marriage? Had to be the marriage, because Heather Stratton was a completely different person.

Shit, Rob should tell her who he was. He *needed* to tell her.

Chapter 7

Relief spilled through Heather's veins, and she took another deep breath just to rid herself of any lingering apprehension. Officer Rob was exactly what she needed. And apparently he was right in sync with how she needed it too. How she'd gotten so lucky, she had no idea, but she was running with it.

With one final turn and dip, the song ended, and she and Rob came to a stop at the edge of the dance floor. She smiled up at him. "Thank you. That was awesome. Can I buy you a drink?"

"No, but I can buy you one." He led her off the dance floor toward a table with a handful of people around it. "Hello, friends. This is Heather." He placed his palm on her lower back and glanced down at her. "Heather, these are some of my good friends. You already met Jeff."

Dominant, charming, funny, good-looking, *and* a great dancer. Jackpot winner. God she hoped he was good in bed too. Heather waved at the man and woman. "Hi. Nice to meet you."

"Hey there." The woman with pretty red hair smiled. "I'm Rayna, and this is my boyfriend, Derek."

"Really nice to meet you both." Heather turned to Jeff. "You too, Jeff."

"I'm always nice. No matter what these chicks say." Jeff winked.

"Nice and obnoxious are not the same things." Derek chuckled. "Have a seat, Heather. Looks like we need to get you a drink."

"Oh, actually, I think I might still have my beer over there where I left my friend—" She pointed in the direction of where she'd been seated with Kim. "She might be worried. I should probably get back over there."

"How about she join us too?" Rob smoothed his palm along her back to her hip. "I'll walk over with you. Derek, you want to see if you can wrangle another chair?"

"Affirmative." Derek nodded.

"Okay, sure." Heather smiled.

Rob took her hand in his. "Lead the way."

Heather wove her way through the crowd. "I feel kinda bad. I left her over there for— How long were we dancing?"

"Eh, I think we were only on the floor for three songs. Maybe ten minutes? Fifteen tops."

"Okay, that's not so bad. I hope she's not upset." She smiled back at him then turned to see Kim talking to another couple.

"Hey, girl! Wondered where you went. Come here, meet mah friends!" Kim waved her over. "Heather, this is Sue and Dominick."

"Hi there." Heather shook their hands. "This is Rob."

"Oh, hell, I know this guy." Kim got up and hugged Rob. "I didn't know you knew Heather. I just met her."

"Really? I've known her for years." Rob winked at Heather.

Kim rolled her eyes. "Well, aren't you the special one?"

"Damn straight I am." Rob grinned.

Yeah, he was definitely funny. And she was definitely going to enjoy her luck while it lasted. Heather laughed and reached across the table for her beer. She took a sip. "Ooh, not so cold anymore. But it's still pretty yummy."

"Let me see." Rob took the glass from her and took a sip. After he swallowed, the scowl on his face was priceless. "Is that coffee?"

"Yes! I love it."

He wrinkled his nose but took another sip. "That's…" He sipped again. Licked his lips. "I think it *might* be good. Can't tell if I need to heat it up and toss some cream in it or get it on ice." He took another sip. "Yeah. Let's get a cold one to be sure."

Heather laughed harder. God, she hadn't laughed this much in forever and a year. And she couldn't stop smiling either. "Definitely."

"Kim, I'm stealing the blond bombshell from you. Come on over to the table near the dance floor when you get done over here."

"Got it." Kim glanced back toward Rob's table. "Nice, Derek and Rayna are here. Jeff too. Then again, Jeff's usually here."

"True story." After setting down her beer, he took Heather's hand and turned to move through the crowd.

Heather followed behind him. "The blonde what?"

"You heard me." Rob tipped his chin in her direction, gave her a wink, and kept moving.

"Nicest compliment I've had in a really long time." Her face warmed, and so did every inch of her skin again. Jeez, the physical effect he had on her was profound…but wholly welcome.

He stopped and turned to her. "Hmm. That's not good." He touched the ends of her hair hanging over her shoulder. "Let's go get that fresh beer, and then I'll see if I can help you raise that bar."

After they were back at the table with his friends, the waitress came over. "Refills anyone?"

"Hey, Little Bit. We're gonna need a whole round here." Jeff circled his hand above the table.

"Dearest Bethany, can you get my blond bombshell over here another one of those coffee beers?"

Bethany laughed. "Sure."

Heather rolled her eyes, and her face went up in flames. She pressed her fingers to her cheeks and glanced at Rayna.

Rayna was smiling from ear to ear. "It's nice to see someone get as red as I do. We should start a club."

Heather fanned her face. "It's terrible, I know, but he's cracking me up."

"Rob's a sweetheart. How long have you two known each other?"

Rob leaned over. "Since high school. Can you believe that?"

"Really?" Rayna smiled.

Heather's eyes went wide. "He's kidding."

"Nope. Totally not kidding." Rob tipped his glass of beer to his lips.

Whoa, what? Wait. Was he being serious? Confusion pulsed through Heather's veins. "Rob?"

He shrugged, and the whole table got quiet. Heather just stared at him, waiting for him to say something like "Gotcha! Just kidding." Instead, his eyes stayed locked with hers as he took another swallow of his nearly empty beer.

What the hell?

* * * *

"It's okay." Rob set his glass down. He hadn't the first idea how to tell her about their shared teen years without it seeming weird or like he'd tracked her down with some crazy agenda. But dropping it on her like he'd just done had not been his plan.

Then again, he didn't have a plan...hence why she was now looking at him like he was an asshole instead of smiling like she had been before. "Seriously, I don't expect you to remember me."

Okay, maybe he was a little bit of an asshole. Was there a reset button somewhere he could just hit? *Jesus...smooth operator right here.*

Bethany brought the fresh round of drinks they'd ordered, smiling with her usual girl-next-door manner as she distributed them. Heather's eyes stayed on him the whole time. *Fuuuuck!* He needed to fix this.

Rob handed her the fresh glass of beer he'd ordered her. "No kidding, Heather. It's no big deal."

"But it *is* a big deal." She frowned and looked down at her hands.

The expression on her face was more sad than mad, which Rob couldn't quite understand. Shouldn't she be pissed at him or at least a little annoyed? Christ, even mildly offended would be better than sad. He placed his palm on her upper arm. "Hey, hey. Really. It's all good. I didn't mean to upset you."

She shook her head, looking up at him. "I knew a lot of people in high school, but I also wasn't the nicest girl. Tell me your last name. Maybe that will help?"

He chuckled. "Caldwell, but trust me, I was pretty forgettable."

She blinked, shaking her head again. "I'm so sorry, Rob. I don't remember you. I wish I did. And I don't believe you could ever be forgettable."

Rob blew out a long breath because now he really felt like an asshole, with a capital *A*. Okay, time to get real. "Can I tell you something?"

"Yes. Anything." She shifted to face him.

He stepped in front of her. "You're right, you weren't the nicest girl in high school"—she cringed, but he continued—"but you seem pretty nice to me now. Actually, you're different, very different. So, I say"—he took her hands in his—"let's forget about high school because that was, shit... fifteen years ago, right? Yeah, let's forget about that uncomfortable time in everyone's life and just go with me being the cop that pulled you over a few weeks ago, and you're the gorgeous blond bombshell I kept running into until I finally got you in my arms on the dance floor."

She smiled, the corners of her eyes crinkling, making her breathtaking. "I can do that, I think."

"Uh oh...there's that doubt again." When she went to respond, he stopped her. "Hold up. Before you say anything else, let me get some clarification first. You doubting you, me, or us?"

"Me! Definitely me. Oh God, I mean..." She raised her brows. "I'm being cautiously realistic, that's all. I feel horrible about not remembering you, never mind the fact that most of the time I'm appalled at myself because I was a spoiled little bitch my entire teenage life and into my early twenties. I don't think I should be let off the hook so easy for any of that, that's all."

"Is that the reason you want to be punished?" Holy hell, the road to Heather Winters just got twisty and bumpy and possibly required caution. She blushed and looked away. Rob passed his thumbs over the top of her hands. She looked back to him, and he dipped his chin. "Is it?"

"Not the only reason. Just one of them. Is that bad?"

Rob let go of her hands, parted her thighs, and slid between them to get closer to her. He bent to her ear. "It's not bad, it's just complicated. What concerns me is, if you pick the wrong kind of guy to do the punishing, it could also be dangerous."

She slid her hands up his sides. "Are you the wrong kind of guy?"

He pulled back to look into her eyes. "No. I'm absolutely the right kind of guy."

"Good. Then I pick you."

She gave him another slow blink, and his dick went stone-hard behind his zipper. He might be the top in their little escalating situation, but hands down, Heather held all the power.

Yes, Rob was absolutely the right guy, and he was going to give her whatever the fuck she needed.

However it was that she needed it.

Chapter 8

With her keys in her hand, Heather stepped up to her front door. Rob was right behind her. Since they'd left the bar, save for holding her hand in the Lyft to her house, and just now when he put his palm on her lower back, he hadn't touched her.

She'd liked all that touching she got from him when dancing and just hanging in the bar and wanted more of it. Was he withholding now in order to build the sexual tension, or because he was having second thoughts? God, she hoped he wasn't having second thoughts.

She definitely was, but not because she didn't want him. Heather 100 percent wanted him, was attracted to him for sure. But also, she genuinely liked him, and if this was only going to be a one-night stand, liking him could get in the way.

As Rob placed his hands on her hips and snugged up behind her, she fumbled with the key. "Shit."

"Here. Let me help." He slid one hand up her side, onto her extended arm, and down to her hand.

Covering the back of her hand with his palm, he helped her slide the key into the lock and turn it. Molten heat spread from where he'd touched her on her side and even her arm, along her skin, and settled deep in her tummy.

As cliché as it was, Heather's knees went a little weak, and when she pulled the key free of the lock, she let her head fall back against his shoulder.

Rob opened the door and walked them both inside. With the front of his body tight against her back, Heather heard the door swing closed behind them. He had one hand on her hip still, and he pressed the other to her stomach. "You ready for this?"

"I think so, yes."

"You think so?" He dragged his hand higher, stopping just below her bra. With his thumb, he traced the underside of her breasts through her shirt. "More doubt? Do you need more time to think about it?"

Every inch of her skin was alive and sensitive. And she still had all her clothes on.

"No—"

He traced the lower half of her breasts again, and Heather sucked in a harsh breath before shaking her head.

"No, I don't need more time. I'm ready."

Rob smoothed both hands up her fabric-covered chest, cupped her breasts with his palms, stroked her hard nipples. "Tonight isn't for punishing—"

"But—"

"No. Let me finish…." He paused, and Heather clamped her lips closed. Even though her stomach had dropped and a lump had lodged itself in her throat, she nodded. He continued. "Tonight is for getting comfortable. For finding our way around each other." He pinched her nipples through the thin fabric of her blouse and bra, tugging the tight points away from her body, and she let out a harsh breath. "For just a little bit of pain too." He ran his nose along her ear. "But all of it is for pleasure. Punishment will have to wait for a night. Understood?"

The low gravelly sound of his voice was pure sex, vibrating through her and settling in her clit. Heather nodded. "Yes."

After letting go of her nipples, Rob turned her around. He wrapped one arm around her, then brushed her hair away from her face with his free hand, stroking her cheek. His gaze roamed over her face, before he stared into her eyes. "Heather Winters…I can hardly believe my eyes, hardly believe you're real."

His intense expression as he looked at her and the words he spoke made her heart squeeze. Her face warmed, and a shiver raced down her spine. He looked at her as if she was amazing. Like she was so much more than she really was.

God, the way Rob was looking at her made her think, maybe almost believe, she was special.

But she wasn't.

What Heather was, was damaged goods.

For the love of all things holy, she needed a release, an epic one. Because what she knew deep inside was that there was only ugly darkness. Still. And she needed to purge all the pent-up turmoil roiling inside her constantly, but she wasn't going to get that.

Not tonight, anyway. Maybe not ever again.

* * * *

Rob stroked his thumb over her bottom lip. The woman was more beautiful now than any memory he had of her. But maybe it was because the real thing was always so much better than a fantasy. He was glad she didn't remember him. He'd rather have this fresh beginning with her.

God, he hoped it was a beginning and not one night.

Clearly, she'd been scarred in some way by her marriage, and she'd paid some steep emotional price for it. He had no idea what she'd gone through, and maybe someday she'd tell him, but whatever it was, it'd changed her. But that change meant that now, there was so much more to her than Rob ever thought possible.

People changed as life had its way with them, him included. This was the version of Heather he wanted to get to know. He'd just have to make sure she didn't get away.

He stroked his thumb over her bottom lip again and then slid his fingers into her hair, bent his head, and brushed his mouth over hers. She let out a soft exhale. Rob slid the tip of his tongue out and stroked over her bottom then top lip. This time, a little moan emerged from her, and she pressed her palm to his chest.

He hadn't expected to be this tender with her, especially with all the buildup at the bar, but he didn't want to rush this moment. Raising his hand from her waist, he cupped the other side of her face, brought her to him, and pressed his mouth to hers, shifted only a little, and nipped at her bottom lip.

Taking little sips, the tips of their tongues touched and retreated, growing more intense, more heated from each pass, each stroke. With Heather's body pressed fully against his, Rob slanted his mouth over hers, and her soft lips gave way, parting for him, and he dove inside with his tongue, exploring and tangling with hers.

He tasted a hint of her beer and the mint she'd sucked on when they left the bar, but more, he tasted heaven. Heather was pure fucking heaven.

She moaned, rose on tiptoe, and wrapped her arms around his neck. Rob slid his hands around her waist and then down to her ass. Cupping her bottom, he slid his long fingers between her thighs, grazing the soft skin exposed below her short-shorts. She moaned and rocked her pelvis forward, and sucked his tongue into her mouth.

Goddamn…his dick was a steel rod, the head pulsing inside his jeans. Gripping her ass hard, he lifted her, and she wrapped her legs around his waist, grinding against him. *Fuuuuck!* The lady was hotter than a firecracker on the Fourth of July, and Rob was so ready to be burned into sweet oblivion by her.

He broke from her lips. "Bed or couch?"

She blinked, a dazed look in her eyes. "Bed."

"Got it. Which way?" He nipped her chin and nuzzled the soft skin on the side of her neck.

She tipped her head back and moaned. "Um...through the entryway, then down the hall. Last door on the left. God, you feel good."

Looking to his right, Rob shifted her and walked in the direction she mentioned. She had a nightlight in the hallway, so there was no need to flip on the hallway light. Or any lights for that matter. Though he definitely wanted to be able to see her body when he got her naked. She was fucking beautiful, but more, because for right now, she was his.

Rob wanted to see, in full detail, all that was his.

Chapter 9

"The bed's to the right." Heather caressed the soft, short hair on the back of his head with her fingertips and nuzzled the side of his neck. The scent of sun on his skin, along with a hint of clean soap and cologne, was intoxicating. She ran her nose along his ear, breathing in more of him. "You smell so damn good."

"Bet not as good as you feel—or taste."

He bent forward, and a second later, Heather felt the soft mattress against her back. Hovering over her, Rob pressed his lips to hers again, his tongue sweeping and exploring deeper than he had in the entryway. Kissing her as if every touch of their lips, their tongues, was as precious as a dying man's last drink of water.

Heather felt every bit of their shared touches and breaths, from the top of her head to the tips of her toes, and everywhere in between. Not even physically inside her yet and he'd settled deep within her core. Her clit throbbed in response.

Heather ran her hands up his sides, tugging at his shirt, needing to feel his skin. Rob rose off of her, pulled his shirt over his head and tossed it aside. She watched him as he looked around the room and—

"Don't move."

"Okay." Heather lay still, keeping her eyes on him as he stepped away from her.

God, she loved that he'd turned out to be dominant, though most cops were, she guessed. Or assumed anyway. No idea if he was a real deal Dom, but that didn't matter. She simply needed him to be strong enough to handle dishing out what she was desperate for.

He might be being gentle and tender with her for now, but she could tell by his clipped orders, the way he was touching her, he'd be able to get the job done. Adequately. She just needed to be patient.

"Do you have a lighter for these?" He turned toward her, holding one of her candles. "I don't want the lights on, but I still want to be able to see you."

"In the little wooden box on top of my dresser."

The lid creaked as he lifted it. "Got it."

After lighting every candle she had in her bedroom, he put the lighter back in the box and came back to her on the bed. But he didn't crawl onto it. Instead he stood at the edge and stared down at her. Which was fine, because Heather was doing her share of staring too.

His bare chest was also bare of hair. Two nickel-sized areolas that she couldn't wait to suck into her mouth stood out against his pale skin. And, God help her, he had a thin line of brown hair bisecting his lower abdomen below his navel, trailing down into his jeans. She'd be running her tongue over that, too, as soon as she got the chance.

Rob raised one of her legs, pressed his lips to the inside of her ankle before he untied and pulled off her sneaker and sock. He did the same with the other. Bending forward, he slid his palms up the top of her bare legs to her hips and then unbuttoned her shorts, pulled the zipper down before sliding the soft denim down her thighs and off her legs. Taking her hand, he helped Heather sit up, and gently, as she raised her arms, he slid her shirt up and off.

He did all of this in silence. With his body language and actions, what he wanted her to do was clear enough. It was also clear he didn't want her to speak. If he did, he would've told her to. Clad in only her bra and panties, she lay back down and gazed up at him. Heather focused on the rise and fall of his chest as he breathed and gazed down at her in silence.

Did he like what he was seeing? Still in her early thirties, Heather was in good shape, especially since she hadn't had any children.

A pang of grief sliced through her chest like a hot knife, and she looked away from him, resisting the urge to rub at the phantom pain behind her sternum.

"Hey, hey. You okay? Where'd you just go?" Rob climbed onto the bed, planting his fists into the mattress on either side of her shoulders, holding himself above her.

Please, make it stop... Please? She nodded. "I'm good. I'm right here." Heather swallowed the lump in her throat. She wasn't good or fully present, but she wasn't that far away either.

Forcing herself back into the moment with him, she ran her fingertips down his chest to his tight abs, and back up again. "You have an incredibly nice body."

He frowned for a moment before his gaze roamed over her face, as if he was checking to see if she was being honest. She wasn't. Not entirely anyway. Regardless, she needed to stay focused, not get into the "whats" and "whys" for which she was the way she was now.

Rob shifted his body to the side of hers, planted his elbow in the mattress, and propped his head in his hand. "Leave your hands at your sides, please." He pressed his fingertip lightly to her chin, then traced a line down to the dip at the base of her throat. "Mmm. You're good at that, aren't you?"

She placed her palms flat on the comforter and gazed up at him. "Good at what?"

With a calm expression, Rob continued his finger's journey, lightly tracing along one collarbone and the other. "Deflecting. Hiding."

"Not much different from most people, I guess. We all wear masks." When he drew little circles on her sternum, skimming the edge of her cleavage, Heather moaned and her stomach tightened.

"Fair enough. You think I have a mask too?"

"Maybe." Jesus, the light touches were almost torture. As her clit throbbed in time with her pulse, she licked her lips and fisted the blanket in her hands.

"What if I said I don't care for masks, and if you want to take yours off, I'm willing to help you?" He trailed the tip of his finger over the fleshy mounds of her breasts above her bra. "Would you want that?"

Heather didn't get a chance to answer—which was fine since she had no clue what to say to his proposition—because in the next breath, he'd tugged a bra cup down and traced a circle around her tight areola. Heather sucked in a harsh breath and bit her bottom lip.

"I'd want that." Rob pulled the other cup down and did the same to that nipple. "In fact, I bet you'd want it too. You just don't know it yet." He sighed through his nose, and in one motion, he rose, bent over her, and sucked one hard, distended nipple between his lips.

Searing heat from his tongue spread through her veins. With a moan, Heather arched off the mattress, wanting to give every bit of herself to him and take all he was willing to give.

He was setting her on fire, but she'd burn alive before she asked him to stop.

* * * *

With one very perfect, very pebbled, tiny pink nipple against his tongue, Rob closed his eyes and savored the taste of her. The scent of her skin filled his lungs. A feminine, lightly floral aroma from whatever perfume she wore reminding him of all things soft and pretty. He wanted to curl himself around her and hold on to her forever.

That's the effect Heather had on him. That's how she made him feel.

She also made his cock rock-hard. With one look from her, heavy lust pulsed hot in his veins. That had always been the case. She'd forever been a fantasy, but now she was beside him, now she was real. Heather was half-naked, panting and moaning for him, and she was better than any fantasy he'd ever conjured of her. She was fucking perfect!

"*Rob...*" A breathy moan followed after his name as it left her lips, and then one of her hands was on the back of his head.

He pulled from her sweet nipple and blew a light breath over the hardened nub. Her areola tightened further, pushing the distended peak higher. Jesus, her nipples were *outfuckingstanding*. He let his gaze roam from her breast to her eyes, enjoying all there was to see. "Where are your hands supposed to be?"

She pulled her lips between her teeth, and he felt her hand leave the back of his head. Yes! Fucking perfect. The head of his cock pulsed hard in his jeans. God bless America, he was going to enjoy every minute of this night with her. "Good girl."

Shifting so his weight was off her, he pulled one bra strap down her shoulder and did the same with the other. He coaxed her to roll to her side toward him and gave her a soft kiss on her cheek before undoing the clasp on the back of her bra. After she returned to her back, he slid the loose fabric down her arms.

Her breasts were the perfect handful, tipped with pink areolas, barely the circumference of a quarter. Yep, better than any fantasy he'd ever had of her...or anyone else for that matter. Rob grazed the distended tips with his knuckles, reveling in the sound of her harsh intake of breath. "You like your breasts played with?"

She nodded. "Yes."

"Nipples?" He flicked his thumb over one peak, then the other.

"*Mmhmmyes.*"

"Do you like them pinched? Tugged?" He rolled one nipple between his finger and thumb, pulling at it just a little.

"Oh God! Yes."

Rob let go and slid his hand down to her stomach. "How hard? Show me."

"Hard as you want to give it."

He shook his head. "Show. Me."

"Yes, sir." Slowly she raised her hands from her sides, skating them over her stomach and the rise of her breasts and took each nipple in her fingers. She pinched them and tugged them away from her body.

Definitely harder than he'd expected. He liked that though, that he could push not only her limits of pain tolerance, but his own at giving it. "You like it rough?"

"Yes." She licked her lips. "As rough and hard as you want to give it."

"A true masochist?"

She shrugged one shoulder. "Maybe, I guess?"

"Hmm...you guess? All right, then I 'guess' we'll find out soon enough, won't we? Besides, I'm not sure if I'm a true sadist, so you get a pass on that one." He winked. "Raise your arms over your head, please."

With a small smile, she did as he asked.

"Good girl." Rob got up long enough to shed his shoes and jeans. Leaving his boxer briefs on, he climbed back onto the bed and straddled her thighs. "Are you always so compliant?"

Another small smile arched her lips. "Yes."

He chuckled. "Guess we'll find out about that soon enough too." Rob ran his palms up her sides to her breasts and traced circles around her nipples with his fingertips. Soft, slow, mesmerizing circles, around and around, again and again. Her sharp inhales and whimpers were all he needed to know she was getting more and more aroused by the stimulation.

So was he. Rob continued, and as she trembled beneath him, her nipples grew so hard they could probably cut glass. He bet they ached too. Too bad he didn't have a set of nipple clamps handy. He'd have to improvise. Rob pinched both tips hard and tugged them. "Do you think you could come from nipple play?"

"Fuck!" Heather arched and let out a cry.

"Is that a yes?" He twisted and pulled on her nips again. She gasped for air, thrashing her head side to side. He'd never been with anyone who could come from nipple play, but he was sure willing to try. "A no?"

"*Mmmnnnooo*...God! Fuck!"

He smirked, loving how easily he'd driven her this high. "I bet you want to come though. Probably need to. I bet your panties are soaked through too." He bent forward and licked once over each nipple before shifting down her legs to her ankles.

"Let's see." His cock throbbed, leaking pre-cum onto his underwear. She wasn't the only one needing to come, but no way he would let himself orgasm until he'd given her release. At least twice.

Rob slid her panties down her hips and off. After dropping them on the floor, he paused a moment, admiring her body. A thin layer of blonde curls covered the front of her mound, but she was bare below that. "So gorgeous. Spread your legs for me."

Heather raised her knees slightly and parted her thighs. The small hood of her clit was nestled between two perfect, pale pink labia. Rob licked his lips. "Good girl. Now, show me."

After smoothing her hands down her body, she grazed her petite clit with her fingertip before spreading her labia apart. The mouth of her pussy glistened from her arousal like a sweet treat just for him, and Rob had to swallow. "Do you want me to lick all that pretty wetness for you?"

"God, yes."

"Dip your fingers in your pussy, get them nice and wet, then rub your clit. Show me how you like it." Rob palmed his length through his bottoms. Fuck, he was beyond aching to be inside her. But seeing this was worth the wait.

"Yes, sir." With a moan, she did as he asked, panting as she slid two fingers inside that pretty cunt, withdrawing them and rubbing her arousal over her clit.

Tight little circles and even pressure. Rob watched, caught in a trance. All he could manage was to squeeze his hard length though his boxer briefs. She was so fucking hot, so off the charts sexy—

THWAPP!

Heather let out a whimper, and Rob's eyes went wide. She'd slapped her pussy, and he had to clench every muscle in his body because he nearly came at the sight and sound of it.

"Fuck, little girl! You do like it rough."

"Yes." She spread her labia apart and slid two fingers inside again, then returned to her clit. This time rubbing more vigorously. "Told you... Oh, fuck..." She arched, raising her hips off the mattress.

Jesus, he was about to lose all of his control. Rob slid his boxer briefs off. "Condom, Heather."

She froze. "I...I don't have any."

"Shit. Let me check my wallet." Rob grabbed his jeans, pulled his wallet from the back pocket and opened it. No condom because fuck his life. "Fuck. I don't have one either." He sighed through his nose and put his wallet away. Screw it. "It's fine. We can do other things."

"But I'm clean. I haven't been with anyone in a year. It's okay...unless." She bit her bottom lip.

He lay on the bed between her parted thighs and lightly stroked the hood of her clit with his thumb. They didn't need to fuck. As far as cock in the vagina went anyway. They could do a lot of things to pleasure each other all night long. "Unless what?"

"Please don't take this wrong."

"It's all good, little girl. Say it." Rob slid his thumb down to her cunt and circled the opening. Jesus, she was soaking wet. "You can say anything to me."

"Unless you're not clean, or haven't been tested in a while."

"Hmm." Rob licked his thumb, and the sweet taste of her exploded in his mouth. Oh, yes, definitely going to be eating this fine pussy. "I've been tested. And I've been off the dating train for a few months. We're good there. But what—"

Fuck it. He was done talking. Mesmerized by what lay before him and no longer willing to hold himself back, Rob inched forward and licked through her slit.

Fuuuuck!

Heather's knees jerked higher. At the same time, she gripped his head and moaned.

Dragging his tongue over her opening, he licked through her folds again and then laved at her clit. Stroking the nub over and over again with his tongue. She was pure ambrosia on his tongue and lips.

Her body writhing beneath him, she rolled her hips, grinding her cunt against his face, taking as much as he was giving. And Rob was nowhere near done giving.

Chapter 10

"*Rob.* Oh my God, yes. Like that. Just like that. Don't...stop." Heather arched off the mattress, so near to climax she could practically taste it. Sweat coated her skin, and the tension building inside her body made her limbs tingle with the desperate need for release.

Rob pulled away and—

THWAPP!

"*God!*" The sting from the slap to her clit and pussy radiated through Heather's core, and her cunt clamped down on the two fingers Rob held inside her. He curled the tips, stroking the inner wall of her channel, and sucked her clit into his mouth again.

And that's when her orgasm broke free, crashing down and drowning her. She slammed her head back onto the mattress. "*Fuck! Fuck!*"

Wave after sweet wave rippled through her. All of it, heaven.

He rose from between her thighs and rested on his knees. Heather looked down her trembling body and watched as he stroked his gorgeous cock.

"You taste sweeter than honey." He licked his lips. "Want to fuck you so bad right now. My dick is throbbing."

Well, yeah, she needed to be fucked. He'd stimulated her body for sure, but more so her mind to the point of madness. Heather was desperate to feel his length buried deep inside her. She licked her dry lips. "Please? I need you."

Slow stroke. From root to head. Then down his shaft again. "Are you on the pill?"

Heather closed her eyes and swallowed, trying but failing to push down the pain rising in her chest.

The question caught her off guard, but then again, she should've anticipated one like it. After all, it was a perfectly valid question. They were both in their very early thirties, and for all intents and purposes, healthy. For most people their age, pregnancy was a real possibility.

But not for her—though Rob didn't know that.

After drawing in a deep breath, she managed to settle the thrum of sadness pulsing in her veins. Heather opened her eyes and focused on him. *No, there's no need for the pill because my uterus and ovaries are a fucking mess and I can't have babies...* "We're good. You can't get me pregnant."

She didn't want to lie to him, but she sure as hell wasn't going to tell him the truth. It wasn't any of his business anyway.

With a cocky grin, Rob tipped his head to the side. "Don't say that. You make it sound like some sort of a challenge. Like maybe—" He slid his other hand down and cupped his tight sac, massaging and stroking the tender skin. "*Mmm.* Maybe I need knock you up just to prove I can." Rob licked his bottom lip, and then winked at her. "Kidding, of course. I'd never do that. Just, cut me some slack and let's blame that little declaration on the caveman inside me."

Heather almost laughed, because yes, he *was* being funny, but the bile in the back of her throat burned like she'd been stabbed with a hot poker. Christ on the cross, she was pathetic. For fuck's sake, even a god of fertility couldn't get her pregnant. And that was a fact.

When a woman's ovaries didn't function or act their age, the chances of knocking said woman up were damn slim. Her ex had been declared "above average" as far as fertility went. Yes, Charles was perfect. Lucky him.

To be doubly sure, though, that same woman's body would also reject the very few frozen embryos (using the only viable eggs she'd produced in five years) she'd attempted to have implanted in her womb four years ago. Too many failed in vitro attempts to count.

So there was no challenge to win.

There was no prize, and there would be no babies.

End of story.

Somehow, Heather managed to shove all of the pain and heartache filling her chest away. Nothing short of a miracle, really. But that was likely because being numb to it all was so much more bearable.

She blinked and focused on the beautiful naked man kneeling between her ankles. "You know, there's a lot of truth in joking."

"Sometimes, sure. We can debate that later if you want." Rob knee-walked forward, positioning himself right between her parted thighs. He tapped her clit with the engorged head of his cock. "I'd much rather see how your sweet cunt looks wrapped around my dick."

Sucking in a breath, Heather's stomach jumped and her clit spasmed. "I'd like to see that too."

Rob ran the head down to the entrance of her cunt, dipping just the tip in and spreading her wetness back to her clit. She drew in a sharp breath and bit her bottom lip.

Again he tapped her clit with the head before sliding once more to the mouth of her pussy. "Goddamn, I bet your tight cunt is going to feel like a satin glove stroking my dick. So sloppy wet for me, I can barely stand to hold out any longer."

"Don't hold out." Heather arched, tipping her pelvis back. Her veins filled with lust and desire and an ache she needed satisfied. "Fuck me, Rob. Please?"

After positioning the head at the mouth of her pussy, Rob caught her gaze and guided the bulbous flesh fully inside her. Heather let out a high-pitched cry followed by a deep groan as he pressed deeper, filling her narrow channel and stretching her walls with his long, thick erection.

Rob drew out, and pressed in. And out and back in again. Slow, even thrusts. Again. Again...

This was heaven.

And this was hell.

She'd wanted him to take her rough, to spank or even flog her ass until it burned bright red, and she wanted him to take her by the back of the hair and fuck her as hard as he could from behind, banging his solid pelvis into her scorched ass cheeks. But that wasn't what he was giving her. Surrendering herself to the sensations and feelings his fat cock were enticing from her body, Heather squeezed her eyes closed and gripped the bedding beneath her.

In and out. In and out.

In. Out. In—

Oh, *God.*

God!

Fuck, he was killing her, inch by inch, with each tempered pass. The sensual drag of skin along skin had every nerve in Heather's body tightening. No, what he was doing, how he was taking her, wasn't what she wanted.

But it was exactly what she fucking needed.

* * * *

"Look at me, beautiful." Rob raised Heather's legs in the air, propping her ankles on his shoulders. Sliding his cock deep inside her hot core once more, he pressed his thumb to her clit and rubbed tight circles.

Heather gasped and opened her eyes. "You're… Oh, *fuuuuck.*" She yanked on the blanket beneath her. "*MmmnngggGod…* Killing me."

"Killing you? Hmm." He knew what she meant, but he wasn't giving in. Keeping his movements consistent, Rob drew out and slid back in. Her tight cunt clenched around his shaft each time he penetrated her. The feel of her sent bolts of arousal down his spine, settling in his balls. His orgasm hovered, but he was holding it at bay, and would do so for as long as he could handle it.

But it wasn't easy. The noises she made were both a sexual torture and music to his ears. The way she exhaled or inhaled. The way she moaned, her little whimpers and cries, and the way she arched and shifted her pelvis, taking his prick deeper… All of it was by far the hottest fucking thing he'd ever witnessed.

He could tell she wanted it harder, but he wasn't going to give her that. Maybe later, or the next time. For sure, there would be a next time. But this time, he planned on fucking her slow and steady and 100 percent thoroughly.

Heather Winters may not have known who he was before tonight, but from this point on, she would always remember him. There were a ton of ways to leave a mark on a woman, the kind of mark that made her know she belonged to someone and had been branded in the best kinds of ways. He ran his hand down her thigh to her hip and gripped the flesh there. "You need to come? Tell me, beautiful."

"Yes. So close." She licked her lips. "Please?"

"Pinch those tight nipples for me."

With no hesitation at all, Heather grabbed the stone-hard tips and tugged them. "I need it harder. Please?"

Rob dragged his length out to the tip and, slowly, slid back in again, ensuring she felt the ridge of the head, and then his shaft fill and stretch her.

A low, guttural moan came out of her, and she closed her eyes again. Rob grit his teeth, beating back his climax. Just a little longer, just a little more. She'd come; he knew she would.

Rob's balls pulled up tight, and his cock swelled harder. Fuck, she felt amazing. He slid her legs off his shoulders, shifted his knees wider and crouched over her. Without breaking pace, he pressed his pelvis to hers and moved in and out of her, rubbing her clit with his pelvis.

With her face cradled in his palms, he gazed down at her. "I know you want it harder. But you don't *need* it harder. Tonight, all you need is this." He brushed his lips over hers. "Feel m—"

She moaned and caught his bottom lip in her teeth.

Rob chuckled but didn't break from stride. "Feel me, Heather. Let it build." He pressed his lips to hers, sweeping his tongue deep into her mouth.

Moaning, Heather wrapped her legs around his waist and rolled her pelvis, meeting his steady thrusts. Over and over, they moved together until Rob couldn't hold back any longer.

She was shredding his control as her tight cunt stroked his dick, giving him as much pleasure as he could only hope he was giving her.

"*Fuck.*" His orgasm tingled at the base of his spine. He speared his fingers into her hair and gripped the soft strands tight in his fists.

Her soft breasts pressed against his chest as their damp bodies slid against one another. Heather tipped her head back, arching beneath him and rolling her hips. "Don't stop. Oh God, *Rob. Yes.*"

"*Come* for me, beautiful." Unable to hold out any longer, Rob sped up just a little, thrusting his pelvis forward and back, grinding against her, burying his cock as deep as he could inside her core. Tugging her hair a little harder, he stared at her. "Look at me and come for me, Heather. Now."

She opened her eyes, and Rob let his control go. Pulling his pelvis from hers, he slammed back into her. Skin slapped against skin as he gave her everything. Harder, faster—

"*Yesss.*" Heather's orgasm struck, and she let out a loud cry. Arms and legs wrapped around him already, she tightened her grip.

Rob covered her mouth with his and drove his tongue between her lips. One, two, three more strokes and he gave in. His orgasm shot from his dick, spurting his release deep inside her.

Still caught in the throes of his climax and half out of his mind, Rob jerked from her mouth and cunt, rose up and, stroking his shaft, spurted three more times onto her belly and tits.

He needed to mark her.

Needed to claim what was his.

Rob had to leave a mark so deep on Heather, so permanent, she'd never forget him. Because she'd definitely left her mark on him.

There was no going back from that now.

Chapter 11

Heather blinked a few times, adjusting to the dim light from the rising sun filtering through her window sheers. As foreign as it felt, ease and contentment flooded her system from head to toe. Amazing...

This was the best part of waking up too early. Two bodies spooned together, warm and snuggly beneath the blankets, not wanting to let that warmth go and hey...*bonus!* Realizing she didn't have to lose it, she could just go back to sleep and stay in her little cocoon.

Intent on doing just that, Heather yawned, burrowed a little deeper into the blankets, and pressed a little closer to the heat from the body curled against her back. It'd been a really long time since she felt peaceful. And safe. Yeah, she also felt safe.

She hadn't expected Rob to stay the night, and to be honest, she hadn't wanted him to. Sleeping next to someone was way too personal. Not that sex wasn't intimate, it certainly could be with the right person, but if it was only a casual fling, it was just sex. A biological function driven by a mutual desire for pleasure.

And Rob was only supposed to be a casual fling.

Unfortunately, what they'd done together in her bed last night felt a whole lot more than casual. And the cuddling he'd done with her was for sure *way* more than just a hookup.

One-night stands didn't come with cuddling. It wasn't allowed. Primarily because female hormones kicked in after an orgasm, and when a person added cuddling to that mess, all logic and reason was nullified and insides turned from lust-driven to mushy, lovestruck goo.

But worse, the sleeping over was the cherry on top. Or the kiss of death, depending on what a person was looking for. In Heather's case, although she really liked how good his warm, sleek body felt against hers, she wasn't looking for anything more than sex, and it was probably best if sh—

Rob shifted, snaking the hand that had been perched on her hip down and up to her stomach, pulling her tighter to him, pressing his pelvis, and his semi-erect cock, against her ass.

Heather let out a sigh and closed her eyes. Why did the man have to feel so damn good? To make matters worse, she hadn't had any discomfort during sex with him. The gobs of endometrioses in her uterus often caused that complication, but with Rob, so far anyway, it wasn't a problem.

Anyone else on the planet would think that was awesome. But sending him home, letting him go, would be so much easier if she were having pain. Still, maybe if she turned a little to her left, she'd be able to ease away from him? Okay, yes. That's what she…

For the next hour—but probably only ten minutes—Heather managed to move away. Inch by slowly executed inch, Heather made a clean getaway. Which now sounded and felt like a stupid, childish thing to do. But she couldn't be bothered about that. Right now, she just needed some space to clear her head.

Tiptoeing around the bed, she made her way to her en suite bath and closed herself in. After taking care of her bathroom needs, she stepped in front of the mirror and turned on the cold water.

Without looking at her reflection, Heather bent forward, cupped her hands under the flow of water, and pressed her palms to her cheeks and forehead. The coolness felt like a healing balm to her aching head.

Pulling open the medicine cabinet, she grabbed the bottle of ibuprofen and shook out two, bent and drank from the tap. And Arizona water still tasted like dirt…she definitely needed to get a water treatment and softener system installed.

Shaking her head at her wandering brain, she padded over to the door. Cracking it an inch, she peeked out at the form in her bed. Why was he still here? But more, why didn't he leave last night?

What kind of guy *wanted* to cuddle and sleep over? Ugh, another stupid thought. Some guys liked to cuddle; there was no harm in that. As far as the sleeping over went, Heather had to admit, they were both no less than dog tired, and he likely didn't want to make the drive home after the mind-blowing sex. That was all there was to it.

And Lord above, the sex had been mind-altering. A chill raced through her body…not from the air-conditioning. Regardless, or in an effort to pretend her body wasn't reacting to the memory of how he'd brought her so high she thought she might shatter, Heather grabbed her robe hanging on her bathroom door and slid it on.

Being as quiet as she could, she opened the bathroom door and moved over to the easy chair in the corner. She could just leave the bedroom, go lie down on the couch. She needed space, distance, but not that much space and distance.

After sitting, she pulled her knees up against her chest and stared at him. In her bed.

Her bed.

Sleeping.

So soundly, it was as if he belonged right where he was. He didn't, of course. But what if he did? God, why was her mind wandering like this? Thinking things that weren't even a thing? Heather cringed and bit her bottom lip.

She was the definition of fucked-up. No way Rob had any clue she was this much of a head case. He never would've talked to her if he did. As it was, she was "that one girl" from high school everyone hated. Or loved. More like...loved to hate.

Except that was the least of it. There was so much more—

"Come back to bed, Heather."

With wide eyes, Heather straightened, as if a metal rod had fused her spine. Guess he wasn't sleeping so soundly after all.

Rob pulled the covers back on Heather's side of the bed, then patted the mattress. "Come on, beautiful. It's early still."

First instinct was to rise and do as he asked. But she managed to get a choke hold on that little idea and anything else that might require an intervention. And Heather's side of the bed? As if the other side was his? So stupid. But maybe it was his side? Fucking hell, what was she doing, trying make herself more miserable?

He shifted, rose on an elbow, and extended his hand. "Heather? C'mon, baby. Get out of your head and come sleep some more. You'll feel better. I promise."

How the hell did he know?

Goddammit it!

Ugh! He was probably right.

Okay, he was for sure right. But, whatever. Yes, she needed more sleep. Who didn't? Bottom line: getting back in bed with him, letting him hold her, curl against her, make her feel safe, was fucking terrifying. And absolutely not what she needed.

So then why did she want to go to him so badly?

Because.

Just...because.

She didn't need it—him. But she wanted him. Want and need were two different things. And some wants weren't logical. This was definitely one of those things. Drawing in a deep breath, Heather got to her feet, untied her robe, and let the soft material slide off her shoulders and fall to the floor. With another deep breath, she focused on taking one step at a time, making her way to her bed...

And into Rob's waiting arms.

* * * *

Rob wrapped his arms around Heather and pulled her against his chest. "I gotta say, you have some fantastic A/C in this place."

She let out a soft chuckle. "Thanks, it's new."

Her warm breath skipped over his upper pec muscle, and a chill zipped down his spine. He slid his palm down her back. "The A/C? Hope you got good deal. Not a cheap appliance to have to buy in AZ, that's for sure."

She giggled. "No, the whole house is new."

He'd already known her home was a new build, but teasing her served as a distraction to whatever dark place she'd gone in her head. "In that case, I really do hope you got a good deal. I mean a whole house? Shew... the market is good here, but that's an even bigger appliance to buy."

Heather tipped her head back, a perfect grin adorning her lips. "You're teasing me, aren't you?"

"No, ma'am. I'm completely cereal." Barely able to keep his expression blank, he squeezed her side. "Houses and appliances are really cereal subjects, young lady. I'd never tease about something like that."

She rolled her eyes. "Uh-huh. Sure."

"Oh no! First you doubt yourself, then you're doubting me? When I'm being completely cereal, even? Pfft...where does it end, bombshell?"

Now he got a full laugh from her, and Rob couldn't help but laugh with her. After a moment, she shifted forward and gave him a soft kiss. Rob closed his eyes and let the warmth from her sweet lips spread though his body.

He pulled her tighter against him, and the feel of her soft curves melting against his body kicked his desire wide awake. Rob could take her again, have more mind-numbing sex, but somehow, he knew that doing that wouldn't get him the closeness he was seeking to find with her. The sex was amazing, unbelievable even, but this intimacy was even better.

Drawing back from his lips, Heather tucked her head under his chin and let out a soft moan.

Relief that maybe she'd let go of whatever had been plaguing her a few minutes ago spread through him, and he stroked her back. "Better?"

"Were you this funny when we were kids?"

Rob blinked, reconciling her abrupt change in subject as he focused on the light filtering through the sheer curtains. Obviously, she wasn't willing to so much as admit she hadn't been in a good place a few minutes ago. There was no point in forcing her to either. Rob sighed through his nose. "Maybe? I guess that depends on who you ask."

She smoothed her palm down his shoulder to his upper arm. "Right, but you had friends, I'm sure. Did they think you were funny?"

Rob shrugged. "I guess they did? I mean, it's not like I set out to entertain them with my wit and cheesy lines."

After another little laugh, she pressed a soft kiss to his collarbone. "What about your parents?"

Parents? Well, damn, the last thing he wanted to do was talk about his parents while lying in bed next to a gorgeous woman who he might still be totally infatuated with. Plus, naked. "Uh, I mean, of course, Mom thinks I'm hilarious. Dad thinks I'm a smart-ass. Not so much anymore, just old habits I suppose. It's all in good nature though."

"Well, if it counts for anything, I think you're funny." Heather smoothed her hand around his waist to his lower back.

Tingles erupted in the wake of wherever she touched him. It was wonderful, and annoying, and amazing, and torture...and Rob didn't want her to ever stop putting her hands on him.

Letting out a sigh, he trailed his fingers up her spine and then stroked the back of her head with his palm. Her hair was soft against the rough skin of his hand. Hell, every part of her was soft and sweet, warm and tender. A dichotomy to what she was in high school.

Though, all of that shit when they were kids could've been a front. Maybe she was always like this, sweet and soft, but similar to many teens, she wore a facade? There was no way for him to know, unless she opened up to him, confided in whatever the truth of her life really was.

Except, trying to dig into that part of her might prove disastrous. Heather wasn't just any woman, she was the woman he spent most of sophomore and all of junior and senior year secretly in love with. Heather Winters wielded a power over him he was sure could be turned against him. Especially if she turned out to be just as cruel as she was all those years ago.

Of course, it was possible that she might not even be aware of the power she held at all. Or that she'd never use it in cruel ways, or to harm him. There was just no telling which. So, yeah, Rob needed to be careful. Proceed with caution at every turn would be the course to follow where his blonde bombshell was concerned.

"I meant to ask you this earlier—" She yawned. "Excuse me. Sorry. Anyway, you're a K9 officer?"

"It's five thirty in the morning, beautiful. You're allowed to yawn." He pressed a kiss to the top of her head. "Yes, I'm a K9 officer."

"I love dogs."

Rob stared blankly into the dim light from the windows. Of all the things she could say to him, she had to say the one thing that was pretty much like shooting Cupid's arrow straight into his heart. She loved dogs. A goddamn direct hit.

She.

Loved.

Dogs.

Fuuuuck! He was so screwed.

Chapter 12

Heather ducked her head under the hot spray of the shower and rinsed the shampoo suds from her hair. She'd slept nearly all day. But worse, she'd done it with Rob beside her. Cuddled up against each other—as if the two of them hadn't a care in the world, and definitely no responsibilities.

They just…slept.

All. Day.

Together.

Side by side. And in each other's arms.

Heather groaned and reached for the conditioner. It was wonderful, true. But it was also horrifying. And stupid. And irresponsible. And…

God, cuddling while sleeping was by far the most intimate act two human beings could partake in. She'd partaken, all right. And done so only knowing Rob a few hours.

Though, he knew her.

Sort of…

Technically he didn't really *know* her, since they weren't friends in high school, or even acquaintances, so none of that really counted. But he *knew* who she was, so that had to count for something, right?

Except—*ahhh no. That really didn't count either, soooo there was no point in using it as an excuse. Ugh!*

Heather blew out an exasperated breath and poured a generous amount of body wash onto a cloth. Smoothing the creamy soap over her chest, she tried to get a grip on her neurotic and beyond irritated brain.

She was selfish. Very selfish. Because even though she knew it was wrong to open this intimate door with him, she wasn't sure she was ready to close it yet. When it came down to it, Heather had no business letting anyone get this close to her, not with what a fucked-up hot mess she was.

She'd wanted it though. In a big way. Maybe even needed it too.

So, instead of sending Rob home, they were going to order dinner from Grubhub, eat it while sitting on her brand-new sofa while watching a movie on her new fifty-five-inch flat-screen.

Date night at home was what Rob kept calling it. God help her. How the hell had she gone from a one-night stand to let out a little steam and have fun, to a date night in less than twenty-four hours? Hot mess mode in full effect. Pathetic. Totally and utterly pathetic.

Truth be told, the sex had been out of this world, but now she was feeling the effects of it internally. Endometriosis had a way of either making sex painful during, or dishing out a nice amount of deep discomfort after. She'd take the "after" versus the "during" any day, but yeah, she was feeling it now.

Heather finished in the shower and wrapped up in a towel. After stepping into the steamy air of her bathroom, she dried off and glanced around her closet. May as well pull out all the stops and go au naturel. See if she could maybe scare him off.

Yoga pants. T-shirt. Fluffy socks.

Yeah, baby. Talk about sexy. Plus, it was more comfortable on her tummy. Satisfied with her chosen attire, Heather pulled the towel off her head and combed out her hair. Rather than blowing it dry, she pulled it up in a ponytail. Makeup was definitely a no go.

Blowing out a breath, Heather flipped off the light and headed through her bedroom and then down the hall to her family room. As she reached the entrance to the kitchen and great room area, the doorbell rang.

Rob sprang up from the couch, and as he got moving, he caught a glimpse of her—by way of a double take—and stopped mid-stride and smiled. "Well, hey there, beautiful."

Yeah, he was insane.

She dipped her chin. "Grab the door. I'll get the plates."

He strode toward her, all lean and sexy. "Deal."

Hooking her around the waist, he bent and planted a kiss on her lips. As he swept his tongue inside her mouth, she moaned. And melted. How could she not? Fucking hell, he was an outstanding kisser. It was as if every nerve in her body came awake, dancing under her skin the minute his lips touched hers.

Rob let out a sexy-as-hell deep moan and pulled away. "So, so sweet. Don't think I'll ever get enough."

Well, damn, she'd heard that before. Heather licked her lips as he strutted off on his way to her front door. He'd get enough, eventually. She'd be foolish to actually believe anything different than that.

Clearing her throat, she moved to the cupboards and pulled down two plates, then grabbed silverware, serving spoons, and two linen napkins. Setting everything on the center island, she moved to the fridge.

Rob came back in and set the bag of food down near the plates.

She glanced over. "Beer or wine?"

"Hmm, how about water?"

"That works." She grabbed a water bottle for him and a bottle of beer for her. "Ranch or Italian vinaigrette?"

"Both. I mix them."

"Ew. Really?" She pulled both bottles of dressing from the fridge door.

"No ew. Yes, really." He hip-bumped her once she was beside him—which, due to the height difference was more like his hip, her waist, but whatever—and shot her a sexier-than-sin grin. "School's in session for you, bombshell. Just sayin'."

A laugh escaped that she was helpless to stop as she set his water bottle in front of him. "School? When did cops become teachers?"

"Let's see." Rob pulled the lids off their entrees and added servings to each plate. "Ever since forever, is when."

"It's true what they say then? Cops are *really* smart people." She grabbed the container of salad and dished some onto their plates. "I mean, I can definitely tell by your proper use of the English language."

He grinned. "We can learn you civilians real good, uh-huh."

She laughed again. "Nuh-uh. No sir. I don't need no learning here. Especially about salad dressing." Heather picked up the bottle. "Ranch is a thing of gods. Italian falls second every time. I'm certain that mixing them would be a sin."

"Roman or Greek?"

She grabbed a tall glass from a cabinet, glancing at him. "Huh?"

"'A thing of the gods.' What ones? Roman or Greek?"

Heather frowned for a moment, before realizing what the hell he meant. Moving back to the island, she poured her beer into the glass. "Clever, Officer Rob. Very clever."

"Only around you." He winked and then did just what he mentioned. Mixed ranch and Italian dressing on his salad. When he was done, he picked up his plate, napkin and silverware. "You ready for our date night at home?"

Eyes wide, and convinced he was not only clever, but maybe a little crazy too, she sipped her beer, swallowed, and set the glass down. "I think so, yes."

He dipped his chin and tilted his head to the side. "Oh, yeah. There's that doubt, I mean 'cautiously realistic,' aka bad habit you have, again. Tsk. Tsk. How about you couch that while we break in your new couch and television?"

Heather stifled her grin. "Yes, sir."

"Mmmm." He bent and pressed a quick kiss to her forehead. "Good girl. That's what I want to hear."

A thrill zipped down Heather's spine and arrowed straight to her clit. Phew, the man could give her that stern look all day long, but if he did, she'd be parading around in wet panties the whole time. And the "good girl" thing just added fuel to an already blazing inferno.

Heather set down her glass and gathered up her dinner, napkin, and silverware and made her way to the couch. After retrieving his water bottle and her beer, she sat beside him. Both of them rested their feet on her coffee table and placed their plates on their laps.

Rob turned on the television and cable box. "Any suggestions of what you want to watch tonight?"

She took another sip of her beer. "No clue. You?"

"Hmm. What's your favorite movie?"

"You mean of all time?" She cut a meatball in half with her fork. "I honestly don't know. Favorites are so hard for me. I can never narrow one down."

"Totally get that. Favorite anything is hard for me too. How about when we were kids? What were some of your favorite movies from then?"

"Oooh. Let me think." She scooped a mouthful of baked macaroni and a chunk of meatball into her mouth. "There were so many from then."

"Try and narrow it down to your top five." He shoved a forkful of ranch- and vinaigrette-coated salad into his mouth. "Mmm. Heaven," he said around a mouthful of lettuce.

Heather laughed. It was amazing to see just how comfortable the man was in his own skin. Oddly, she felt nearly as comfortable. Not talking-with-a-mouthful-of-food comfortable yet, but damn close. Maybe even closer than she thought. "Okay, top five. But it might take me the entire meal to come up with them."

"Should we Google movies from '99 to 2003?"

"I was just thinking that!" Eyes wide, Heather pointed her fork at him. "Nice! We're already sharing a brain?"

"I'm not sharing anything." She laughed and bumped his shoulder with hers. "Get out of my head, will you?"

"Not a chance, bombshell. Not a damn chance." Rob leaned over and gave her a brief peck on the lips. "Mmm, that pasta tastes good. Not as you good as you, but still."

Heather felt her cheeks get warm. The compliments and attention he gave her was so contrary to what she'd grown accustomed to in the past five-plus years, it made hearing them feel almost uncomfortable.

Sad, very sad. Heather wanted to take those kind, sweet, and sincere compliments from him to heart. Every one of them.

She just wasn't sure she knew how anymore.

* * * *

Rob scanned the lists of movies from 1999 to 2003 on the IMDB site from his phone. Talk about a shit ton of films. "Okay, yeah. Lots to choose from. This could be dangerous ground we're treading on."

Heather smiled, lips pressed together as she chewed. She swallowed and sipped her beer. "Okay, so pick three from each year."

"Three? Seriously? Awfully confident now, aren't you." He laughed. "Okay, here's three from '99."

She placed her hand on his arm. "Wait. Wait. Pick one chick flick, one comedy, and one drama."

"Demanding too? Phew." He shook his head. "I've created a monster over here." Rob laughed again, loving the easy banter with her. Also loving how she giggled and smiled each time he pulled her pigtails.

"Demanding isn't my strong suit. How am I doing so far?" She smiled and forked in a mouthful of noodles.

"Oh, I see. Well, it's early yet. You'll have to wait a little longer before I'm able to assess you." Rob took a mouthful of his ravioli.

"I see. Well, Officer Rob, please tell me the three. The suspense is killing me."

He sipped his water. "Okay, I have another idea. You ready for it?"

"Hit me." She dug her fork into her pasta.

"We pick three movies from each year. We put them on a list, and then twice, maybe three times a week, we have date night at home until we finish the list." Rob forked up some of his salad.

Knowing he was risking freaking her out, Rob chewed and watched the expression on her face go from curious to fear, maybe? Then back to curious, then confusion? Holy shit, what a sight it was seeing all those emotions, plus a few he couldn't label, working through her brain.

"Well, I guess?" She sipped her beer. "I mean, I guess that could be fun, right?"

Rob's eyes went wide. "Oh no! Cautiously realistic, again? So soon?"

"Whatever." She rolled her eyes and forked up some salad.

He laughed. "I see how it is." Unlocking his phone, he glanced at the list for '99. "Okay, let's see. Chick flick, hmm. *10 Things I Hate About You*? Oooh, wait, *Girl, Interrupted*."

She set her fork down. "Hang on a second, just because *Girl, Interrupted* had women in it does not mean it was a chick flick."

Now it was Rob's turn to roll his eyes. He knew she was right, but teasing her was too tempting. "Okay, well fine. Then what's your definition of a chick flick?"

"Seriously? Are you that much of a guy?" She scooped up a meatball.

"Last time I checked, and considering you spent last night up close and personal with my manhood, we both know I'm a guy." Rob ate a large chunk of ravioli.

Heather busted up laughing. "Did you just say 'manhood' as in, your dick?"

"Damn right." Leaning to the side, he brushed his lips over the hair covering her ear. "You know I'm all guy, and my manhood is all about your sweet, chick flick spots."

She let out a soft exhale. "I guess I can't deny how much I enjoyed your manhood."

Nuzzling her neck, Rob let the scent of her skin and hair seep into his lungs. "Still need you to tell me what defines a chick flick."

Heather cupped the back of her head in her palm. "Romance. A love story. And a happy ending."

He slid her hair away from her neck and ran the tip of his nose over the shell of her ear. "Does there always have to be a happy ending?"

"Yes." She let out another soft breath. "Of course."

"Got it." Rob pulled back. "See? All I need is just a little information and I'll always get you what you need."

Heather's eyes were soft, and she blinked once, all slow and sexy, before taking a sip of her beer. Rob's "manhood" went rod-hard in a nanosecond, and the need to adjust the stiff length in his jeans nearly overwhelmed him. He cleared his throat. "Yeah, okay. Just so you know, dinner. Then movie. Then I fuck you."

Heather's eyes went wide before a devious little grin arched the corners of her mouth. Rob glanced at her lips and groaned. Yeah, he was definitely going to fuck between those fine lips later too.

God help him, she had lust pouring through his system like a fire hose on an open hydrant. Clearing his throat once more, desperate to regain some of his threadbare control over himself, Rob tore his gaze away and glanced at his phone screen. "*Notting Hill.*"

"Yes!" She brought her hands together and pressed them to her chest. "*Loved* that movie."

He nodded. "Perfect. All right, now a comedy…let's see."

Heather leaned toward him and peered at his phone. "*American Pie.* Hands down, best comedy back then." She smiled.

Rob laughed and yanked his phone away. "I thought I was picking."

"Oh, don't be silly." She reached for his phone, but he pulled it away before she could grab it. "Hey! No fair. We're both picking. Aren't we?"

He laughed, dodging another attempt from her to grab his phone. "Hold up, you always change the rules in the middle of the game?"

Then, the most fucked-up thing happened. Heather pouted. She fucking pouted those sweet lips of hers, and everything inside Rob went soft. Except for his dick. That stayed rock-hard. Damn…

Rob schooled his features, doing the best he could to appear unaffected. He doubted it was working but still, he had to try. "That's not going to work on me, bombshell." *Fuck, it's totally working.* "If you think you can just pout and get what you want because you look cute and sexy, all wrapped in one gorgeous package, then you are sorely mistaken." *I swear on my life, you look at me like you are right now, any time of the day and night, and I'll give you anything you want.*

Jesus, he was fucked.

"Okay fine. You win." Heather picked through some of the lettuce on her plate with her fork before she looked back at him and tipped her head to the side. "You know, there were a whole bunch of nice things packed into that elaborate explanation for why you don't know how to share your toys."

Rob gasped and then, unable to hold back, laughed. "Share my toys?"

"Yep." She took another bite. Mouth full and chewing, she said, "Not very nice."

Rob laughed harder. God, he liked her. A lot…so much more than he ever expected he would. The urge to confess his feelings welled up like high tide during a hurricane, but somehow, someway, he managed to hold his tongue. Instead he bumped shoulders with her. "Would you forgive me if I said I was going to pick *American Pie* anyway?"

She sipped her beer and shrugged a shoulder. "Maybe."

"Tough crowd." Rob chuckled. "Guess I better pick a really good drama then." He held up his phone, perusing the list. "Wait, do you want to pick it?"

She stuck her tongue out at him. "Nope."

Rob laughed again, couldn't help it. But then the most amazing thing happened, Heather laughed too. Rob shook his head with a smile. These first moments together. They were easy. The banter. The volleying back and forth. All of it, easy and right.

In truth, he didn't care what movie they watched, or for that matter, if they watched any movie at all. Rob was just happy—actually he was downright giddy and elated and now suffering a case of the serious feels just to be sitting beside her.

Eating dinner with her.

Laughing with her.

Having this time together to just be… Not that he knew for sure, but something told Rob it was what she needed.

Chapter 13

Rob pulled up in front of Heather's house and killed the engine in his patrol truck. Taking a moment, he stared out the passenger window at her front door, as well as the reflection from the hall lights she had on.

Their first official date night had been the night before, and, of course, he'd stayed over. In fact, aside from the short time he'd left her place to go home and check on Tricks, Rob hadn't left her house since running into her Thursday night at the Whiskey Barrel.

Unfortunately, Saturday started his work week, so he'd been forced to leave early that morning in order to get a few things done before his shift started at noon. Plus, he was already pushing it being away from Tricks for so long. His canine had a dog door to get into the backyard when nature called, and a large self-waterer and feeder, so there were no worries there, but still, his partner in the back seat got lonely too.

Instead of going back home, Rob was back at the scene of the crime—aka, exactly where he wanted to be. He'd texted back and forth with her on and off throughout the day, just checking in. Saying hi, nothing too serious. Aside from the minor errands she'd gotten handled while he was working, she'd planned to go to the gym later tonight, which was something she apparently did often. Less people there, which was how he felt too.

He checked his watch; nearly eleven p.m. Lucky for him, he hadn't had a lot of paperwork to get done, else it'd be closer to midnight and she maybe would've headed to the gym anyway.

During one of their text exchanges, he'd suggested they take a run around her housing complex instead of the treadmill at the gym. There was a nice trail that led through and around the perimeter of her neighborhood. Plus, she could meet Tricks, as the dog would come along for the run too.

Heather had agreed, and Rob had been…well, he'd been like a teenager to where his excitement level was possibly, maybe, probably a little bit over the top. More like stupidly over the top. Jesus, he was hooked already.

With a sigh, he glanced in the back seat at the dog. "You ready, partner?" Tricks sneezed, then licked his chops. Rob chuckled. "Yeah, I know. I'm hungry too. But first, you meet Heather. Then we run. *Then* we eat."

Tricks harrumphed/grumbled a low bark and then sneezed again. Rob grabbed his duffel bag, angled out of the truck. Shifting, he opened Tricks's door. After the dog hopped down from the back seat onto the street, Rob led him around the patrol truck to the sidewalk and removed his police harness.

The harness was the main thing that let Tricks know it was time to work. But when the harness was off, his partner became more like a pet rather than a canine officer of the law. Not that a police dog was ever not a police dog, they just knew when it was time to work and when it wasn't. Harness off meant off-duty. Simple.

Rob squatted down so he was eye level with the animal, smoothed his palm over Tricks's head, and continued down his back. "All right, listen up. Be a good boy. Mind your manners, and I'm sure she's going to love you."

He held his palm out, and Tricks placed his paw in it.

Rob wrapped his fingers around the canine's paw. "I'm serious. I know you're going to love her too. Believe me, she's something else. Just don't be nervous. Act natural."

One ear flopped down, his big head tipped to the side, panting. Damn dog almost looked like he was smiling. Rob chuckled and straightened. "I guess that's as natural as a dog can get. Let's go."

Walking up her driveway and the brick path to her front door, Rob ignored the nervous energy bouncing through him. He knew he should probably slow his roll with her, maybe not be so eager to see her. But, why? He knew what he wanted, and he wasn't a man who was interested in wasting time.

It'd been years since he'd had a serious relationship, but he'd dated plenty since, and yeah, even had a few flings over the years. But he didn't play games. If he wasn't interested, he didn't lead people on.

Though he'd been really into a handful of women over the years, none compared to the way he was intrigued by Heather. Maybe it was his past infatuation with her, or maybe it was just the way she captivated him now.

He couldn't be sure, and he'd be a fool not to wonder. When it came down to it, maybe it was both things. Their past and their present.

That could be okay too.

* * * *

Nervous energy bounced around Heather's mind and body like some sort of supersonic ping-pong ball. Her one-night stand had turned into a three-day affair. Or maybe it was two days and this was their third? She'd lost track. Point was, they'd left one-night-stand territory days ago.

And the sex? Holy saints in heaven and all the fallen angels in hell, the sex had been *unbelievable.* Rob had done things to her last night, after their date night at home, that she'd been praying he'd do Thursday night but hadn't.

Case in point: her ass cheeks were no longer pink with palm prints from the spankings he'd given her, but they sure as hell felt like it. Could a girl get a hallelujah? Because, yeah, that had been all that and a bag of chips. Plus dip.

A bolt of lust zipped through her at the memory, tightening her stomach. At the sound of a car door closing, Heather was yanked from her lust-filled thoughts and rushed to the window. She pulled the curtain aside. Letting out a slow breath, she zeroed in on the police SUV parked *right* in front of her house.

Hard to miss the damn thing. And, jeez, what the hell were the neighbors going to think was going on at her house? Of course, Kim would know *exactly* what was going on and with who.

Shit. Heather watched as his tall, lean figure came up the driveway and continued along her walkway toward her front door—his very large, nearly all-black police dog by his side like an animal shadow.

And then the doorbell rang.

Heather jumped. Which was stupid because, duh, it wasn't like the bell ringing was a surprise. She was just so far into her thoughts that she was, in fact, startled by it…. "So stupid."

Heather stepped back from the window and rushed to the door. Swinging it wide, she was greeted by man and canine giving her their own special brand of puppy dog eyes. Between Rob's gorgeous face and his dog's adorable floppy ears, Heather forgot all about her apprehension and fears and practically melted into a puddle of goo.

"Hey there, beautiful." He extended his hand down toward the dog. "May I introduce you to Tricks?"

She'd never owned a dog but had always wanted one. Something was different about the animal sitting so intently beside his owner. The intelligence she saw in this canine's dark brown eyes told her he was so much more than an average dog. Logically, he had to be above average since he was a police dog, but still.

She glanced at Rob, then back at the dog. "Can I pet him?"

"Of course."

Gazing down, Heather took in the animal's clear eyes, long snout, thick chest, and dark fur. The only gold on him were his legs. She'd never seen a nearly all-back German shepherd.

His coloring was gorgeous. But, wow, his eyes told a whole story to her. Amazing.

Rob squatted down. "Go ahead, he won't hurt you."

"Okay." Shoving her reluctance aside, Heather bent forward and raised her hand, keeping it palm down, and let the dog smell her knuckles. After he did, she smoothed her fingers along the top of his head, between his ears. "He's so beautiful. And big."

Tricks blinked a slow blink and let out a little moan, as if thanking her for the kind words. She let out a low chuckle. Either that or he was being a ham. Either way, it was pretty damn cute.

Heather had never been close enough to a service dog to know if they all had a look in their eyes like Tricks did, so there was no way for her to know for sure. But she was willing to bet what she saw was particular to Tricks, something special about him. There was something special about his owner too.

"So, you think you want to let us in and then we can get ready for that run?"

Heather's cheeks grew hot, and she straightened. "Oh my God! I'm so sorry." She stepped back so they could both enter. "Please come in."

Rob moved forward, and Tricks moved with him. After dropping his gym bag on the floor, he wrapped an arm around her waist and rubbed his nose over hers. "It's all good, baby."

"He really is beautiful." Heather gazed up at Rob and once again fell under his spell. She glanced at his lips....

"Mmm, yeah. I missed yours too. Gimme." Rob bent and pressed a soft kiss to her lips.

When he swept his tongue inside her mouth, Heather moaned and pressed her body tighter against him. Instant heat and lust sped through her, making her clit tingle. Did they really have to go for a run? Maybe they could get their workout in via sex...in every room of her house—

But, wait, what would the dog do when they were having sex? Would they lock him out of the room? No, that would make her feel bad. Would he stay in there with them? Okay, no, that was just weird.

Heather pulled back from the kiss as a gallon of ice water pulsed through her veins, effectively drowning her lust. She cleared her throat and patted his chest, but he didn't let her go. "That was nice. But I think we better get ready for that run. Don't want to fall behind in my goals."

"Goals?"

"Yes. Five miles."

"Five? Dayum, girl!" With a big smile, he bent and gave her another quick peck before stepping back from her. "All right, let's go."

"Tricks is coming too, right?"

"Absolutely. Just need to grab his water bottle." Rob bent to his bag.

"He has his own water bottle? That's sweet." She felt something wet touch her fingers, and as she pulled them away, she glanced down at the dog, who'd moved right next to her. She smiled. "Hi there. I think he licked me."

Rob looked up from his crouched position. "More likely he nosed you."

Heather frowned. "Nosed me?"

He straightened and gave her one of his sexy-as-sin smiles. "Bombshell, you act like you've never been around dogs before. His nose is wet. He touched your hand with it. No biggie."

Her frown deepened, and her face got hot as embarrassment crept along her spine. "Sorry. I didn't know." She shrugged. "I love dogs, but I've never had one before. Can't say I've spent a lot of time with them either."

"For real?"

"Yes, for real." She forced her mouth to not frown but couldn't manage to swallow the unexpected lump filling her throat.

Rob's brow creased. He took her hand in his and pulled her to him. "Hold up, no need to be sorry for that." Rob caressed her bottom lip with his thumb. "No need to frown either, baby. So, you don't know dogs. No big deal." He pressed a gentle kiss to her lips. "Tricks is awesome, and he'll break you in good. In fact, he'll spoil you for all other dogs going forward."

Heather melted from his sweet words, his soft touch, and tender kiss. She closed her eyes and licked her lips, savoring the taste of him. If she wasn't careful, she was totally going to fall for him. And his dog.

Gazing at Rob again, she let herself release a breath. "I'd like that."

Rob pressed a kiss to her forehead. "Me too." Then he swatted her ass before stepping away. "Let's go, woman. We got a goal to make and it's barely cooled off outside."

Heather chuckled and rubbed her butt cheek. "Tease."

"Oh, trust me, I don't tease. You ought to know that after the last two nights."

"This is true." Heather slipped her cell phone in its armband case and secured it around her upper arm. "Any preference for music?"

"Nope. Whatever you got works. I'll be behind you."

She stepped outside, and he followed. "Behind me? Why's that?"

He closed the door, and Tricks sat down beside Rob's feet. "Aren't you going to set the alarm and lock this?"

"No to the alarm. Yes to the lock. I have the app on my phone to auto-lock it."

"You should set the alarm too. But I like that you got one of those new smart lock systems. Brains and bombshell sexy." He grinned. "Double whammy right there." Raising his arms over his head, he bent side to side, stretching.

Heather shook her head and grinned. "You're funny. I don't set the alarm when I leave. I set it when I'm home at night, and especially when I go to sleep. Call me crazy, but if someone breaks in, they can take what they want from me. It's just stuff. All replaceable. But I don't want fools doing that when I'm alone in there sleeping. I'm not so replaceable, you know?"

"Definitely not."

"Glad you agree." She tapped her phone screen and locked the door and then pulled up iTunes. She'd just have to go with shuffle rather than one of the typical playlists. The songs she usually listened to while running might actually bum Rob out. Might bum the dog out too. She glanced up at him. "Anyway, why are you running behind me?"

He was staring at her, a look in his eyes she couldn't quite decipher. All she knew was that it was soft and it made her insides feel warm…and in the next moment, the expression was gone, replaced with a flirty grin.

"Not ashamed to admit, it's so I can stare at your perfect ass the whole time." Rob did a few more stretches.

Heather blurted a laugh and bent forward and touched her toes. "You didn't get enough staring in last night?"

"Bombshell, I will *never* get enough of your perfect ass. Ever." He looked down at Tricks. "Watch, she doubts me, partner, but eventually, she'll get it."

Tricks harrumphed, and his ears perked up.

"Yep, exactly what I'm saying." Rob glanced at her. "He agrees with me."

Heather smiled as heat spilled through her body. He was sweet to her…even when ogling and talking about her ass. It wasn't derogatory. He wasn't objectifying her. Deep in her gut, she knew his compliments were rooted in sincerity.

What struck her and made her heart go soft was that he was sweet with his canine too. Jeez, what would this man be like with babies and kids? Instantly, her smile evaporated and another lump filled her throat.

God, when was she ever going to learn? Babies, kids...they were blessings that happened for other people. Not for her. Never for her. Yes, Rob would have kids someday, for sure. And yes, he'd be an incredible, sweet, fun, and loving father. Not a doubt in her mind.

Unfortunately, Heather wouldn't be the woman he had them with.

Chapter 14

"This is one of my favorite lunch places to eat in Chandler." Rob angled out the driver's side, came around his 4Runner, and opened the passenger door for her. "It's super healthy too."

Heather stepped out and smoothed the front of her white sundress. "The menu looked really good when I checked it online."

Six days of seeing her and Rob still couldn't get enough. With a smile, he took her by the hand and crossed the street. "Checking up on me now?"

"Do you need checking up on?"

"Ooh, feisty today, I see."

She laughed. "Nah, I was just curious."

"That's a shame. I was going to suggest an appropriate punishment for the feisty." He opened the door into the restaurant.

Heather's eyes were wide, and she paused in front of him. "Oh? What sort of punishment?"

"Have I told you how pretty that dress looks on you?"

"Yes. And you're very charming, but you're also avoiding my question." She smiled and leaned into him, rose on tiptoe and brushed her nose over his.

Cute, so fucking cute. Without another thought, Rob hooked his arm around her waist and pulled her tight against him. Letting his lips graze her ear, he whispered, "How about you move your fine ass inside and we can order, and then I'll tell you."

She pressed her palm to his side. "Yes, sir."

Oh, yeah. Totally in sync, and his dick just got hard. Eating, then fucking her when he got her back to his place when they were done. He needed to have a full meal because he planned on giving both of them a workout and burning a whole ton of calories.

Before she stepped away and did as he asked, the soft scent of her perfume filled his senses, making him feel a little drunk on her. Jesus, she was an amazing submissive. Not that he was some sort of professional Dominant by any means, but still. Whatever he asked her to do, she did. And whatever he wanted to do to her, sexually, she accepted.

It was as if neither of them could get enough of each other, but more, there seemed to be no sexual boundaries. At all. Last night, she'd shown up at his place with a flogger. He never used one before but was all for spanking her with it. However, that wasn't enough for Heather. No, she'd asked him, very sweetly, if he'd also spank her tits and hips and ass, and even her cunt with it.

Mind. Blown.

Rock-hard cock.

So, yeah, he'd done all that, *gladly*. He'd started with her ass, and when she turned over, he'd swatted her tits. Fuck's sake, her nipples, which were already hard, had grown even tighter with the first hit. By the time he slapped the suede strips down on her cunt, she'd come hard. Arching and moaning and writhing on the bed.

Mind blown. Again.

When they were both sweating, and she was panting and whimpering with skin a pretty shade of pink from the lashings he'd given her, he set the flogger aside and lay on the bed. Pulling her trembling body over his, she straddled him and rode his prick until they both exploded.

Fuck, the whole session had been out of this world intense, and hard-core as hell. Rob had played a lot in his past, but with Heather it was so much more.

The whole time he was buried inside her cunt, her eyes were glazed over, like she was in some sort of trance. Though that didn't keep her from moving her body on him in a way so much more erotic than he could've ever dreamed up in his best fantasies.

Just thinking about it now had him wanting to drag her out of the sandwich shop and back to his place.

"Can I get the Zen Bowl, please? No onion though." She glanced down at the cooler. "Just a regular drip coffee." She looked back at Rob. "You know what you're getting?"

He cleared his throat and moved beside her. "Mmhmm." Rob placed his hand on her lower back. Touching her was something he couldn't not do. Hell, there was no reason not to. "I'll take the Balanced Bowl, with steak, please. And just a water for my drink."

After paying for their lunch, Heather fixed her coffee at the side station. Rob led them over to a table situated against a long booth bordering the entire sidewall of the restaurant, two- and four-person tables arranged in front of it. He indicated for her to sit on the booth side, and rather than taking the seat across from her, he slid next to her.

"This is a really cool building. I had no idea it was here." She glanced around, a sweet smile on her face.

"Agreed. There are photos over there and down the hall of what it used to look like. It was a bank originally, I think. Check out the vault door over there." As he placed his palm on the top of her leg, he motioned with his chin toward the glassed-off area. With his fingertip, he traced little circles on her inner thigh.

Heather sucked in a sharp breath, jerking her gaze back to him when he traced a little higher. Her golden, toned legs were so soft, he couldn't help himself. When standing, her sundress came mid-thigh, but when sitting, it rose a bit higher. Lucky him.

He gave her a grin. "Was there anything you wanted to do today? Any errands you need to run?"

She licked her lips. "Well, I was thinking of maybe going to check out some more living room furniture."

"More furniture?"

"I want a chair for that one corner. Maybe for reading...or something."

Their food was delivered, and Rob moved his hand from her thigh long enough to spread his napkin on his lap and grab his fork. After taking a bite, he placed his palm back on her thigh. "That makes sense. Something really comfy would be nice."

She cleared her throat. "I think so too." She sipped her coffee and then forked up a mound of fluffy scrambled eggs from her bowl.

"That looks delicious." Rob watched her lips as she chewed and slid his fingers a little higher. Keeping his voice low, he bent to her ear. "Spread your legs, just a little for me, beautiful."

With a little moan, probably only he could hear, Heather chewed her food but did what he asked. Fuck, he was in serious heaven. Rob forked up another mouthful of steak. Never before had he done something so brazen in public. Especially being a cop.

Public sexual indecency was something he'd arrested others for, not something he did. How far would she let him go? Could the couple across from them see under the table? Did he want them to see? Maybe he did....

Okay then. Talk about a fantasy he didn't know he had. Sliding his fingers a little higher, he gently stroked the tender skin at the edge of her panties and bent to her ear again. "Are you wet for me?"

"Yes."

"Is your clit throbbing?"

"Yes." She moaned and took another small bite.

Rob slid his fingertip over her panty-covered clit. The dampness of the fabric had his mouth watering. "Sure you weren't being feisty? The punishment might be worth it."

She cleared her throat. "You know, come to think of it, I was checking up on you. Being a cop and all, anything outside of donuts and coffee would be a huge stretch. I needed to be sure."

Rob laughed and shook his head. "Good one." He stroked once more over her clit before sliding his hand away. Picking up his fork, he took another big bite and took his time chewing. When he'd made her wait at least a couple minutes, sufficiently building her anticipation, he leaned to her ear again. "Get up and go into the ladies' room, take off your panties, then come back here to me."

Heather set down her fork, put her napkin on the table, and got to her feet. Rob watched as she walked away, her skirt swaying in time with the movement of her hips. After drawing in a deep breath, he took a swig of his water.

When she got back, her cunt would be bare for him. Rob wasn't sure if he was going to play with her wet pussy or not. It'd be hard not to. Or maybe he'd have her sit with her legs parted. Only barely though...

God help him, the idea of others seeing what was his aroused him in ways he hadn't anticipated. He drummed his fingers on the table, unable to keep himself still. Excitement coursed through his veins, making him hyperaware of his surroundings.

Fuck, this was so over-the-top he could barely stand it.

Yet, he wanted it. All of it.

* * * *

Heather pressed a wet paper towel to the back of her neck. Sweating was just oh so attractive. Rob was the reason she was sweating, so he couldn't actually complain about it. Not that he would.

Shoot, he'd probably run his tongue along every inch of her skin, claiming he was thirsty for her. And wasn't that just the most amazing thing on the fucking face of the earth? A man who actually *wanted* her? Really and truly all of her?

She honestly hadn't realized how much she'd needed this kind of care from someone. The attention Rob was giving her was like being fed after being starved for days on end. A person could become so hungry eventually, they no longer felt the pangs.

That had been exactly where Heather was before meeting him. But not anymore. And the Dom/sub play? Good God Almighty, she'd died and gone to amateur BDSM heaven. For real. She even had the flogging marks on her skin to prove it.

Heather tossed the paper towel in the trash can and stepped back from the counter. She ran her palms up her hips, pulling her dress up as she did, then, hooking her fingers in the waist of her panties, slid the cotton and lace down to her ankles.

After stepping out of them, she tucked them in her purse.

A thrill zipped down her spine. Heather had never done *anything* like this before. Spanking? Yes. Bound to a bed or chair? Yes. Having her orgasms withheld or forced? Yep, that too. But never, ever, *ever* had she been indecent or naked in public.

Never had she done anything sexual in public either. Except, well, like many, she'd fucked in the back seat of a car as a teenager her fair share of times, but that didn't count. That was not the same as having her pussy bare in public so that strangers could see it. Or more, seeing it while it was played with.

Heat bloomed over her skin, and her heart pounded in her ears. Blowing out a slow breath, she gave herself another moment to dig deep and find an ounce of courage. To say she was nervous would be an understatement. More like fucking terrified was a more realistic description.

Considering her clit was throbbing in time with her pulse, she was also aroused as fuck. And wet, she was beyond wet. Come to think of it, every time she'd been with Rob she soaked right through her panties and stayed that way for the duration. Her body had never been that responsive with anyone else.

Especially her ex-husband. Even when her ex had used the flogger on her, Heather's favorite thing, she hadn't gotten as wet as she was last night with Rob.

Was this what people meant by sexual chemistry? If so, she and Rob had it in spades. It would certainly explain her physical reaction to him pretty much every minute she was next to him.

Or…maybe it was just that she was in her thirties? Didn't people also say that women hit their sexual prime in their thirties? They did, and that was probably it. Honestly, she'd prefer it all be about her hormones and not Rob.

After all, she liked him. And she didn't want to like him. Heather wasn't supposed to like him. She was only supposed fuck him and be on her way. Except, dammit, he was really funny and cute and sexy *and* gave her incredible orgasms.

Every damn time he touched her.

He was probably going to make her come sitting in a sandwich shop in downtown Chandler, Arizona, *for the love of God!* Another thrill zipped down her spine, and her cunt clenched in reaction.

Fuck's sake, she didn't need courage. What she needed was another spanking and an orgasm. What she needed was sitting out there waiting for her. Or his dick was anyway. Because…needing Rob's dick was far safer for her heart than needing *him* personally, or as a person.

Right?

Yes.

Sure.

Right. Heather stifled a groan and rolled her eyes. "Okay, enough self-talk." Turning, she opened the door.

She paused another second and tried to calm her racing heart. *Let's go, lady.* Heather took one step and then another, and as she walked, her inner thighs brushed together. They were coated with the wetness from her arousal. The smooth slide of skin serving only to kick her arousal into overdrive.

Finally reaching their table, Heather sat, tucking her skirt under her ass before she settled on the vinyl booth. "Hi."

"You okay?" Rob rested his palm on her thigh.

Tingles spread across her skin from where he touched her, and every inch of her body felt alive. It was a shocking reminder that she was, in fact, alive and breathing. She just hadn't felt that way in so long she'd forgotten what it was like.

Yes, blood flowed through her veins and air filled her lungs. Her heart was dead yet continued to beat. It'd take a lot more than physical attention and awesome sex to bring that thing back to life.

However, if she were going to be honest, since meeting Rob, life didn't seem so dark anymore. Maybe now it was only a little gray. She smiled and placed her palm atop his. "Actually, yes. I'm okay."

"Good." He leaned in and pressed a kiss to her temple. "Eat before it gets any colder."

"Yes, sir."

"I'm going to refill your coffee for you. On my way back, show me how pretty and pink you are under that dress." Rob gave her temple another kiss, grabbed her coffee and slid out from behind their table.

Tingles broke out between her thighs. Her cunt clenched in little spasms, and her stomach pitched tight. Heather crossed her legs, desperate for some relief. And then uncrossed them, remembering she needed to leave herself exposed for Rob to see.

Staring at his back as he fixed her coffee, anticipation smoldered like a slow burn. He turned and with slow, deliberate steps made his way back to their table. His eyes stayed locked with hers until she watched his gaze travel down, down, down…

The moment he could see her bare pussy, Heather felt it. It was as if that slow burn turned into an inferno.

Rob licked his lips.

Her channel clenched in rapid spasms. Her clit pulsed hard and fast. Fuck, she was going to come just knowing he liked what he saw, and that she was giving it to him. Every part of her was hyperfocused on him. His desire, his pleasure, his needs. And also, what he'd give her as thanks for satisfying all his deepest fantasies.

Pleasing him pleased her. When she gave him whatever he wanted, she got the payoff too. She got the reward, and as such, the release. So Heather would give him this. Her bare cunt…in public. And later, she'd get what she needed.

She'd get fucked, in the best possible way.

* * * *

Rob swallowed past a dry throat and slid into the booth beside her.

She hadn't taken her eyes off him, and until he had to walk around the table to sit, he hadn't stopped looking at her perfect pink pussy. Instantly, he'd gotten hard for her. No way that wasn't going to happen.

Rob looked over at her now. She blinked and then licked her lips. God, this woman. She'd done what he asked. Her cunt was wet and his dick was throbbing. Yeah, *goddamn,* this woman! She'd done *exactly* what he'd asked.

After he adjusted his hard-on as discreetly as he could, he placed his hand on her thigh, his fingers curling on the inside of her leg before he slid his palm up, and up until his pinky grazed her wetness. Rob leaned to her ear. "Fucking gorgeous."

"Thank you." Her voice was low and had gone husky.

Fuck, that was hot too. He shifted so his mouth was close to hers. Close enough to kiss her. "How long can you stand it?"

"As long as you say I have to." Her lips brushed his as she spoke.

Rob snaked out his tongue and touched her top lip before dipping and dragging his top lip over her bottom one. Little tastes, little teases, that's all. But it was a lot. "Leave your legs spread and let's see how long we can both stand it."

She nodded, and with that he gave her a soft but quick kiss. Settling beside her, his pinky grazing her wetness, he picked up his water and took a long drink. After he set it down, he gathered some of his breakfast onto his fork. "So, did you go to college after high school?"

Her eyes went wide, as if the question caught her off guard. Likely, it did. Save for his pinky touching her sweet pussy, it was time to eat and chat. Normal with a good sprinkle of kink added to it. Perfect. She'd get it. He knew she would. He chewed and waited for her to answer.

Heather wiped her mouth with her napkin. "Um, I did. Yes." She sipped her coffee and set it back down. "In Maryland. You?"

"Nope. No college for me. I went for the PD, failed the first physical test, and then spent several months working out, building my strength, endurance and body, before I retested. Obviously, made it that time." Rob smiled and wiggled his pinky, grazing her clit.

Heather's breath hitched.

Rob's dick throbbed.

"What did you major in?" He forked up another bite.

"Nursing. I got my nursing degree, my RN."

"No shit? You're a nurse?"

"*Was* a nurse. I haven't worked in the field in a few years. Don't even have my license in Arizona."

"You going to do that here?"

She shrugged. "Maybe? I haven't decided yet."

He bumped her shoulder with his. "You should. Nurses and cops make awesome couples."

She let out a light chuckle. "No way. Where'd you hear that?"

"Telling you, some think it's doctors and nurses that go together. But, nope, they're wrong. Cops and nurses all the way." He took a swig of water. "Besides, no need to hear it. I got a living and breathing example in my life. Dad's retired PD, and Mom's over at St. Joseph's in Glendale, refuses to retire."

"Your mom's a nurse? Wow…"

He glanced at her, and before he could answer, something in her eyes had changed. *That's not right....* Almost like the light went out of them, taking the warmth he'd seen there with it. He gently squeezed her thigh. "Hey, babe, you o—"

"I'm fine." Heather looked away, staring out at the few people in the restaurant.

Not fine. She was absolutely not fine. What the fuck just happened? "Heather...look at me." She sighed and did as he asked. The darkness was gone from her eyes, which was good, and there was a small smile on her face—but it wasn't or didn't look like a genuine one. Rob frowned. "What's up, babe?"

"Nothing. All good. Really." She took a mouthful of food, chewed a moment, then spoke around it. "What was the police academy like? Was it hard?"

Hmm. Great redirection. Fine, he'd play. "It was hard as fu—"

Abruptly, she crossed her legs, closing his hand and fingers between them. Rob's eyes went wide and so did hers. Then she blurted a laugh. Rob shook his head, unable to keep the smile from his lips.

He had barely enough room to wiggle his fingers. Just enough to catch her wetness and tease her clit.

With her eyes glued to his, Heather bit her bottom lip.

Rob let out a slow breath and moved his fingers again. The slightest shift, up and down. Up and down. Not even a half inch in either direction. But enough to build it. Within both of them. "You almost done eating?"

She glanced at her plate. "To-go box?"

"Reading my mind, bombshell." After sliding his hand free of the sweet grip of her thighs, Rob got to his feet. Before he stepped away, he leaned over the table toward her. "Keep it where I can see it."

With wide eyes, she swallowed, her throat bobbing with the action before she nodded.

Fuck him, he couldn't wait to get her out to the truck.

Chapter 15

Rob jerked the passenger door of his SUV open, and Heather climbed in. He was around the front and inside the vehicle on the driver's side before she had even reached for her seat belt. She eyed him and held her hands out for the to-go containers. "Here. Let me take those."

"Stick them in the back seat." After handing them to her, he started the engine and backed out of the parking space and hit the gas, launching them forward.

The tires squealed, and Heather couldn't stop the giggle that bubbled out of her. "In a hurry?"

He glanced over at her when he stopped at the traffic light at the end of the road. Before she could track the movement, he snagged her by the wrist and pulled her toward him and right to his lips.

The kiss was hard and wet and hot and delicious. His tongue swept into her mouth, taking from her, and, boy, did she let him take. Heather's stomach pitched as lust rolled through her, settling right in her core.

A second later, he jerked from her lips. "Definitely in a hurry. Need to get inside your heat."

Heather slid her hand down his stomach and landed on the hard ridge of his cock behind his zipper. "You could go just a little slower, no?"

His brows rose. "Slower? You feel how hard that is for you?"

With a low moan, she pressed the butt of her hand against the length, stroking him as best she could through the denim. "Yes, I do. The jeans are in my way." She pouted. "Unzip for me, please?"

The corner of his mouth twitched, but he didn't open his pants for her. Now he was going to torture her more? Dammit, she shouldn't have asked. She should've just taken. Like he did.

Heather needed this, needed the distraction in a big way. His comment about doctors and nurses *not* belonging but cops and nurses being the optimal struck her hard in a couple of different ways, both confusing.

Much as she didn't like it, it seemed that every time they were together and *not* fucking, he wanted them to get to know each other. As in move their budding whatever-the-hell-they-were-doing-ship forward.

Which meant that eventually she'd have to tell him more about her life. Which was why keeping him naked was the better route. And right now, if she could only… God, their roles had been reversed. She was the guy, and he was the girl. Hello, stereotype much? Jesus.

Stay on task: hard dick, six o'clock. Bending to his ear, Heather licked at the small lobe and smoothed her palm back up the length, then tugged at the top button of his pants. "I want you in my mouth."

He grunted—a sound she felt run straight through her—before he tipped his pelvis forward, raising his ass in the air just enough for her to get the button undone, and thank Judas, pull the zipper down.

She hadn't yet had the pleasure of feeling his gorgeous cock between her lips, and now was her opportunity. She was taking it. It was also her chance to chase away the thoughts that had invaded her mind.

Pressing her lips to his neck, Heather slid her hand inside the waistband of his boxer briefs and found the warm, satin-covered steel length of his shaft. She moaned and wrapped her hand around the girth. "*Yessss* so, so hard."

Rob groaned and took one hand off the wheel, resting it on her back, before sliding his palm lower. "Get up on your knees, baby."

As she moved her lips down his neck to his chest, and then past his stomach to his groin, she did as he said. Tugging his boxers down just a bit more, she revealed the bulbous head and her mouth watered.

With his length tightly sheathed in the grip of her palm, she drew in a soft breath, taking in his scent before tracing her lips with the soft skin of the crown.

His cock jerked, the prominent veins pulsing against her hand as another groan rumbled out of him. This one making her clit throb in response. "Don't tease me, bombshell."

She wasn't teasing; she was taking in everything that was Rob. The way he smelled, clean soap and a hint of male musk. She loved it—or at least liked it a whole lot. And then, how his soft skin in contrast to his stiff girth felt in her palm and against her mouth. Now, it was time to taste him.

She traced her mouth with the head again, this time painting her lips with the drop of pre-cum that had emerged from the tip. She moaned, tingles spreading down her thighs. He tasted almost sweet, sweeter than she'd ever tasted before. His cock jerked again, and Heather licked the new drop that appeared, desperate for more.

"*Fuck.*" With a growl, Rob gripped the fabric of her dress and tugged it up her back, revealing her ass and her pussy.

He slid his hand down her spine, over her bottom and between the juncture of her thighs. And then she had his fingers, stroking her cunt. Dipping two in her core, spreading her wetness to her clit.

"Oh, God." Heather rolled her hips. Whimpering, she sucked the head of his dick between her lips.

Rob hissed, and she felt the SUV accelerate. "Fuck, *fuuuuck.*"

Fuck was right. *This* was exactly what she wanted—needed. She moaned around his thickness and sucked him to the back of her throat, drew him out, then back in again, swirling her tongue around the rim of the head with each pass.

Jesus, he tasted good, felt even better. Heather gripped the root of him and fed his length into her mouth until her lips met her hand. Like heaven on her tongue.

She loved this, loved giving him this. But most of all, loved how giving it to him took her away from everything she didn't want to think about.

A few short turns, a few sharp stops, and she felt the bump and figured he'd pulled into his driveway because they'd stopped moving. A second later, she lost his fingers at her core, and she heard him put the truck in park.

She took him deep again.

"Baby…" He let out a groan. "Heather. Off. Now."

She shook her head, slid her mouth up and sucked the crown, hard. Wanting another taste of his sweet pre-cum.

Rob growled, and a second later, his seat slid back with a hard jerk, away from the steering wheel. A half a second later, she felt his fingers fist in her hair, which he used to urge her off his dick.

Keeping her lips tight, his cock pulled free of her mouth with a soft slurp. Another thrill zipped through Heather when he grunted. Dazed, Heather looked up at Rob. His face was flushed, he was panting and staring at her with a look in his eyes so feral, she felt it straight to her core.

Lunging toward him, Heather sucked his tongue into her mouth as she straddled his hips.

And then she had him again, but more. So much more.

In one motion, Rob cupped her ass in his palms, spread her cheeks apart, and Heather slid down, his cock filling her core. A shiver raced up her spine and her stomach tightened as every nerve in her body was triggered by his girth.

Jerking from his lips, she cupped his neck in her hands. "*Yes.* God, yes."

"Ride it, bombshell." Rob pursed his lips, the corner arched in a sexy-as-hell grin.

Oh, yes. She'd do just that. Heather pressed her forehead to his and rolled her pelvis back and forth, grinding her clit against him. Rob held tight to her ass, helping her move, teasing and tracing where her cunt rimmed his prick with his long fingertips.

"Baby..." With a moan, she sucked his bottom lip and kept moving.

Rob growled, gripped her butt cheeks hard. "*Fuck.*"

Heat swirled through her, the tension building, growing.... Her orgasm was rising fast, and she closed her eyes. "So, so good. Don't stop."

"Fuck."

Harder.

"Baby, oh God...*don't stop.*"

Faster.

"*Fucking hell.*" Rob let go of her ass with one hand and tugged her dress down, revealing one breast, and rolled her hard nipple between his fingers.

Heather let out another moan and rocked her pelvis, riding. Riding until she couldn't see, smell, or feel anything but him.

And he gave her more.

Rob slid his wet fingers back and circled her anus.

"Oh God!" Heather jerked, her climax breaking free and crashing over her. Her clit pulsed, her cunt clenching in rapid spasms as wave after wave overtook her and she kept moving on him.

Panting, Heather let her forehead fall to his shoulder. Riding it out, whimpering and moaning, knowing he was close. Giving him as much as she could. Giving him everything she had left in her.

"*Heather...*" Rob let go of her breast and locked his arm around her waist, lifting and holding her to his body as he thrust his pelvis up, slamming into her until his orgasm hit. "*Fuuuuck.*"

With one final thrust, he yanked her down, burying his cock deep. As each pulse of his orgasm rolled through his shaft, jerking within her channel, hot cum spurted inside her. And she wanted every drop.

She kept her forehead to his shoulder and listened to him catch his breath. God, this was beautiful. Almost too beautiful. And that was really, really bad.

Rob trailed the fingers of one hand over her ass, and with the other, traced her spine. Sweet. He was being sweet. Tender. Caring for her. Giving her more beauty.

Heather didn't know what to do with the kind of beauty Rob Caldwell was giving her. It was unexpected and overwhelming. And yet, because of all the happy orgasm hormones flowing through her system, she needed to stop this. Before it was too late.

Problem was, Heather didn't want it to stop, but she didn't know how to continue with him either.

* * * *

"You okay?" Rob pressed his lips to her shoulder and trailed his fingers up and down her spine.

Quiet…it was so quiet in the car. But more, in the middle of the day, in his neighborhood. He glanced out the driver's side window. Middle of the week, early afternoon, save for the rare stay-at-home mom…or dad, people were at work.

Good thing, too, since he'd just banged Heather in his freaking driveway. In broad daylight. In his SUV.

Jesus, he had to be out of his ever-loving mind. Yet, he'd done it.

Shit, truth was, he'd do it again, because it was just that fucking good.

Her fingers twitched where they rested on his neck, but she hadn't answered him.

Rob moved his other hand from her ass, up her spine and stroked her hair. "You sure you're okay?"

"Yeah." She shrugged.

Rob frowned and felt it in his gut. Something was wrong. Just like in the restaurant for brunch earlier…Heather was not okay.

Fuck.

Chapter 16

"Hi." Rob smiled. "Caldwell?"

"Yes. Right this way." The young hostess smiled and indicated for him to follow her through his family's favorite pizza restaurant.

"Robert!" His mother stood and waved him over.

"Thanks. I see them." Rob smiled at the hostess and moved past her to the table. "Hey, Mom." He bent and kissed his mother's cheek and then clapped his father on the back. "Dad. Sorry I'm late."

His mother smiled up at him. "Hi, honey. No problem. You're earlier than we expected."

"I just ordered an Italian beer for me and wine for your mother." His father held the drink menu up to him. "What're you having tonight?"

"Give him a chance to sit, Danny. Sheesh." His mother elbowed his dad in the ribs.

"Ouch!" His dad chuckled. "Then the waitress can bring bread too."

Rob laughed. Coming around the table, he took one of the empty seats across from them. "Where's Josh?"

"You and the bread. You'll get all the carbs you can handle when your pizza comes." She waved her hand at Rob's dad and rolled her eyes. "Your brother is running late too. But he should be here soon."

"Gotcha." Rob picked up the menu and glanced at the lists of drinks.

Friday family pizza night was a weekly thing, and Rob made a point not to miss it. Though last week he'd missed it in favor of being with Heather. Tonight, she was out with Kim and he was going to meet her afterward, along with Derek, Rayna, and Jeff. Maybe Tish, Rayna's best friend, was coming too.

Jeff had relayed that last part. The guy apparently had it really bad for the woman, but she apparently didn't have it bad for him. Anyway... Rob glanced across the table at his parents.

"Which is why we need bread." His father leaned forward, elbows on the table, hands clasped together.

"For God's sake, you don't need the bread." Again, his mother rolled her eyes. "You act like you never eat." She leaned over and patted his father's stomach and laughed. "Proof right here that you eat."

"I may be fat, but I'm happy." His father smiled at Rob's mother.

She smiled, shook her head, but then leaned and gave his father a quick kiss. Rob smiled too, and refocused on the menu. It wasn't as if it'd changed since the last time he was there. But whatever.

The waitress came over and, true to his word, his father ordered bread. Rob ordered an Italian beer, the Menabrea Blonde. Because, yes, Heather was *his* blonde, and the beer made him think of her. He was still a dork at heart. Maybe if things progressed as he hoped, he'd bring Heather for family pizza night in the future.

"Sorry I'm late." Rob's brother came around the table and greeted their parents. Then circled back around to sit.

Rob gave his brother a one-armed hug. "I beat you here."

"Show off." Josh grinned. "Did you order bread?"

Mom threw her hands up in the air. "God help us with the bread."

Dad started laughing and so did Rob.

"What'd I miss?" Josh looked between Rob and their dad.

"Just the usual."

The waitress returned and set Rob's beer down. Rob thanked her and took a swig.

His dad slid the drink menu Josh's way. "Quick, before she leaves. Figure out what you want to drink so we can order dinner."

Josh took the menu and glanced up at their waitress. "Sorry, just give me a second."

"No problem." The young waitress smiled, blushing. "Take your time."

Josh glanced at Rob. "Are we getting something different than the usual?"

"Nope." Rob took another swig of beer and eyed the waitress.

The girl had her eyes glued to his brother. Not surprising, his brother possessed the kind of looks and body that were cover-model worthy. He and Josh had the same features. Both blue eyes. Both brown hair, but Josh's was a little lighter. Add in that the guy was a fireman and built like a muscular Mack truck, and ladies lined up around the block. Guys lined up too.

The girl cut her eyes to Rob, and he smiled. She smiled back, obviously not caring that she'd been caught staring, and went right back to looking at his brother. Rob chuckled. Pretty girl, for sure, and definitely crushing on Josh. Too bad she was probably way too young.

"We're getting the same pie we always get." His mother grabbed a piece of bread from the basket, buttered it, and handed it to their father. "Why? Did you want something different?"

"Nope. Wouldn't dream of it." He looked over at Rob. "What are you drinking tonight?"

Rob picked up the empty bottle. "Menabrea Blonde."

"Nice. Yeah, I'll take the amber, please?" Josh smiled.

"Coming right up." She smiled and tucked a lock of hair behind her ear.

Rob stifled a chuckle. Although she stayed by Josh's side, she took the food order from their mother. When that was done, she finally stepped away. It was cute, seeing a girl with a crush. The best part was, the only reason seeing women (or men) fawn over his brother wasn't annoying was because Josh wasn't an asshole. The guy was never rude to people, and he never let the attention go to his head.

Josh grabbed a piece of bread and spread some butter on it. "So, what happened? You had to work last week?"

"No." Rob set his glass down, unsure if he was going to share about Heather or not. Although it wasn't like there was a reason to *not* share. "I was…well…I met someone, sort of, on Thursday night and then Friday night, we had a date."

Their mother frowned. "You *sort of* met someone? Robert, what does that mean exactly?"

Rob glanced at his mom and shrugged. "I guess a better way to say it is I got *reacquainted* with someone I went to high school with."

The waitress brought Josh his beer, he thanked her, and then when no one said anything else, she walked away. Josh focused on Rob again. "Really? Who?"

Rob cleared his throat. "You remember Heather Winters?"

Josh's brows rose. "Gorgeous, prom queen, mean girl, Heather Winters?"

Rob smirked and shook his head. "That'd be the one."

"Dude, how could I *not* remember her? She was smokin' hot and as cruel as they come."

"Cruel? I'm not sure that sounds too good, Robert." Mom buttered another piece of bread.

"I don't know, Rebecca. The smokin' hot part sounds pretty good to me." Their father laughed, but when their mother slapped his arm his eyes got big, feigning innocence. As usual. "What? Come on. I'm kidding." Still chuckling, he bent toward her. "You know I'm kidding."

"Killing me, Danny." She laughed, too, but rolled her eyes. "You know what happens to young men who have a dirty mind?"

"Yes, they become dirty old men." Dad tickled her side.

She laughed and then let out a little squeal before swatting his hand away. "Stop. Come on, now." She cleared her throat. "You're making a scene."

"I know, angel." Dad bent toward her again and pressed a kiss to her cheek. "I'm your dirty old man though. Huh?"

Mom glanced between Rob and Josh, and shook her head. "He's incorrigible. I swear."

Rob couldn't help but laugh. Seeing his parents' flirtatious banter, or at least his father flirting, his mother just trying to keep him on the appropriate side of the street, was always entertaining.

But it was a sign of where they were in their relationship, their marriage, after thirty-five years together. Not perfect by any means. Nothing ever was. Dad drove Mom nuts, and she did the same to Dad, but they still loved each other. Were still loyal to one another.

It was the kind of relationship Rob had always wanted for himself, and maybe now he'd found it.

Rob leaned forward, resting his forearms on the table. "She's still gorgeous, yes, but what's better is she's not mean anymore."

"Jackpot." His Dad smiled.

"That's a relief. You don't need to be with anyone mean, Robert." Mom nodded. "You might be a tough cop, but your heart is sweeter than most."

"Aw, you're sweet? Soft and squishy too?" Josh placed his hand on Rob's shoulder and squeezed, trying but failing to keep a straight face. "Can I be you when I grow up?"

"But you already are, *Joshy.*" Rob laughed and shrugged his brother's hand off his shoulder. "Don't play like you didn't rescue a kitten last week."

Josh cleared his throat and got serious. "All part of the job, man." He puffed his chest out before shoving a piece of bread in his mouth.

"Uh-huh. Anyway…"

"Are you going to see her again?" Mom took a sip of her wine.

"Ah, yeah. I've been seeing her all week, actually."

Mom set down her glass. "Wow. Things are progressing quickly, then? Be careful, son."

"He knows what he's doing, hon." Dad sipped his beer. "He's a grown man."

"Every day this week?" Josh swirled the beer in his glass. "Nice."

Rob glanced at his brother. "Yeah, well. What can I say? I like her. She's a lot different from how we remember her when we were kids. But then again, aren't we all?"

Josh clinked his glass against Rob's. "You can say that again."

"You're hearing me." Rob looked at his mom. "Don't worry, okay? We're just getting to know each other."

Dad put his arm around Mom. "It's fine. Don't worry about it. When do we get to meet her?"

Rob sat back. "I don't know. I guess, if things keep going well, maybe in a couple of weeks. Maybe more? We'll see."

Josh ran his palm along the top of his short hair. "She meet Tricks yet?"

"Yep, he loves her."

Dad let out a chuckle. "Pfft, well that's not hard. Tricks loves everyone."

Rob frowned. "Except the bad guys."

"This is true." His father raised his beer. "Here's to things working out long-term. And if not, then at least enjoy the ride while it lasts."

"Danny, *good grief.*" Mom rolled her eyes.

Josh laughed.

Rob couldn't help but laugh too. "It's all good, Mom." He clinked his glass with is father's. "Thanks, I think?"

The waitress came over and set the metal stand on the table before placing their large pizza on top of it. After setting plates down for all of them, she checked for refills on drinks. Her eyes still lingering on Josh, she stepped away.

"She's too young, Joshua. Don't even think about it." Their mother served the first piece of pizza to Dad.

Josh's eyes went wide. "I wasn't— I'm not—"

"Uh-huh. Just eat, young man." Mom nodded and dished up slices for each of them.

Rob chuckled. "She called that."

Josh gave Rob the side-eye and then bit into his pizza. Rob followed suit. Life was good, and family pizza night was as expected. Telling his family about Heather wasn't necessary, but he'd really wanted to share.

It added a little more seasoning to the night. Although after he'd brought her up, Rob decided that he didn't need to get into any further specifics regarding where they were in their…relationship.

He'd just wanted to give his family a heads-up…or a small clue that maybe he *might* be a little busy in the future.

At least, Rob hoped he'd be busy.

* * * *

Heather set down the keys to her parents' house on the kitchen counter. "Hey, Mom."

Her mother jumped and whipped around from her bent position at the subzero refrigerator. "Heather! My God, you startled me!"

"Sorry." Heather wrapped her arms around her middle. "I thought you heard me walk in."

With a sigh, Mom turned back to the fridge. "It's fine." She glanced back over at Heather. "I wasn't expecting you. What's up? Bad day?"

"No, not really." She drew in a breath and looked around the immaculate kitchen. It'd been redone three times since Heather was a child. Every ten years, it was remodel time. That's what happened when people had an upper middle class amount of money at their disposal; they got to do what they wanted with it. At least her mother spent it on decorating things, making their world pretty. "I don't know, maybe? I'm okay though. Really." Heather shrugged. "I just figured I'd stop by, see how you were doing."

"Oh? Well, that's considerate of you...I'm, well, I'm fine. Your father's at the office, of course. Working on a big case. You know how that goes. Did you have dinner?"

"No. But I'm not hungry yet. I'll be meeting some friends later, and I'll probably grab food then."

Her mother blew out a breath and came over to the island. She cocked her head to the side and frowned. "You look tired."

"I'm fine, Mom." Heather looked down at her hands, inspecting her cuticles, then shook her head. A laugh threatened to bubble up, but she managed to shove it back down.

It was funny how "fine" she was. So fine that, if she could, Heather would let that laugh out...except her mother would think she'd lost her mind. And maybe she had. But the point was, the standard reply had always been: Heather was fine. Her mother was fine. And Heather's father was probably fine too.

In fact, the Winters family was a great many fucked-up things, but at the top of that list was fine.

Always.

That's how they worked. How they'd always worked, and exactly how they'd continue to work.

"Tell me about these friends. Anyone I know?"

Heather glanced up, torn from her less-than-happy but definitely humorous reflection of reality to see her mom had moved across the kitchen to the opposite counter. "No, they're new. Kim, she's my neighbor across the street. Interesting lady, single mom."

"That's good, I suppose."

"What is? Being a single mom?" Heather frowned as frustration bloomed in her gut, replacing her weird giddiness.

"No, I meant, it's good that she's interesting, that's all. Don't be so sensitive. I worry about you being alone all the way down in the East Valley."

"I'm fine. Really."

Her mother sighed, sounding tired. "Well, that's a relief. But I still worry."

It was a statement Heather's mother often made. She supposed her mother would always worry. The woman would worry for days, but no one ever talked about anything. Mom worried and they were all fine. Not that it mattered if they weren't. There would be no talking about any real feelings. They never ventured much past surface emotions. Anything deeper had no place in their home. Not now, not ever. It was quite sad, for a thousand different reasons.

Which was also what made it so hard living with her parents for the last year after moving back from Baltimore. Heather had been a walking, talking emotional mess. Her father really had no capacity to deal with that level of emotion, and her mother just looked at her with a shit ton of worry...or was it pity? Probably both, but no way to know for sure.

Heather glanced around the kitchen and focused on her mother chopping up vegetables. "What are you making for dinner?"

Mom glanced back at her before returning to her task. "Just a salad for now. I'll probably throw some chicken breast in it. I don't think your father's going to make it home anyway."

"Sounds good." She rested her forearms on the counter. "So, I got a bunch of stuff for the house. I'm nearly all set up. Not everything, of course, but I have all the basics now. You should come by sometime."

"That'd be nice, honey."

Heather stared at her mother's profile. They didn't look alike, not really. Though they were the same height and body type. Maybe a little around the eyes and mouth, but mostly Heather looked like her father.

Mom had light brown hair, no sign of gray yet, but that was because it was colored regularly. In her early fifties, the woman was still a head turner. Definitely a knockout. Heather bent her arms and rested her chin on her fists. "When do you think you can come by?"

Her mother smiled. "Maybe next week? I'll have to check my calendar. I'm on the planning committee for two charity events, and we're down to the last couple months to get things done."

"Oh. Well, you let me know what works." Heather swallowed as disappointment filled her gut like a rising river. She sighed, wondering why the hell she was being so sensitive. Her mother was busy, always had been. The woman didn't work; the volunteer stuff, especially the charities, was her way of staying busy. None of her mother's busyness was personal, and Heather didn't need to take it that way. "Maybe we could have lunch too? There's this cute little sandwich place I went to that I think you'd like."

The memory of Rob beside her in the sandwich shop, playing with her bare pussy, burst into Heather's brain. Her stomach wobbled, her clit pulsed, and she crossed her legs. Yep, she was nuts even thinking about bringing her mother there, but hey, the food was good.

Her mother laughed. "Goodness, that's a look I haven't seen on your face in a long time. Probably since you were a teenager."

Heather jerked her attention back to her mom. "Um, what do you mean?"

"Whatever you're thinking about has you looking happy. A little bit mischievous too."

Heather couldn't stop the grin that arched her lips. "I told you I was fine."

Her mother raised a brow, and the corner of her mouth quirked. "Is this the part where I let it go and not ask anything further?"

Heather tipped her head to the side. Should she tell her mom about Rob? She could, there was no reason not to. Though Heather and her mother had a *decent* relationship, they didn't have what some would consider a close one.

Heather wasn't one to come home from school and gush about her boyfriends. When she met Charles, she'd gushed, but only because she knew her parents would be happy she'd landed a doctor.

Talk about white privilege at its finest.

And now the knowledge that she'd ever cared about such a thing made Heather rather sick to her stomach. God, how she'd changed. None of that shit mattered to her anymore. Then again, it was amazing how crawling through the wreckage of life could alter a person.

Heather just saw things differently now. It wasn't lost on her that she still had a piece of that privilege wrapped around her, considering the fact that she wasn't working—and didn't need to—thanks to her divorce settlement. And then there was the Mercedes she drove....

Rob was a cop, and Heather didn't know how much money cops made, but she had a feeling it sure as hell wasn't what doctors made. His parents both worked, his father also a cop, though now retired, and his mother was a nurse. Nurses made a decent salary, but not exactly six figures.

Heather bet his home life was the opposite of hers. Not that he'd had it hard, she assumed he didn't; she didn't know for sure, but she doubted his mother remodeled the kitchen every ten years.

After everything, the money no longer mattered. The social status didn't either. She wasn't the popular girl in high school anymore. This was real life, and real life was much better than the false facade money or privilege gave some people.

Heather got up and moved to the refrigerator. After grabbing a bottle of water, she closed the door and resumed her spot at the island. "I met someone. A guy—" She twisted the cap off and took a long sip. When she pulled the bottle away from her lips, her mother was staring at her. Heather went on. "Sorry. Anyway, I met a guy. I think we're dating now." She shrugged and let a grin spread across her lips.

Very slowly, her mother set the knife down on the cutting board. "Oh?"

Heather took another sip of her water. "He's a cop. A K9 officer. His dog, Tricks, is a German shepherd. Totally beautiful." Another sip of water. "The dog's beautiful too." Heather chuckled. "So anyway, yeah. We're dating. Pretty sure."

Her mother just stood there, motionless. She hadn't even blinked.

Holy shit, did Heather just short her mother's brain out? She waved her hand. "Mom? You okay?"

Mom jerked yet managed to do it without moving from the spot she stood. "Um. Yes. Of course. I'm fine." She nodded and drew in a breath. "Do you think it's a good idea for you to be dating?"

Heather let out a chuckle. "No, but...I like him. I like how I feel when I'm with him."

"How long has this been going on? I mean you barely moved out of here."

"It's been nearly two months since I moved out. I guess it's been about a week? Or so? I don't know. The days are sort of running together."

Mom shook her head, but in a way where she just sort of jerked her chin to the side. As if she was shocked or floored or offended...who knew which. "Where did you meet him?"

"Funny you ask. Apparently, we went to high school together. He recognized me when he pulled me over."

"You got pulled over?"

Heather blurted a laugh. "It happens, Mom. Relax."

"Did he give you a ticket?"

"No. Let me off with a warning." Heather laughed again and took another sip of water. "I didn't recognize him though."

Her mother put her hand on her chest, drumming her fingers on her sternum, and glanced away as if searching for some answer on the walls, and finally looked back to Heather.

Heather sat there, watching, in complete awe. Her mother was so uncomfortable, and Heather was equal parts shocked and pleased. Shocked because, in truth, she'd hoped, even if just a little, her mother would be excited for her, would want to know more.

Pleased because Heather knew it was because she'd gone from being a well-to-do doctor's wife to now dating a cop.

An under-six-figures-a-year cop.

An intelligent, funny, sweet and dominant cop...with an awesome canine partner.

A cop who made her smile and made her body smile too.

A cop who treated her better in one day than Charles had in five years.

A cop.

And right then, in that moment, Heather decided that she was definitely dating Rob. No questions asked. She was in.

Chapter 17

"So, you two, like, a thing now? I mean, the other night was your one-week anniversary and all. And you're still all glowy like a new bride." With a goofy grin, Jeff knelt down next to his canine partner, Rio.

Rob shook his head, rolling his eyes, but couldn't help his own grin. "Yes, Nelly, it's officially been somewhere around ten days. Let's talk about you? Tish give you the time of day yet?"

"Oh, that was harsh. *So, so* harsh." Derek pulled his baseball cap down low. "Mad points, brother."

Rob chuckled and fastened Tricks's harness.

Jeff got to his feet and rested his hands on his hips. "Ladies, please." Jeff sucked his teeth. "Tish is an independent woman. She doesn't give the time of day to just anyone."

Derek raised his brows. "Did you just insult yourself?"

"Nope." Jeff frowned.

"Uh-huh." Derek chuckled as his canine partner, Axle, paced back and forth beside him, but finally settled on his haunches, panting. Derek glanced down at Axle, then focused on Jeff again.

Jeff rolled his eyes. "Okay maybe. But all I mean by that is, I'm giving her space. She knows where to find me." He glanced at Rob. "Still waiting for you to answer my question, Rhonda."

"No comment, Nelly." Rob grinned. "Come on, we training or what?"

"Fine. Be stingy. It's my turn on the runway, anyway." Jeff moved to the exit and turned back. "This isn't over, ladies." In a show of typical Jeff theatrics, he swooped the nonexistent hair from his shoulder, spun around, and sashayed off with Rio by his side into the warehouse they were using for training.

Derek laughed and Rob did too, but not until Jeff was out of earshot. No need to feed Jeff's goofball ego. Having him there always made training more interesting—maybe entertaining was more accurate. Better was having both guys with him. It wasn't often they got to train together, so when the opportunity came up, they always made an effort to be there. Different PDs, but that didn't matter. It kept them in sync. Kept their dogs in sync, too, and that was never a bad thing.

Barely two minutes later, they heard vicious and high-pitched barking from Rio as he'd undoubtedly found the decoy drugs hidden somewhere in the vast space.

"Got it." Derek grinned. "Anyway, *soooo*…are you?"

Rob glanced at his friend. "Am I what?"

"You and Heather. Are you official or still getting comfortable?"

Jesus, how to answer this question? Rob sighed. "Wish it was that simple, you know? For her? We're getting comfortable. For me? I'm all in."

Derek smiled. "Yep, that's how it was with Rayna. She was unsure and guarded. Maybe timid would be a better way to say that."

Rob nodded. "Exactly, except, Heather is not at all timid. But she is definitely guarded."

Derek smirked. "Yep, totally get it. Not easy. But down in my bones, I knew she was the one for me, so I held on. If you feel that way about Heather, hang in. She'll get there too."

"I appreciate that. It's crazy, because at first it was just the infatuation from high school, the chance to be with someone I'd always dreamed about. But now?" Rob switched the leash he had attached to Tricks's harness to his other hand. "After spending the last week with her, I realize she is not at all the person she was when we were kids. Thank fuck for that, though, because she was a bitch then. But now? God, she's so much more, so much…I don't know, better than I ever imagined."

Derek nodded and clapped Rob on the shoulder. "I hope things work out, man. Truly. I like how she looks on you."

"Thanks." Rob nodded.

The clacking of Rio's nails on the concrete floor brought their attention to the doorway. A moment later, Jeff appeared and strolled into the room. "The drugs have been found. He's breaking record times too." Jeff's grin spread from ear to ear, but then he sobered and frowned, looking between Rob and Derek. "*Haaaayyy!* Did you ladies bond without me?"

Derek rubbed Jeff's arm. "Sweetheart, you know you're my queen. Rob is just my backup call."

Rob blurted a laugh. "You two, yeah. My turn." He looked back when he reached the door. "I'm not anyone's backup call. I'm riding front seat or nothing, bitches."

As Rob walked away from his two laughing friends, he chuckled and moved into the warehouse with Tricks for his round of training.

Talking about Heather was a fantastic distraction, which kept Rob calm, soothed him in a way he'd only just begun to experience. That calm rubbed off on Tricks, so heading into the training situation they were in, Tricks was completely at ease, or as calm as could be expected, considering the animal knew he was going hunting.

As he neared the edge of one of the floor-to-ceiling metal shelves, Rob gave Tricks the German command to heel. "*Fuss!*"

The dog came to an immediate stop and then sat, quietly panting.

His canine never failed to amaze him. Alert, but totally calm. Ready to attack, yet looked as docile as a teddy bear. Rob squatted down and ran his palm over the thick fur at the back of Tricks's neck. After another heartbeat or two, Rob commanded Tricks to go on, to search blindly. "*Voran!*"

The dog practically launched into the air, taking off at a steady trot in search of the scented decoy they used to teach the dogs how to find drugs. Holding tight to his leash, Rob followed as Tricks rounded one corner then another, down a couple more aisles, deeper inside the warehouse, until finally he came upon his target.

Burlap sacks filled with twenty pounds of uncooked rice, stacked neatly on top of each other, on a pallet. Tricks zeroed in on them, practically skidding to a stop before jumping up and sniffing at the sides, yelping and barking with his aggressive alert.

"You find something, Tricks?" Rob came up beside his partner.

The pile was about five layers, and likely the master trainer had buried the decoy deep, probably damn near in the middle. Rob was the lucky son of a bitch who got to drag bags off, one by one, as Tricks went apeshit scratching at the bags. Barking, yelping, wagging his tail.

Rob pulled one bag down to the floor. "What'd you find? Is this it?"

Tricks nosed the sack on the ground before going back to the stack, clawing again at another bag.

"Not that one? Okay, this one?" Rob pulled that one down too.

On it went, bag after bag, and as they went and the scent got stronger, Tricks got more and more amped up, yelping louder, jumping and clawing, even tearing some of the bags until Rob got to what he hoped was the final sack with the decoy.

Continuing to encourage the animal, Rob gave him the command for search. "*Such!*"

Tricks yelped and clawed into the sack, the burlap fabric tearing, rice trickling out onto the ground. "Get it boy. Find it!"

A moment later, a boatload of rice spilled out of the mutilated sack, and when Tricks stepped back, doing as trained, not touching or biting into the decoy, Rob looked down and saw that half the rice was gone and the decoy had been exposed.

Tricks sat back on his haunches and sneezed.

Rob pulled Tricks's reward toy from his pocket and tossed it to him. "Good boy!"

Tricks caught the stuffed toy and immediately started chomping it.

Catching the edge of the toy, Rob tugged, playing with Tricks. "Good find! Kick ass. Good boy!"

Still praising Tricks, Rob grabbed the decoy out of what remained of the rice sack, and with his partner at his side, wandered back to the room his buddies were waiting in. Derek was up next for a search drill with Axle. Then Jeff would go again. Rob was on duty but had a few more hours before his shift was over, so he'd likely run only one more drill and head out on patrol for the last few hours.

When the night was finally done, he and Tricks would head over to Heather's. She wasn't expecting him tonight, and he hadn't expected to see her either. But after gabbing about her with Derek, Rob had decided he wanted to see her.

He missed her face, and her lips…pretty much all of her.

* * * *

The doorbell rang, and Heather nearly jumped clean out of her skin. Worse, almost dropped the box of cereal she was holding, mid-pour into a bowl. With a sigh meant to both calm her now-racing heart and the instant annoyance that shot through her at almost losing some perfectly good Fruity Pebbles, she set the box on the counter.

After refastening the bun she'd pulled her hair up into, she shuffled toward the front door in her pink fluffy slippers. There was only one person it would be this late at night, okay, maybe two. Likely it was Rob, but it could be Kim.

Or maybe a serial killer? A polite one, of course, who was ringing her bell. Waiting to chop her up into a million pieces. Right.

The bell rang again, and then a knock sounded on the metal panel. Fucking hell, whoever was at her door at nearly eleven o'clock at night needed a syringe full of patience in their ass.

Heather covered her mouth, smothering the snort/laugh at the stupid joke she'd made, and kept her footsteps light as she got close to the door. Placing both palms on the cool panel, she rose on tiptoe and peered through the peephole.

Rob...

Heather's heart skipped a beat, this time from the instant attraction she felt each time she saw him. He was just so damn pretty, those blue eyes of his a killer. And his body was freaking amazing.

Staying quiet, she took advantage of the opportunity to just watch him as he focused on his phone, doing something she couldn't see. Her phone chimed on the table with a text. For the love of God. Heather laughed. Why didn't he just call her?

She stepped back and hit the four-digit code into her alarm keypad, unlocked the door, and opened the way for him. His lips parted to say something, but she cut him off. "Hey. So, confused because I thought we weren't seeing each other tonight." Movement caught her eye, and she glanced down. "*Aww,* you brought Tricks?" She squatted down, scratching the fur under the dog's ears.

"Well, he wanted to see you."

Heather looked up at Rob from her knelt position. "*He* wanted to see me, huh?"

"Yeah, you should've heard him. Thought I was gonna need a set of earplugs. I mean, he *would not* shut up about the matter until I agreed to come over."

Heather straightened and crossed her arms, leaning against the doorjamb. "Really? That's...wow. What was he saying?"

Rob rolled his eyes. "Come on, babe, don't make me try and do an imitation of dog speak. I seriously suck at it. Just trust me, the animal whined like he'd transformed himself into one of those fluffy little dogs I could fit in my pocket."

She gave him an exaggerated frown. "Aw, what do you have against little dogs that fit in pockets? They're cute."

Rob grunted. "Bah, they're not even a whole dog. More like a quarter of one. Petite novelties, bombshell. That's all."

"I happen to like petite things. In case you haven't noticed, I'm kind of petite myself." She straightened and placed her hands on her hips. "And, wait, are you saying I'm a novelty?"

"Nope. You"—Rob hooked his finger in the front of her yoga pants and pulled her close to him—"could never be a novelty. But just to be clear, I'm well aware and happen to be *quite* fond of your petite-ness."

"Is that so?" Warmth rushed down her spine at the husky tone in his voice. Heather swallowed past the dryness in her mouth and slid her palms up his arms. "So, you want to come in?" And, damn, she sounded just as husky.

"Affirmative." With one arm around her waist, Rob lifted her off the ground and walked them into her house.

Heather let out a giggle-squeal, and once the door was closed behind them, he let her slide down his body but didn't let her go. Instead, he bent and pressed his mouth to hers, swept his tongue inside.

His kiss was aggressive, yet his lips were soft, pliable. He slid one hand up her back and cupped the back of her neck, holding her, controlling the kiss but giving it thoroughly and completely.

God, this man.

He just did it for her, in so many ways. And she loved that. But mostly, the thing that did it was how he held all the control. Every bit of it, and the relief she felt, knowing Rob had the wheel was also—

He slid his other hand across her lower back, dragging his blunt fingernails over the thin fabric of her shirt. Heated lust flowed through her veins, and she melted against him.

God.

God...

Oh, yes, he did it for her.

When he pulled from her lips, Heather was panting and so wet with arousal she was ready to climb him like a tree. Maybe lay him down right there in her entryway. Dazed, she touched his bottom lip with her fingertip. "Mmm."

"You hungry?" Rob opened his mouth, and when she slid the tip in, he bit down gently.

"Mmhmm." A slow smile spread across her lips. "You?"

"Definitely." Rob grinned and bent to her ear. "Food, then I fuck you."

Heather rolled her eyes to the ceiling—even though she felt his words arrow right to her clit. "Yes, sir."

"Bombshell, even when you're being a good girl, you're still naughty." He gave her bottom a sharp but not hard swat. "Come on. Feed me." He stepped back and looked down at the dog. "Tricks, come."

Heather smiled and let him lead her by the hand to her kitchen. Tricks followed right beside them. "I was just about to—"

"God bless America, Fruity Pebbles? Seriously?" Rob picked up the box.

Her face got warm. "What? I like them. They're good." Annoyed at herself that she felt embarrassed at such a stupid thing, she snatched the box from him—only because he let her, she was sure—and stepped around him.

With a frown, Heather tipped the box and finished filling her bowl from earlier.

"Tricks. Down." Rob came around her other side and faced her, leaning against the counter. "Lots of sugar, you know? Really bad for you too."

Heather frowned and ignored him. Was he seriously going to lecture her about cereal? Seriously? She looked away from Rob and saw that Tricks had laid down at the end of her large island. One ear was flopped down, the other still at attention. His dark eyes soft but intent and focused on her. Such a beautiful animal.

Rob pressed his front to her back. "Bombshell?"

"What?" She looked away from Tricks and grabbed the half gallon of milk she'd taken out before and unscrewed the cap. She needed to chill. She sounded like some sort of queen bitch from the land of sugar cereal ready to bite his head off. Shit, was she getting her period?

He wrapped his arms around her waist and ran his nose along her neck. "Can I tell you a secret?"

Heather drew in a slow breath…the way he was touching her, the low tone of his voice, she couldn't care less if he was being all Mr. Healthy Pants officer of the law, she just wanted to see how good he looked naked in her kitchen. Except, Tricks was watching them and… "Sure."

"I love Fruity Pebbles."

"You're so mean." Heather busted out laughing and swatted his arm. "Then why were you teasing me?"

Tricks sneezed and followed it with a little half whine, half yawn as he got to a sitting position.

Rob laughed too. "You thought I was serious?" He nuzzled her neck. "Only thing better than Fruity Pebbles is Chocolate Fruity Pebbles."

Heather blurted a laugh then cleared her throat. "You mean Cocoa Pebbles."

"Yeah, that's what I said."

Still in his embrace, she shifted her head to the side and glanced back at him. "No, you said choco—" Okay, Queen Bitch of Cereal Land, take it down a notch. It so did not matter what the cereal was called. And clearly she was PMSing. Heather blinked and forced a smile. "How about I get you a bowl?"

He kissed the tip of her nose. "How about you get a spoon so you can start eating, and I'll get a bowl for me."

Her smile went from forced to soft, and all at once she wanted to kiss him. No way in hell he hadn't glommed onto the fact that she was a tad bitchy, yet he was just rolling with it.

The man was perfect.

Seriously.

Did. It. For. Her.

It'd been somewhere over a week since they'd started— *Oh God, she was really doing this*...yep, dating. So, really, it was early still, and he was on his best behavior. After a few months of her insanity, he'd be gone. For sure.

But right now, she had him. After Heather picked up the spoon she'd pulled out earlier, she turned in his arms to face him. She glanced at Tricks, who'd laid down again, then returned her focus back to Rob. Bowl in hand, she scooped up a spoonful. "I have a better idea."

He looked at the spoon filled with colored crunchy sugary goodness, then back to her. "You want to share?"

Heather nodded and pulled her lips between her teeth. She raised the spoon to his mouth. Rob's eyes flashed with equal parts softness and desire before he parted his lips and she slid the spoonful inside.

He chewed, and she scooped some for herself.

They stood that way, leaning against her kitchen counter and Tricks lying on the floor at the edge of the island, sharing her small bowl of Fruity Pebbles until they'd finished it.

After sipping milk directly from the bowl, she pulled it away, and Rob caught the drip running down her chin.

With his tongue...

Oh, yes, maybe she'd get to see him naked in her kitchen after all.

But...Tricks. She didn't know if she could have sex with the dog watching. It was just too intimate and weird.

Rob moved his lips to the side of her neck and found her breast with his hand, tweaking her nipple through her thin tank top.

And Heather forgot all about the dog watching them.

Chapter 18

Rob took the empty bowl from her and set it on the counter. He focused on her again. Jesus, every time he saw her, took in her features, his breath was lost. *So fucking beautiful.*

But more so now that he'd distracted her from whatever grumpy mood she was in and she had lust pumping through her system. At first he'd thought maybe she was upset that he'd stopped by unannounced. After a few minutes, he was pretty sure that wasn't it.

Could be female time of the month related. If so, he wasn't a stupid man; he wasn't going to ask her. He'd find out one way or another soon enough.

Rob cupped her face in his palms and bent to her mouth once more. This time, he flicked his tongue over her bottom lip and did the same to the top, coaxing her open. "Give me your sweet tongue, baby."

Heather touched her tongue to his and let out a soft moan, one he felt deep in his gut. Rob gave her his own moan, curling his tongue around hers, before covering her mouth with his and kissing her deep. Needing to feel more of her, he ran his hands down her sides and pulled up her thin top, revealing her breasts to him.

Her skin was as smooth as satin, and another moan escaped him when he palmed both her bare tits and flicked his thumbs over her pebbled nipples. Placing his palms under both of her arms, Rob picked her up and set her on the counter in her kitchen.

Pulling from her lips, he pressed his face to her sternum and just breathed her in. God help him, he couldn't get enough of her. Heather wrapped her arms around his head, holding him to her. Soft and warm. Sweet and—

She stroked the hair on the back of his head. "Honey… I'm sorry but…"

He pulled back and looked up at her. "What's up, babe?"

"Tricks is just…" She bit her bottom lip and glanced at Tricks. "Is he going to watch us? I mean, is it weird that I'm kind of freaked out about that?"

Rob chuckled. "Well, he's not a person."

She blew out a breath. "Well yeah, I mean, I know he's not a person. But it's like he knows what we're doing."

Rob flicked his thumbs over her nipples again. "He might know. He's male and smart, but trust me, he's not going to join us. Unless…wait—" He tipped his chin down, raising his brows. "That's not your thing, is it?"

"Oh my God, no!" The horrified look that came over her face was hilarious, and Rob couldn't contain the laugh that burst out of him.

With the cutest frown on her face, Rob finally managed to get his fit of laughter under control. How the hell did she even make frowning adorable? He shook his head, unable to hide his smirk. "You can relax, I'm totally kidding. You should see your face." He chuckled. "Even when you know I'm kidding, it's like you don't trust it and then get annoyed and agitated, and I think that's beautiful."

"Ugh, you are so mean." She shoved at his chest, half laughing, half pissed. "And being annoyed at you makes me beautiful?" She shook her head and pushed at him again, but of course, he wasn't budging. "I swear, Rob. Move so I can get up."

Still laughing, instead of moving away as she'd ordered him to do, he wrapped both arms around her and held her closer. Bending forward, he rubbed his nose over hers. "Stop, Heather. Come on, I'm just pulling your pigtails. That's all."

She gripped the sides of his shirt. "I'm literally half naked and you're teasing me? So annoying. I swear, just…" With a growl, she shifted and in the next second, Rob felt her teeth in his trap muscle.

"Did you just gr— *Ouch!*" That's what he got for trying to hold her still or keep her from moving away from him. But damn, he was sure she'd growled too. "Look at you getting all feisty now."

"You earned it." Heather nipped his earlobe, and as she pressed kisses along his jaw, she slipped her hands under the hem of the back of his T-shirt, and sliding up, she dug her blunt nails into his lats and then around and down onto his abs.

It didn't hurt, though he could tell she was trying to do any damage she could manage. He'd take it, whatever she wanted to throw his way. "Do your worst, but I get to return the favor when you're done getting this frustration out of your system."

"Fine by me." Heather bit his bottom lip before sucking it.

Rob let out a growl and flicked his thumbs over her nipples. With a moan, Heather moved her lips down his throat, nipping and sucking as she went.

"Need this off you, please?" Straightening, she tugged at the hem of his shirt, urging him to remove it.

He yanked the shirt up and off his body, tossing it to the floor. Heather leaned back on one hand and reached to his chest with the other. With one fingertip, she traced a line from his bottom lip, down his throat, between his chest muscles, and then farther through the center of his abs.

Her eyes had tracked her movement, but when she reached his waistband, she raised her gaze to his. "So beautiful."

"So are you." Rob's dick was already hard behind his zipper, and now, with every touch, with every look from her, it ached and throbbed. He cradled the side of her face in his palm and stroked his thumb over her bottom lip.

Leaning toward her, Rob took her mouth in another deep and wet kiss. As he devoured her mouth, he urged her back, and Heather lay flat on the counter, her legs coming around his waist.

Taking her by the hips, Rob slid her toward him until her body met his and his pelvis was pressed against her cunt, their clothing the only thing stopping him from fucking her.

Rob rolled his hips, and Heather gasped into his mouth, raising her knees higher. He pulled from her lips and trailed kisses along her chin to her throat and down to one firm breast. Glancing up at her, Rob sucked the tight nipple into his mouth.

Heather arched beneath him, cradling his head in her arms. "Rob…baby, please?"

"Please what?" Gently, he circled the pink nub with his tongue and rolled his hips against her core.

"Make him go…to the guest room, or the backyard, or—"

Rob bit the tip and tugged it with his teeth, stretching it from her breast.

"*Fuuuuck.*" Heather arched, a sexy moan oozing out of her.

A moan so sweet and full of need, Rob's cock jerked in his jeans.

Rising off her, Rob rolled her other nipple between his finger and thumb, tugging the erect point away from her body. Heather arched, hissing through a moan at the sweet sting of pain he was giving her with nipple play.

At the same time, he cupped her pussy through her yoga pants. A bolt of lust zipped down his spine, settling in his balls. "Fuck, bombshell. You've soaked through your pants."

"Keep pulling on my nipples like you are and I'm only going to get wetter. I need you inside me." She swallowed and rolled her pelvis off the counter trying to get more contact with his hand. She glanced to her right, in the direction of Tricks. "But...please, baby? Please send him out?"

Rob smoothed his hand up her stomach. "Okay, babe."

She sat up. "I'm sorry."

"Hey, no sorrys. It's all good." He pressed a kiss to her forehead and stepped away.

Last thing he wanted was for her to feel uncomfortable about Tricks. Rob knew the animal being in the room was no big deal, and eventually she'd get that too.

But for now, he had no problem giving her what she needed.

* * * *

Heather watched as Rob led the dog down the hall. She heard a door close and assumed he'd put Tricks in her guest room. She sighed as a mix of relief and guilt went to war in her tummy.

Could she be any more of a pain in the ass tonight? Obviously her hormones were off the charts, the spike causing her irrational, grumpy side to emerge and take center stage.

Rob emerged from the hall, looking all sorts of gorgeous, and moved toward her.

She swallowed. "Babe, I'm sorry. I'm being crazy, I think."

He waved his hand at her, brushing off her comment. "Stop. He's fine. We're fine." With a devilish smile, he parted her thighs and wedged himself between her legs. "Now, where were we? Ah yes..." Rob bent in and pressed his warm lips to hers again, kissing her with slow, dragging sweeps of his tongue across hers.

As he kissed her, he urged her back so once again she lay on the counter. He moved his lips down to her throat and tugged the waistband of her yoga pants down and off her legs. Her heated, exposed skin tingled from the cool air in the room, and all Heather could think about was how good he felt...how good he always felt.

Breaking from her mouth, he rubbed his nose over hers again and fiddled with what she figured was his jeans. And once more she had his lips and tongue. As the blunt, bulbous head of his cock pressed against her still-wet core, Heather closed her eyes and moaned.

Rob slid the swollen head inside her channel. "There you are."

"*Ohhh.*" Needing to anchor herself, she gripped the back of his neck and moaned as she exhaled a breath through her nose. As he pressed deeper, feeding her body his cock, Heather's pussy flooded with arousal. "*Ohhhh, God. Fuuuuck.*"

Rob's blue eyes were locked on hers as he seated himself to the root inside her core. "Wanted to fuck you on this counter since the first time I saw it." He drew out and slid back in. "Then again, pretty much want to fuck you anywhere and everywhere."

"Baby…" Ripples of pleasure slipped through her. Heather let go of his neck with one hand, slid it down his side and gripped his ass. "You gonna talk or you gonna fuck?"

He smirked. "Woman, you trying to get spanked?"

"Maybe."

He drew out and then drilled back in again, this time with a little more force. "See, the thing is, you can try and top from the bottom all you want. But at the end of the day"—he drew out and slammed deep—"I still own this cunt, and I still make the rules."

Oh, God, yes. *Yes,* he did.

He made *all* the rules.

And she'd let him.

Especially when he was fucking her hard. So hard her teeth clacked together and she nearly bit her tongue.

Rob slammed his pelvis to hers. "Say it."

She drew in a breath. "You own my cunt, and you make the rules."

"Fuck yeah." Rob rose off her body, grabbed her legs behind her knees and raised them so they were spread but pressed against her torso. He looked down between their bodies. "Love watching your pink cunt swallow my dick. Love seeing how you take all of me and coat me with your honey."

"Mmm." Speech was not something she was capable of, not with how he was driving her body, taking her higher and higher. And talking like he was to her was nearly enough to send her right over the edge.

Heather gripped his forearms, holding on tight as he drilled into her. The slap of skin on skin, the feel of his balls hitting her ass and how the muscles in his stomach bunched and clenched as he worked his pelvis, drove her arousal higher, her climax.

Rob set nerves inside the mouth of her cunt ablaze as he glided over them again and again, hitting her G-spot with the bulbous head and solid shaft of his prick with each pass. Giving herself over to every sensation, her body was entirely attuned to him, responding in ways she hadn't thought possible.

Heather slid her hand down the center of his stomach, spreading the perspiration from his efforts over his tight abs. Jesus, he was a sight to see. Not perfect, no one was, but to her, he was amazing. His body, his face, his smile...but also, the way he looked at her. The way he made her laugh. The way he teased her and showed up unexpectedly and ate cereal with her and... Fucked her on her kitchen counter.

Yeah, she was going to come for sure, and it was going to be cataclysmic.

Letting go of one of her legs, Rob licked his thumb and pressed it to her clit. Circling, circling...

"Oh, God!"

"Feel you, Heather."

Her clit pulsed. "Oh, *fuck. Fuck.*"

"I want all of it."

"*Rob!*" She raised her head off the counter, and her orgasm hit like an earthquake.

He slammed inside her and froze, his cock buried to the hilt. "Yeah, baby. Fuck yeah, milk it from me."

Heather's climax plowed through her, and her body shook with the effects.

A moment later, Rob let out a guttural moan and fell over her. His cock jerked, pulsing inside her with each wave of his climax. Heather wrapped her legs around him, holding him to her body.

Spurt after spurt of his hot cum filled her, coating her, branding her. Making her his. Heather liked that. Being his. Being marked by him. At least in the sexual, dominance kind of way.

But maybe, just maybe, she'd also like belonging to him in an emotional way too.

Chapter 19

Rob heard the telltale sound of a car door closing. He glanced down at Tricks, who was currently laid out like he hadn't slept in days. "Was" being the operative word because his partner heard the car door too.

The animal had raised his head and with ears at full attention was looking back and forth between Rob and the general direction of the front of the house.

"Yep. She's here." Rob jerked his chin toward the door. "You go let her in, 'kay?"

Tricks yawned, a hint of a whine peppering it. Once he was up on all fours, he bent, stretching his front paws forward, sticking his ass in the air before stepping forward and stretching his back legs out behind him—all while moving toward the door.

Rob laughed and kicked his recliner closed and got to his feet. "If you only had those damn thumbs, huh?"

Tricks stopped right in front of the entrance and sat, panting, tongue hanging out to the side of his mouth, tail doing a fantastic sweep job on the tile and essentially blocking Rob's ability to open the door.

She knocked.

Tricks's tail wagged faster.

Rob rolled his eyes. "You want to move aside, dude? I mean, I get it. I'm excited, too, but neither of us will get to have fun Heather time if you don't move your big arse out of the way."

She knocked again.

Tricks shook his head, then yawned again, this time moaning through the whole thing—as if *he* was offended?

"Don't get your panties in a twist. You'll live…now move aside, Mr. Sensitive Puppy Pants." Rob gently nudged Tricks over with his shin. Amazingly, Tricks stayed sitting at complete attention, eyes on the wooden panel as Rob opened the door.

"Hi." Heather hit him with one of her big and bright smiles, but a hot second later, as if Rob wasn't even there, she turned her gaze to Tricks. "Aw, hi, baby boy." She stepped into the house and bent to Tricks, who immediately stood and backed up as she moved with him.

"Uh…" Rob chuckled. "Hi to you, too."

As Heather moved past him and into the house, Rob closed the front door, turned, crossed his arms and leaned against the wall to watch as she petted and loved on his canine partner instead of him.

He wasn't exactly jealous of the attention Tricks was getting over him, but damn if a kiss from her *before* she laved all that sweet loving on Tricks would've been nice. Then again, he was currently and happily staring at her ass while she was bent over—so that was a benefit for sure.

Heather dropped her purse on the ground, went to her knees, resting her ass on her heels. Tricks nosed her chin before running his face over the tops of her legs, giving her a garbled moan and flopping over onto his side, nearly falling on her lap.

Heather burst into a fit of laughter as she shifted to her hip, landing near his hind end, but continued running her hands down Tricks's side. "Are you trying to cuddle with me? You're so funny." She laughed again. "You might be a little too big."

Tricks chuffed and rolled back to his feet, pivoted and rolled once more, this time so his head was facing the same direction she was. With his front paws outstretched so they were touching her knees, he licked his jowls and kept right on panting.

"Sweet boy." She scratched around the back of his ears. "That should be your name, huh? *Yes, it should.* Not Tricks. Nope. Nothing tricky about you, you big softy." Still petting his ears, Heather bent forward and pressed a kiss to the top of the dog's snout, then slid down, resting on her elbow so she was nearly eye level. "He looks like he's smiling. It's the craziest thing."

There was something so very surreal about watching this woman, who he definitely had feelings for, show his canine the amount of love she was right then. She and Rob had been seeing each other about three weeks now. Things had been great. They got along really well, the sex was out of this world, and she loved his partner.

Except she'd yet to really talk about her past or her marriage, divorce or…anything personal, really. He'd tried a few times to broach the subject, sharing various things about his past, his family, opening up bit by bit. So far she'd not gone there with him.

Not wanting to push her, he'd backed off last week and kept their time together light. Eventually, if things kept going like they were, she'd trust and share. He hoped anyway.

Rob circled around to the other side of Tricks and got down on the floor. Lying out on his side, he leaned on his elbow, mirroring Heather's position. With his eyes locked on her, he ran his hand down Tricks's side. "That's part of how he got his name. He always looks like he's smiling. Like he knows some sort of secret or joke that just got played."

She smiled. "Why not Joker then?"

"Joker seemed too...I dunno, typical maybe? I settled on Tricks instead. It's more mysterious." He smiled at her over the top of dark fur.

"Can't argue with that." She smoothed her hand over to Tricks's side and found Rob's, lacing her fingers with his as they both stroked down Tricks's thick fur.

Rob smiled. "Did you have a good day today?"

"I did. It was a long day of rearranging boxes in my garage."

Rob furrowed his brow. "Hon, you only have maybe three boxes in your garage."

"I know." She pulled her hand away to smother a yawn but then laced her fingers with his again, their linked hands resting on Tricks's side. "I was going to move them into the guest room closet but they took up too much space. I thought maybe the attic. Turns out, I can't really put stuff in the attic of this house, so I decided just to put them back in the garage."

"Babe, it's Arizona. Does anyone use their attic?"

She shrugged. "Well, my parents used the one over their garage, so I guess I tho—"

Tricks pawed Heather's breast and let out a little doggie grumble as if to remind her that he was still cuddled up to her and she needed to be paying attention to him, not Rob.

Heather burst into laughter. "He's totally copping a feel!"

"Hey, ya perv." Rob leaned over Tricks and gently tugged on his ear to get his attention. The dog looked over at him. "Paws off my girl, yeah?"

Tricks chuffed, laid his head back down.

"Awww, don't be jealous." Heather smiled and bent close to Rob. "And...your girl, huh?"

Shit, he hadn't exactly meant for that to come out, but that didn't make it any less true. She was his girl, even if she hadn't quite gotten to the same place he was yet.

Rob swallowed, her lips so close he should kiss her and let the little comment fall on the floor, or he could just...own it. Choices, choices. He could always do both. "Yeah. My girl." He closed the inch separating them and brushed his lips over hers before pulling back. "You okay with that?"

She looked down, her lashes dark against her skin, and licked her lips. A beat passed, and then she met his gaze again, an expression on her face he couldn't quite decode. "Yeah, I think I'm okay with that."

Rob raised both brows. "Did you just go cautiously realistic on me again?"

"Wait... No. I just mea—"

Without getting to his feet, Rob pushed himself up with the arm he was leaning on, and shifted himself over the top of Tricks, clearing his long body completely, before planting his other arm on the ground beside Heather, coming down on the ground beside her.

Placing his free hand on her side, he rolled her to him. "You just what?"

Her eyes went wide. "Holy upper-body strength, Batman." Tricks got to his feet with a grumble and then sniffed at the back of Heather's hair, nosing her a bit. Letting out a little laugh, she glanced over her shoulder at him. "It's okay, baby boy. I'm okay."

Rob rolled his eyes. Safe to say Tricks had decided Heather was now under his protection. Which was more than Rob could have ever wished for. It was awesome, actually, but Rob wasn't going to linger on that right now.

He watched as Tricks trotted away from them and flopped on his side onto his big dog bed. Rob refocused on Heather, who was still looking at the dog. "He's fine, but listen—"

She turned back to Rob and gave him an exaggerated eye roll. "I know what you're gonna say, but there's no need. It was just a bad word choice. Seriously. I'm sure. Totally and completely sure." She nodded as if there was no more need for discussion.

"Hmm..." He kissed the tip of her nose. "We have a good thing going. But I want to make sure you feel that too."

Her lips curved into a small smile. "I feel it. I didn't plan it, but I feel it."

"I get it. I can't really say I planned it either. But now that..." Okay, maybe he needed to just button things up now, mainly his lips. Finishing his sentence wasn't necessary. He more or less got the answer he wanted.

"Hey, no fair. Finish what you were going to say, please?" She frowned, a small crease forming between her brows.

"It's all good, bombshell." Rob let his gaze roam over her features, then smoothed her brow with his thumb. "We're good."

"Hmm." She frowned again, but this time added a pout. Not a fake bratty one either. A real one. One that hit him in the gut. Rob wanted to finish his sentence, he truly did. He wanted to tell her everything that he felt for her—everything he'd always felt for her.

If she looked close enough, she'd see everything. Yet, he didn't want to spook her. Ultimately, Rob wanted things to keep progressing in the positive direction they were heading, which was now at the point where she officially became his girl.

Heather Winters was Rob Caldwell's girl.

Wow...

* * * *

As Heather gazed into Rob's eyes, her heart jumped into her throat. She could see everything he wasn't saying in his expression. And she wasn't sure what to do with it. Mostly because over the past three weeks, she was feeling it too.

Rob smiled, cupping the side of her face in his palm, and stroked her cheekbone with his thumb. "I'm glad you're here."

"Me too." Heather pressed her palm to his chest, over his heart. "How was your day off? Do anything exciting?"

"You mean besides vacuum dog hair and run errands?" He traced a line down the side of her neck. "Nope. Though the night is looking up now that you're here."

She smiled. "Your first night off, right? It's a weeknight, but do you want to go out?"

"Couple of folks are heading down to the Dry Desert Brewery for their beer-tasting and trivia night, but I wasn't feeling up to it. I'd rather stay in with you, maybe order some takeout. Eat, talk, and maybe watch a movie if we feel like it."

Heather furrowed her brow. "You want to talk? What kind of dude are you?" She laughed. "Guys don't want to talk."

"Right, right. I forgot. I'm supposed to be a brainless caveman, slumped on the couch watching Sports Center and drinking a beer. Hand down my pants." Rob tickled her side.

She let out a squeal, squirming against him. "*Nooooohmyyyygod no! Stop!*" Through her laughter, Heather sucked in a breath.

Still tickling her, Rob nuzzled her neck, making a snorting sound as he thrust his hips forward like he was humping her leg. "Is this better?"

"*Gahhhohhmygodddd stoppp.*" Heather blurted another laugh/squeal and gripped his shoulders. "*I'm gonna pee!*"

"Whoa, whoa. Easy there." He pulled back. "No peeing, bombshell."

"Well…" She cleared her throat and wiped a tear from laughing away. "If I do, it'll be your fault."

"You started it." He shrugged. "With all your 'dudes don't talk' mess."

She laughed again. "Fair enough, but I'm just saying. The men in my past weren't fans of communication. You're like a whole new experience for me."

"Ah, yes, the dreaded ex."

"And my father."

"Right, right." He smoothed his hand down to her hip. "I get it. I got my work cut out for me." He shrugged. "I'm up for it."

"Jeez, when you say it like that, you make me sound like I'm a chore." She raised both brows.

"Yeah, well. Good thing I don't mind chores, right?"

"Wha—" Half gasping, half chuckling, Heather slapped at his chest. "So wrong."

This time it was his turn to laugh. And, God, seeing Rob's beautiful smile and full laugh was something Heather didn't think she'd ever get tired of witnessing. The genuine sound rippled through her. Her heart went soft and her belly got tight.

Rob pulled her closer, his body still shaking with his chuckles. Heather sighed and rolled her eyes. After another few beats, his laughter settled, and she pressed her nose to his neck.

He'd been wrong when he guessed her ex—at least half wrong anyway. Charles had been fine with communication in their first few years. It wasn't until after she'd pulled away from him that he finally gave up and stopped talking to her.

Rob stroked down her back and back up again, with his fingertips. His touch soft and affectionate.

Sweet, always so sweet.

She didn't deserve such sweetness.

Truth was, she was the one who had an issue communicating. There were so many things she kept to herself, like pretty much her entire life after high school. Rob had asked her about her life. Her marriage, but more obviously, divorce.

She hadn't really given him much at all. And she definitely hadn't shared the fact that she hadn't been able to have babies. Maybe she could open up about the marriage, but as far as her reproductive past went, or lack of it, she wasn't sure she could, or ever would share that with him.

Besides, they were just dating. Not getting married. Certainly not making a life together, so what difference did it make if he knew or not?

What was she supposed to do, share about the nights she'd spent drunk in the bathtub? Heather swallowed, remembering all too well, even though she'd been blind drunk, how those nights were, what had gone down. Getting plastered was the only way she'd been able to cry. Otherwise, she walked around like a zombie, mostly dead inside.

Just…existing.

Another failed round. Hell, not even a real round considering the fact that *that* time the eggs, all two of them, she'd produced weren't viable.

Not viable.

How could that have even been possible?

Poor Charles, he'd knock on the bathroom door and then…

"Heather, I'm leaving. Just wanted to let you know."

"Fine."

"Do you need anything?"

Yeah, a fucking baby! A new uterus? Ovaries that fucking work, maybe? *"Nope."*

"Sweetheart, I'm worried and I think we…I think you *need to talk to someone about this."*

"Go to work, Charles."

A few moments more and then finally, blessedly, she'd hear his footsteps retreating from the bathroom door. She didn't mean to push him away, but it'd started the year prior when the in vitro attempts were failing and, ultimately, retreating into herself and turning away from him had felt inevitable.

He just…he'd never understood what it was like for her. It wasn't possible, no matter how hard she tried to explain it. He was a man. Men were wired differently. Her father was, and so was Charles.

Not surprising she'd married a man like her father. Wasn't that how the saying went? Bitterness filled her throat, and she swallowed it down like bile.

Give those men a set of golf clubs, or some other pretentious hobby, and they were happy. Children were an accessory for men like her ex and father. Take 'em or leave 'em.

God, she wished that were true for her. If only she had been the kind of woman who didn't want kids, didn't care if she had them. But she wasn't. She wasn't.

At that time, as far as Heather had been concerned, Charles needed to go play golf, and in doing so, leave her alone. Alone with all her broken dreams, her broken body and mind.

It wasn't fair to him. At all.

But the cards she'd been dealt hadn't been fair to her either.

She hadn't asked for this fate. Hadn't asked for her uterus to be so filled with endometriosis it made having a normal cycle impossible and pain a constant. She also hadn't asked for ovaries that behaved like she was a fifty-year-old woman. And for no obvious reason either. Both issues being the reason she never would conceive, according to the doctors.

Heather hadn't asked for any of it, yet it was the fate she'd been given. Maybe it was what she'd deserved….

She focused on Rob. "To be fair, Charles was a good communicator. At least the first few years anyway."

He nodded, his chin grazing the top of her head, but said nothing.

She nuzzled his neck as waves of guilt over Charles and loss of the child she still wanted filled her heart.

"You know I'm teasing, babe." He gave her a squeeze.

Swallowing back the tears that threatened to breach her emotional walls, Heather threaded her arm under Rob's and curled it around his side. "Yes. I just wanted to be sure you knew that Charles wasn't all bad. In the end, he may have turned into someone I hated, but he wasn't always like that. I didn't always hate him."

"Understood."

"Plus, it takes two, you know? I'm just as much at fault as he was."

"Right." He stroked her back.

"People cheat for two reasons. They're either a chronic cheater, or they're miserable. Charles was miserable." She closed her eyes, not sure how she'd allowed herself to go down this road and equally unsure how to stop the train of information pouring out of her. "Bottom line, it's important to know, it was my fault he was miserable."

Rob's hand on her back stilled, and she heard him sigh, felt his chest rise and fall as he exhaled, but he said nothing.

For a moment, panic that Rob might think she was a horrible person filled Heather's chest, but thankfully, she washed it away with logic and reality. Maybe it was better that he stayed silent. What could he say, really? "It's okay" didn't really cover it. "Thanks for sharing" would be weird and awkward. And "don't blame yourself" would only be bullshit. Rob was too self-aware to think otherwise.

Another few beats passed and Heather felt his palm on the back of her head. "Thank you for telling me that stuff. I realize it's the past and you likely don't want to shine light on it." He stroked her hair and then cuffed the back of her neck. "But it's *your* past, babe. An enormous part of you, and I want you to know that you don't have to hide any of that from me. No matter how ugly you think it might be."

Relief that he wasn't judging her filled her chest, and she sagged against him. "Okay."

"Okay." He kissed the top of her head. "How about we order some dinner, yeah?"

"Yeah."

After pressing his lips to the top of her head once again, Rob got up off the ground and gave a little whistle. "C'mon, Tricks. You need dinner too."

Heather turned to her back and watched as Tricks got up from his doggie bed, did a big bend and stretch of his front and then back legs, before following Rob into the kitchen.

She blinked and drew in a slow breath. Yeah, she'd just said all that mess about her life and how it was her fault to him. And there he was, acting like it was no big deal.

Yep, sweetness *and* an abundance of understanding.

And she didn't deserve one drop of it.

Chapter 20

"*Rob!*" Heather gasped as the hot sting from the slap he'd just delivered to her pussy lips sent heated tingles radiating through her.

She arched as far as she could off the mattress, needing more of him, needing to come. Her wrists were bound to the headboard, legs to the footboard…and Rob was flat on his stomach, his head buried between her very parted legs.

They'd been together—"dating"—somewhere around six weeks, and this was the first time he'd tied all her limbs. Arms yes, but all four, no. The sex just kept getting better, and if she were honest with herself, so was the relationship. But she didn't want to focus on that. Instead, she gazed down her body and focused on the top of Rob's head.

Groaning, he sucked her clit between his lips and drove two fingers into her channel, making that come-hither motion with them, her body shaking. She needed to come. But he wouldn't let her.

And, God, it was the most intense, overwhelming, horrible and gloriously wonderful torture.

After he'd laid her out and tied her naked to his bed, a few realizations had come to Heather. First, she discovered she hated having her legs bound, and because of that, she really fucking loved it. As a result, her pussy was soaking wet before he even laid a finger or his tongue on her. And also as a result, she'd made a mental note to go shopping with him for a leg spreader.

Second—not so much a realization but further affirmation—the man loved eating pussy. And she loved that he loved it. He was also really, *really* good at it. Pretty much every damn time they had sex, Rob ate her out.

Morning, noon, night, after a run, before she could shower, when she was funky. And it did not matter one iota to him that she was funky. Bottom line: the man ate pussy like it was his last meal.

Third, if he spanked her cunt one more time, she was probably going to come. No matter how many times he told her she couldn't and her body automatically obeyed him. It was gonna happen.

And that was the fourth thing. Her body obeyed him. No matter what. Except for now, at this moment, Heather just knew, if he slapped her pussy again, she was a goner.

He nipped her clit with his teeth, and Heather arched off the bed again. "*Fuuuuck!*"

Rob growled and slipped his fingers from her channel and pressed them to her throbbing clit. "Sloppy wet for me."

"*Yes.*" She swallowed and tilted her pelvis forward.

"Your pretty pussy is nice and pink from slapping it. And your clit is so swollen it's peeking out from the hood. Fuck, I can't take it." He dropped his head and licked over her clit, sucking it before flicking it with his tongue.

Heather whimpered, shifting her hips as much as she could, trying and failing to gain more contact with his mouth. God, she was going to fly apart, or lose her mind.

Rob raised his head and looked at her, a devious grin arching his lips, and went back to rubbing small circles against the hard nub with his fingertips. "You want my cock, bombshell?"

Heather shook her head. "More than anything."

"You want to come on my cock, or do you want to come now?" He slid his fingers down to the mouth of her cunt, dipping them inside and drawing out more of her arousal to spread over her clit.

Heather bit her bottom lip. "Can't I have both?"

He chuckled, then sucked his two fingers between his lips. Before she had a chance to say anything else, those same fingers, along with the others, slapped down, landing on her labia with a loud *CRACK!*

Heather's clit pulsed with hot and sharp bursts and her core clenched down on itself. She let out a loud cry, which turned into a succession of whimpers as the ripples of her small orgasm tore through her.

As the short waves settled, Rob rose up and knelt between her legs. "Mmm." He tapped her clit with the bulbous head of his cock. "Guess my girl is getting both after all."

He pressed forward, eyes locked with her, slowly burying his prick deep, stroking every nerve ending inside her core. Fucking her with his body, but also with his eyes. Every emotion that could be called to life, his eyes awakened in her. Heather moaned, licking her lips. Yes, the sex just kept getting better and better. But the feelings were growing too.

They'd snuck up on her, hiding behind orgasms and spankings and smiles and jokes and cuddling....

God, the fucking cuddling.

With his hands planted in the mattress, his weight on his arms, Rob stared down at her. "You're beautiful when you take my cock."

Heather gazed into his eyes and knew, with every fiber of her being, he meant what he was saying. She didn't believe it would last, but she knew in the moment, he meant it. She clenched her fists around the bindings leading from her wrists to the headboard. "You're beautiful when you give it to me."

He smiled, dipped his head, and gave her his lips and tongue as he slowly, oh so slowly, fucked into her. Rocking his hips forward and back, grazing her clit with each stroke.

The slight contact was like a tease, a small spark not quite big enough to start the fire, yet almost catching each pass. Heather moaned, struggling to shift her body to match his motion, to get more contact, but her legs being bound made it impossible.

And that just made her arousal climb higher. Her legs were spread far enough apart, she just couldn't move or rock against him. She had no choice but to take it how he was giving it to her. And, God, was it good. So, so good.

Dropping down on his elbows, Rob shifted the angle of his hips and thrust forward.

Heather cried out, arching as much as she could as his pelvis ground right against her clit. "There..." She drew in a breath through her nose.

"Where, baby?" Rob thrust forward again. "There?"

"*Yesssss. Godnnngggyes!*"

"Want to feel you come." He nipped at her bottom lip. "Need to feel your tight cunt clench down on me."

Unable to speak, Heather nodded as the small knot of her orgasm grew bigger, tighter, and little bolts of pleasure arrowed from her clit outward. His pace increased, his thrusts a little harder, and she moaned, tipping her head back, pulling hard against her restraints.

And then he took her higher. Rob shifted his weight to one arm and pressed his palm to her breast bone. Heather focused on him again.

With his eyes locked with hers, he slid his hand higher and loosely cuffed her throat. "Come for me." He tightened his hold, and her eyes got wide as her cunt spasmed, clenching on his shaft. Rob groaned. "Felt that. Come for me, my girl. Let me see it, feel your sweet pussy clench me over and over." He bent and nipped at her bottom lip again. "Give me that beauty."

Pulling from her lips, he held her throat and fucked her. Faster, harder, with no mercy. Heat pooled low in her tummy and spread outward as the tingles of her orgasm crested. Keeping his pelvis tight to hers as he thrust his hips forward...drilling his cock deeper and rubbing against her clit.

That hand he had around her throat, the one that said she was his, squeezed just a little more, adding just a bit more pressure, and that was it.

"Yes..." Heather drew in a breath right as her orgasm broke through, obliterating every coherent thought in its wake. Waves of pure pleasure blasted through her so hard, her whole body convulsed with it.

"Fuck, *yes*. There it is, my girl." Rob let go of her neck and with both arms beside her again to support his weight, pounded into her, drilling her cunt hard and fast. It was a possession, a claiming, and it was raw and real.

Less than thirty seconds later, Rob rose off her body, taking his thick cock with him.

Breathless and nearly mindless, she watched as he gripped his slick erection in his fist and jerked the head and shaft until the first white ropey spurts of cum shot out of him, landing on her stomach, nearly reaching her breasts.

"Fuck, yeah...baby. Fuck!" Rob's head fell back, the tendons in his neck stretched tight. His abs glistened with sweat, and the muscles of his torso were solid as a rock. Spurt after spurt shot out of his cock, coating her stomach and dripping down his fist.

Spent, he fell forward but caught himself so his weight didn't crush her. He wouldn't have, of course, and she'd welcome the heaviness of him pinning her down. She wanted to caress his back, his shoulders, maybe even cuddle...but in her current position that wasn't happening.

Instead, she kissed his shoulder, his cheek, and anywhere else her lips could reach. And at the same time, soaked up his addictive scent and taste. Was there anything about him she *didn't* like? Strangely, no. Heather closed her eyes and let out a soft sigh.

After a few minutes, Rob nuzzled her neck and pressed a tender kiss to her pulse point. "Thank you for the beauty."

She opened her eyes and stared up at the ceiling, completely flabbergasted and knocked on her ass. Figuratively, of course. Yes, he'd asked her to give him beauty, and now he just thanked her for giving it to him.

But she was also sure Rob had no idea he'd given her beauty too.

* * * *

"Be right back." Rob pressed another kiss to her lips and rose off the bed, heading for the bathroom. Grabbing a washcloth from the shelf, he turned on the hot water and got the terrycloth nice and wet.

After cleaning himself up, he got a fresh cloth for Heather and took it to her. She was still bound to the bed, all limbs spread-eagle, and she was fucking gorgeous. She opened her eyes when she felt the mattress dip from him kneeling on it and gave him a small smile.

Taking care to be gentle, he cleaned her between her legs and then wiped her stomach and chest down. She let out a little moan, and he bent and pressed a kiss to her sternum. "I probably should've untied you before I went and got the cloth, huh."

"I'm not complaining."

"No? Does that mean you're saying you want to stay like this while we sleep? I could give your arms a little slack and play with you whenever I feel like it through the night."

She pursed her lips, as if mentally debating the idea. But then she rolled her eyes. "No, definitely not saying that. But…for the record, you already can play with me whenever you want, morning, noon or night."

"Is that so?" He shifted closer and brushed her hair away from her cheek.

"Yes, very so."

"Good to know."

She gave him a slow blink.

Rob traced her jawline, then down her throat. "So, I guess I should untie you?"

"Yes." Heather nodded.

"What if I told you I like the idea of having you all to myself." He trailed his fingertip down her sternum. "Always in my bed."

She smiled. "You mean always tied up in your bed? Are you going all stalker-boyfriend on me?"

"Yes, definitely what I meant." Rob rolled his eyes and snorted. "No, not tied to my bed—unless you wanted to be, of course." He grinned. "I take requests."

She laughed. "Just checking. Glad to know you're not going to go all stalker on me."

He kissed the tip of her nose. "Boyfriending, yes. Stalking, no. That's a word, right? Boyfriending?"

"Um, no." Heather laughed. "But there you go again, dazzling me with your proper use of the English language. Superb grammar, honey. I swear, when my hands are free I won't be able to keep them off you."

Rob laughed. "Teasing me while in such a precarious position? I gotta hand it to you, bombshell, you're one hell of a confident woman. I could tickle the ever-loving hell out of you right now."

"This may be true, but only if you want me to pee in your bed."

Rob's brows hit his hairline. "Did you just…"

She nodded. "I totally did."

"You'd pee in my bed?"

"No. Well…not on purpose exactly." She gave him a cheesy grin. "Which is why, if you don't untie me soon, I might have an accident."

He blurted a laugh. "Say no more." Rob shifted to the head of the bed and untied one arm, moved to the other side and untied the other. "Two down, two more to go."

Heather pulled her arms down, cradling them against her chest as she flexed her fingers. "Mmm. Nice."

Once he got her ankles freed up, he helped her sit up and then knelt in front of her on the floor beside the bed. "Take a minute. Let the blood start flowing before you go running off."

She leveled her gaze on him. "Tell that to my bladder."

"Got it." Rob stood and scooped Heather up in his arms. "At your service, bombshell."

She let out a little squeal when he spun around and marched her to the bathroom. He set her down on her feet in front of the toilet. "Safely delivered. You pee, I'll go get you water."

She grinned at him and tucked a lock of hair behind her ear. "Yes, sir."

Rob gave her a quick kiss, turned, and left her alone to take care of business. He was pretty sure Heather hadn't caught what he was trying to say to her. He was serious when he said he liked the idea of having her there all the time.

As in living together.

Yeah, it'd only been six weeks, but his feelings for her ran deep and he knew they were only going to grow deeper. He loved that there was always something to talk about with her. He loved how she teased him, how they joked back and forth with each other. He loved how she loved Tricks and how Tricks loved her right back.

Hell, Rob just plain loved her.

Yet there was nothing plain about that love. Just like there was nothing plain about Heather Winters. She was the bright sun after an Arizona monsoon. She was all the shining stars in the clear desert night sky.

She was so many, many amazing and wondrous things. When Rob looked into her crystal-clear green eyes, he could see everything about her that made her so special.

When he got back to the bedroom with a bottle of water for each of them, she was just coming out of the bathroom.

Locked out while they were having sex, Tricks followed into the room shortly after Rob and went and lay down in his bed. Rob smiled and set her water on her nightstand. "Everything come out okay?"

She rolled her eyes, walked over to Tricks, scratched the top of his head. "Goodnight, baby boy."

Tricks gave a soft moan before Heather stepped away from him and climbed onto the mattress. "Robert, that's like the worst question on the planet."

Rob chuckled and came around to his side of the bed. "You know what? You're right." He slid under the blankets. "I don't even know why I said it. Not like you're going to answer me and say—"

"Nope, and since you mentioned it, do you have a plunger?" She scrunched up her face. "I might've broken it."

"Exactly!" Rob laughed and shut the bedside light off, settling on his back, and motioned for her to cuddle to him. Heather curled up to his side and rested her palm on his chest. Rob covered the back of her hand with his. "Mmm. Now that we've covered that. How're you feeling?"

She yawned. "Tired."

"Me too. You sore at all? Anything cramped up?"

"Nope." She stroked the skin on his chest with her thumb. "You can do that anytime you want. Oh, you know what would be even better?"

"Tell me."

"You tie me up on my stomach, spank the ever-loving hell out of my ass, then fuck me from behind." Her voice was low, husky and laced with lust.

A bolt of heat shot down Rob's spine. Though the room was dark, he glanced over at her. "You want a paddle, a flogger, a crop, a belt, or my hand?"

"Damn...I think you could pick any one of those and I'd be up for it."

"I'll surprise you."

"Mm'kay." She wiggled. "Shit, now I'm horny again."

"Feel free to wake me up in the middle of the night to take care of that." He smiled, let out a sigh, and closed his eyes. "For now, I need a little bit of rest because my mojo tank is on E."

"Whaaa?" Heather laughed. "*Ohhkayyy*, fine. But for the record, I wasn't the one who brought up what toy to use to paddle my ass."

"This is true. But you were the one that brought up having your ass paddled to begin with."

"Touché." She shifted her hand and pinched his nipple.

"You really *do* want to be tied up while you sleep, don't you?" With a snort, he grabbed her hand and re-centered it on his chest. "I thought you were tired?"

She laughed. "Whatever. Go to sleep."

"I'm trying."

"Shh."

"Woman." He grinned, couldn't help himself.

She let a little giggle escape before she shifted and kissed his shoulder and whispered, "Night, Rob."

"Night, bombshell." Rob's grin turned into a smile.

Yeah, he was completely in love with her.

Chapter 21

"That was so awesome!" Heather lowered the footrest on the reclining seat in the movie theater.

"It was. She was a complete badass." Rob gathered their empty candy boxes.

Heather grabbed her purse, the near-empty popcorn bucket, and got to her feet. Stepping out of the row they sat in, she made her way toward the exit. A sharp deep pain hit her lower abdomen, and she stopped moving, drawing in a deep breath.

"You okay, babe?" Rob clasped her upper arm.

Heather swallowed. "Yeah. Good. Just a girl cramps. I'm fine." She smiled, and although the pain hadn't passed, she moved forward anyway. After giving herself another few moments to adjust, she glanced over at him. "I really didn't know what to expect, you know? Hell, Lynda Carter was the original gorgeous Wonder Woman, but that was seventies TV. You and I weren't even alive yet." She laughed. "If it wasn't for clips on YouTube, I'd have no clue."

Bless him, he looked concerned, but carried on with the conversation she was pushing anyway. "I'm not sure I've ever seen a clip of the original Wonder Woman."

She continued to the exit door. "Oh my God, you should for sure look that up." She smiled as they deposited their trash and exited the theater. "I'm glad they went in a totally different direction. Girl power all the way."

Rob chuckled. "It was definitely worth seeing it on the big screen. But superheroes always are."

Still smiling, and ignoring the discomfort she felt, she reached and laced her fingers in his. "So true."

They walked, hand in hand, through the main part of the theater to the exit. Jeez, she was in a great mood. A fantastic mood, actually. And she was determined to not let her damn uterus affect her night with him.

She and Rob had been seeing each other for two months exactly, and they'd gone on more dates than she could count at this point. Tonight was a sort of "anniversary date," though she wasn't the one who called it that.

No, leave it to her incredibly romantic boyfriend to decide they needed to go out on their two-month anniversary. Dinner and a movie. Followed by drinks with friends. Who knew men kept track of such things? Even when she'd first been married and things were wonderful, Charles wouldn't have been able or even willing to mark anniversaries by the month.

Rob was different though. He was a whole new kind of experience for her. And Heather was starting to realize she was incredibly lucky to be with him, even if she wasn't worthy of him.

After the hellacious mess she'd made of her life, marriage, and career, she couldn't possibly deserve someone as wonderful as Rob Caldwell. Yet, here she was, walking beside him. Holding his hand. Sleeping in his bed. And sex for days.

As a result, being in a good mood had started to become almost normal. An amazing thing, really. Heather's wallowing in misery and self-loathing had taken a back seat. Not to say she was cured and she didn't still have down days, because she wasn't and she did. She still had them a lot.

But in between all of that, she now had Rob.

And she had Tricks.

New friends too.

Amazingly, Heather had a life. Again.

It wasn't anything like the life she had before. And she wouldn't say this life was better than the other. It was just…different. But different was okay with her. Honestly, different was probably exactly what she needed.

As they approached their parking spot, Rob hit the key fob and unlocked the 4Runner. Like he always did, he walked to the passenger side and opened her door.

"Thanks, babe." Heather kissed his cheek and angled into the SUV.

"Of course." He closed her in and came around to the other side and got behind the wheel. "You still up for drinks with the crew?"

"Yes, absolutely." She smiled.

He caught her gaze and paused. More than a few heartbeats passed before he broke the soft silence stretching between them. "You're really beautiful right now."

Her stomach got warm, and Heather felt the heat hit her cheeks. "Thank you, honey."

"No. I mean, yes—" He shook his head and smiled. "You're welcome, babe." He cupped her cheek in his palm. "What I mean is you're always beautiful, but right now you look especially so. Different somehow."

She shrugged one shoulder. "I'm happy."

He raised both brows. "Happy?"

"Yep—" She leaned closer to him and let out an easy sigh. "Happy."

"Not even being cautiously realistic about it?"

She let out a short laugh. "Nope."

He smiled. "I like that." He stroked his thumb over her bottom lip. "Happy is a good thing, baby."

Rob's smooth, deep voice spilled into her, sending tingles through Heather's body. She closed her eyes, letting herself feel everything he was giving her. "It is, I agree."

His mouth touched hers. Rob's lips were soft, timid at first. But then, like it had become between them, the smoldering heat exploded into an inferno. Heather let out a moan and clasped his wrist, holding on as he ravaged her mouth.

Jesus, she could kiss him for days. The way his tongue felt against hers made her stomach tight with arousal. And the way he tasted, his flavor speeding through her, was like being drunk on a vintage wine.

Rob let out a strangled groan that she felt between her legs and pulled from her lips. Panting, he pressed his forehead to hers. "Fuck, all I want to do right now is take you home and fuck you senseless."

She sucked in a breath. "You have the best ideas."

He laughed and shook his head. "You're one of a kind, bombshell. Don't ever think different."

Wow...

God, could he get any better? Not even if she conjured him in a dream. She licked her lips. "Does that mean we're not going home so you can fuck me senseless?"

Rob laughed again. "Well, no. It just means that first we're going to celebrate our two-month anniversary with our friends by having one, maybe two drinks. While we do that, I get to show off my beautiful, sexy woman so all the guys present know I'm the luckiest son of a bitch on the planet." He kissed the tip of her nose. "Then, after that, I'm going to take you home and fuck you senseless."

She smiled. "Okay."

"Okay." Rob pulled back, settled in his seat and started the SUV.

She gazed over at him. How come she got to have this second chance? Things were awesome between her and Rob, but seriously, how could things keep going like they were? She was stupid to think they would. After all, what sort of future could there be for them together?

Rob was a young, healthy man. Plus, he was a die-hard romantic with parents who were happily married. He'd want that too. Marriage, kids, etc. Even if Heather was willing to entertain the idea of marriage again, kids were 100 percent a no go. And adoption wasn't an option. Hell, if a person were lucky enough to get a baby, a *healthy* baby, with the way open adoptions had become such a popular thing, they'd have to keep the birth parents in the game. Definitely a no go for Heather.

So yeah, depriving an amazing man like Rob the gift of a family? Hell no. Heather didn't have it in her to do that to him. So, no. Definitely not. They had no future.

This couldn't, wouldn't, last much longer. Eventually, she'd have to find a way to let him go.

Just…not yet. She needed a little more time with him.

* * * *

"Hey!" Rob waved at the table in the far back with all of Rob and Heather's friends. God, he loved that his friends had become "their" friends. With a smile on his face, he kept hold of Heather's hand and navigated around the other patrons and tables in the Dry Desert Brewery toward the group.

She'd gotten quiet in the 4Runner on the drive over, and although he hated it when she withdrew, he'd learned enough about her in the past eight weeks to know that sometimes she just needed a few minutes to sort through something. Or to make up her mind about it. He'd give her that. He'd give her anything.

Another concern was the "girl cramps" as she called them. It was something that seemed to be happening more and more as of late. He didn't press her about it, but he didn't forget about it either. He had no idea if it was anything beyond normal female monthly cycle stuff, but if it was, he hoped she'd tell him.

"Rhonda! You made it." Jeff grinned at them from his spot at the table. "Hey, have I told you lovebirds how adorable you are together? It's like a match made in heaven, for realsies."

"God help me." Tish rolled her eyes. "For realsies? How many guinea slaps to the back of the head are you going to earn tonight?"

"Ay, Mami." Jeff raised a brow and rubbed the back of his head as if she had in fact slapped him there. "You know I secretly love it when you're mean to me."

"It's not a secret if you tell everyone, Jeffrey." Tish stood, leaned toward Heather, and hugged her. "Good to see you, gorgeous. You too, Rob."

Heather shook her head. "You two are funny."

"That's one way of putting it." Rob laughed.

"First round is on me." Jeff slapped his hand down on the table.

Rob grinned. "Best idea you've had yet."

Heather shook her head and focused specifically on Derek and Rayna. "Hello, my favorite couple. Tell me again, why aren't we at the Whiskey Barrel instead?"

Rayna smiled. "Hi to you too. We can head over there in a little bit if you want. Just figured since it's still early we'd be able to have better conversation here."

Derek nodded. "Basically, you can't hear yourself think with the band they got playing over there tonight."

"Got it. Good thinking." Heather took a seat. "I should text Kim and let her know we're here."

Okay, apparently all was well in the land of Heather. Quiet contemplation mood gone and no sign of girl cramp pain either. At least from what he could tell based on her body language. Rob exhaled and took the seat beside hers.

"Already took care of it," Jeff said and slid a menu Rob's way.

Tish snapped her head to look at Jeff. "Took care of what?"

Jeff's brows rose. "I texted Kim. Let her know where we are."

An expression filled Tish's eyes that looked a whole lot like jealousy, but how could that be since she—

"I wasn't aware you had her number." She looked away and shrugged. "Anyway, I need something different tonight."

Jeff frowned but then smoothed his features, sliding a little closer to her. "Is there a problem, Mami? You jealous?"

Tish focused on the menu. "Stop calling me that."

"Only when you stop pretending to hate it." Jeff grinned.

Tish rolled her eyes and looked back at him. "First, I'm not jealous or pretending. You're completely delusional." She poked him in the chest. "Second, my palm is itching to knock you in the back of your head for annoying me."

Jeff looked down at her finger against his chest, and popped both brows, the corner of his mouth arcing into a grin. But he said nothing. Tish rolled her eyes once more and looked away.

"Well, that was interesting," Heather mumbled.

Rob turned to look at his girl and kept his voice low. "It sure was." He pressed a kiss to her temple. "Let's get a beer."

"Going for broke since Jeff's buying." Heather grinned.

Rob chuckled and pressed another kiss to her temple. She smiled at him and placed her palm on his thigh before returning her focus to the beer list.

Their night had been awesome so far. Now, with their friends, it could only get better.

* * * *

Careful to keep her voice low, Heather leaned forward and jerked her chin in the direction of Jeff and Tish. "Yeah, so, any change with those two?"

Rayna and Derek were sitting directly across from her and Rob, and Rayna cupped her hand on the side of her mouth and loudly whispered. "Foreplay."

"Nailed it." Rob nodded.

"Right? That's exactly what I was thinking." Heather leaned her chin on her palm. "I hope he makes his move soon because she's—"

"*Really pretty*. I know." Rayna shrugged. "My bestie is hot, hot, hot."

"Doc, you're ten times that hot as far as I'm concerned." Derek winked at Rayna, and she immediately blushed then bent closer to the table. God, they were cute. "As far as they want us to know, they're no way in hell dating. But as far as all of us believe, based on all that mess you're witnessing right now, they *have got* to be dating."

Rob tipped his head to the side. "Or at least fucking."

Rayna blurted a laugh and covered her mouth, but Heather and Derek laughed out loud, failing to cover anything.

"Ahem, what's got everyone giggling like a gaggle of girls over there?" Jeff leaned forward, which also allowed him to brush up against Tish's arm as well as be a whole lot closer to her.

"Gaggle?" Tish laughed, appearing to "try" to brush him away by wiggling her shoulder. Though Jeff didn't budge. And Tish didn't "try" to shove him off again.

Yeah, Heather was 150 percent sure there was so much more going on with those two. And neither one would admit it. Craziest damn thing.

The whole group of friends hoped Jeff and Tish figured their shit out soon because the constant tension, mostly sexual, bouncing between them was enough to consume the whole table when they were all out together.

"Okay then, moving on. I'm trying a cider tonight. Where's the waitress?" Heather got to her feet and looked around.

Rob glanced at the menu. "Which one, bombshell?"

Heather sat again and pointed to the cider. "Storm the Peach."

"Good choice. That's actually really delicious." Derek nodded and looked back to his menu.

"Have I tried that one yet?" Rayna glanced over at the menu Derek had. Derek put his arm around his woman. "I don't think so, babe. You want to?"

"Um, Heather, can I have a sip of yours when it comes, see if I like it?" Heather smiled. "Of course."

The waitress came over and they ordered a round, plus an appetizer. As they waited and even after their beers and food were delivered, Jeff and Tish continued their banter, but a little quieter than before.

The rest of the group went on ignoring them, which had become the norm.

Rob took a swig of his beer and set the glass down. "You off for the rest of the week, Derek?"

"Actually, for the next two. Finally talked Rayna into getting out of town for more than three days." Derek smiled.

"Not my fault." Rayna rolled her eyes. "I finally have enough staff at the vet hospital."

"Sounds fun! Where are you going?" Heather sipped her cider. "Oh, yum. That *is really* good, Rayna." She passed the glass over.

"Oooh, yum. I definitely want one." Rayna licked her lips and handed the glass back.

"I'll go get you one, baby." Before getting to his feet, Derek gave Rayna a kiss on the side of her head before walking off toward the bar.

"Thanks, honey." Rayna smiled and sat back in her seat. "Too bad your nursing degree doesn't translate to veterinary medicine. I'd love to have you in the clinic with me."

Heather laughed. "Not a bad idea. How long is that program?"

Rayna tipped her head to the side, her brows drawn together in thought. "Eighteen months, I think."

"Sweet. Tricks would get his own private nurse?" Rob grinned.

"Right? As if he doesn't already have that." Heather chuckled. "So, where're you two going on vacation?"

Derek returned and handed Rayna her cider. "Here you go, Doc."

"Thanks, honey." Rayna smiled and took the glass. "We're going to wander around Northern Cal. Check out Napa, then San Francisco."

Heather smiled. "Ooh, fun! Have you been?"

"Nope." Rayna shook her head. "But it's our anniversary, so I'm guessing Napa should be pretty romantic."

"Aww, how long have you two been together?" Heather rested her elbows on the table and leaned forward.

"One year." A proud smile spread across Derek's lips.

Rayna's cheeks went pink, and she sipped her cider. Heather smiled and winked at her friend. Rayna and Derek were happy together, and any fool could see they were a total match and meant for each other.

"That's awesome!" Rob laughed and raised his glass. "A toast to your one year and our two months together!"

"Here, here." Derek raised his glass. Rayna joined him. They all clinked and then sipped.

Heather took a healthy swallow.

Rob set his beer down. "I wouldn't trade a minute of it."

"Me either, man. Me either." Derek put his arm around Rayna.

Rob laughed. "Shit, who knew we were such romantics?"

"I think it's sweet." Rayna smiled at Heather, and leaned closer to Derek.

Heather shrugged. "Not gonna hear any complaints from me. Two badass cops with a romantic side? That's looks a lot like heaven t—"

"Has anyone ever told you that you're a pain in the ass?" Tish stood, her chair screeching behind her.

With a smirk, Jeff leaned back in his chair, raising the front legs off the ground, balancing on the back ones. "Only you. But, sugarplum, I thought you said you liked it when we did it that way."

Oh. Shit.

"Jeff…wow. Did you really just say that?" The look on Tish's face was a cross between hurt and fury as she picked up her drink and downed the remains. After setting down the glass on the table, she turned to Jeff, planted both hands on his chest and shoved him.

Jeff, who obviously had no idea what was coming, still grinning like a fool, tipped backward and, when he hit the ground, rolled ass over teakettle.

And Tish stormed out of the bar.

Ohhhhh, shiiiiit…

"I should probably go after her." Rayna got to her feet.

Derek stood and clasped Rayna around the waist. "No, baby. Let her go. I think it's time to go to the Whiskey Barrel."

Rob looked at Heather. "You want to go with them, or do you want to go home?"

Heather slid her glass away and stood. In the short time they'd been there, her cramping had gotten worse. Not unbearable yet, but bad enough that a heating pad would feel like heaven. "I think may—"

"Isn't Kim supposed to be over there too?" Derek came around the side of the table.

Crap. She'd forgotten. "Yep. We should probably get over there."

Jeff, who'd managed to get to his feet without any of them noticing, came up beside Derek. "So, what's the plan, Shirley?"

Derek rolled his eyes. "The plan is, I'm getting you a muzzle and leash, and you're staying with me and Rob while we pay the bill. Also, hand over your cell phone, that way you don't text Tish and make a bigger mess."

"But—"

Rob raised a hand. "Nope. Shut it." He looked at Heather. "You and Rayna head on over there and find Kim. We'll see you in a few minutes."

"Okay, honey." Heather nodded and turned to Rayna. "Ready?"

"Yes, ma'am." Rayna linked her arm with Heather's. "Why does it feel like we just missed the last five minutes of the final episode in a season of *This Is Us*?"

They walked out the door. "Right? And *ohmyGod*, I love that show."

Rayna laughed. "Me too!"

Heather shook her head and continued on down the sidewalk, arm in arm with someone who she was happy to call a friend. Considering she'd been back in Arizona for a little over a year, the only friends she had were the ones she'd made in the last few months since moving to the East Valley.

All her supposed friendships had fallen by the wayside in Maryland. Her sole focus had been Charles, and soon after him, it'd been all about having a baby. Her world had gotten so small that in the end, there was no one.

A bathtub and bottle of wine only made good companions for so long. Eventually they turned on their user and stole all the light that should exist inside them.

Heather wasn't sure how to be a good friend anymore, but she was grateful for Rayna, for Kim, just the same. Tish was part of that group too. Heather was worried about her because something was definitely up with her and Jeff.

Whatever it was, both were being damn private about it. For sure, Heather could definitely understand that, respect it even. She had plenty of things to keep private herself.

At that moment it was the fact that her pain was back and making itself known in a way that was scarier than Heather wanted to admit.

Chapter 22

"Oh, God!" Heather's orgasm hit with a force so hard, she nearly lost her balance. With her back against the wall in Rob's bedroom and one leg curled over his shoulder, she held tighter to the soft strands of hair on top of his head and rode the waves rolling through her.

On his knees, his face buried between her thighs, he growled and sucked her clit harder, granting her no mercy.

Her hips jerked forward, pretty much of their own volition. Every nerve in her body was sensitive, especially the ones in her clit. "Babe…" Still trying to catch her breath, she licked her lips and looked down at him. "Stop. I can't…"

Rob looked up at her, his expression all satisfied male, and kept his eyes on her as he oh-so-slowly licked through her slit and then swirled his tongue around her swollen clitoris. "You want my cock, bombshell?"

"Yes."

"How do you want it?" Another swirl of his tongue.

She drew in a shaky breath and loosened her hold on his hair. "Whatever way pleases you most."

He nipped at her clit. "What pleases me most is fucking you how you want to be fucked. Now—" He drew his tongue through her labia once more. Licked his lips and moaned as if what he tasted was the most divine thing on the planet. "How. Do. You. Want. It."

Heather's stomach did a flip-flop. He was so sexy when he was like this. His eyes all lazy and filled with lust. His hair disheveled from her fingers running through it. His lips…God his lips.

Ten weeks, and they were still going strong. Rob had managed to get sexier damn near every day they spent together, in bed and out of it. Of course, he'd gotten better and better at making her come too. Moreover, he excelled at making her smile and laugh.

If she wasn't careful, she was going to get attached....

Fuck, who was she kidding? She was already attached. Had been for a few weeks now.

Heather swallowed, slipped her leg off his shoulder before bending forward and cupping his face in her palms. She stroked her thumb over his bottom lip and took in his features. "I want you to put me on my knees... but different."

"Show me." Rob got to his feet.

He still had his jeans on, but had lost the shirt somewhere on their way from the living room to the bedroom. Heather dropped her hands to his shoulders, then smoothed them over and down to his lean, muscled chest. He had such an amazing body.

She bent and pressed her lips to his sternum. At the same time, she dropped her hands to his button and zipper and undid both, freeing his engorged cock. After shifting his pants lower, she slid her hand inside his boxers. The thick heat of him hit her palm and she moaned, trailing kisses down the center of his abs.

She just wanted one taste....

Gripping his shaft, she licked over the head, catching the bead of pre-cum waiting for her. With her tongue coated with him, she moaned. "So sweet. Always so damn sweet."

Wanting just a little more, Heather sucked the bulbous crown into her mouth, and let him go.

Rob growled, and his hand landed in her hair.

Straightening but holding tight to his erection and still stroking the length, she pressed her lips to his. Rob's tongue was demanding, wet and warm, and he tasted of her pussy. And she tasted of him. The mix a heady combination she couldn't seem to get enough of.

Wrapping his arms around her waist, Rob picked her up and walked to his bed. Heather broke the kiss when she felt the soft mattress against her ass. Doing as he asked, she crawled to the center of the bed and got into the position she wanted to be in.

Kneeling, her knees tight together instead of apart, and although she had her arms out in front of her on the mattress, she sat back a bit, almost into a squatting position. She wanted him snugged up behind her, on his knees with his legs positioned on the outside of hers.

Rob seemed to understand exactly what she wanted because as she looked back at him, he climbed onto the bed and moved behind her. "I see where you want it." He stroked two fingers through her folds, front to back, stopping at the mouth of her pussy. Slipping them inside her, he bent forward, his chest to her back, and kissed her shoulder. "Nice and wet for me."

Heather drew in a deep breath as the sensations from his touch rocketed through her. "Always."

Sliding his fingers free, he moved his hand around her waist and down to her clit. "Raise up for me, just a little."

She did, tilting her ass back...and felt the blunt head of his penis. "*Yes.* Right there..."

As the bulbous head filled her cunt, Rob let out a hiss and pressed his fingers against her clit. "Take it, baby. *Fuck*... Slide right down and stuff yourself full."

Heather slid back, impaling herself on his cock until he was fully seated inside her. All her breath left her lungs as every sensation her body was capable of feeling sped through her from head to toe.

And then he started moving, and she had no choice but to move with him. Rob kept the pressure on her clit with the fingers of one hand and grabbed her breast with the other, twisting her nipple between his fingertips.

With his lips pressed to her shoulder, he tilted his pelvis forward and back, and she rocked against him, his shaft sliding deep within her channel. Slow and easy, but definitely not softly. Working her clit and nipple, driving her higher with each thrust.

With a moan that ended in a whimper, she closed her eyes and let this moment, let Rob have her...

All of her.

The glide of his cock inside her, the feel of his big body behind her, his arms encompassing her, brought Heather to a whole new level of pleasure. Her climax rose easily, her body tight with the need to orgasm. A sheen of sweat coated her body, a drop sliding down her hairline. "*Rob...*"

"Tell me." He nipped her shoulder.

She rolled her hips. "Harder."

Rob let go of her nipple and clit and gripped her waist in his palms. "Work your clit."

"Yes." Heather moved her fingers between her legs.

Rob raised her and drove her back down onto him. His thighs slapping against the back of her legs and ass as his cock drilled deep into her over and over.

Heather groaned and rubbed her clit. "*Baby*... Oh, God, don't stop!"

He sped up, slamming into her harder. "*Fuck.* Heather..."

Her orgasm burst through her, and she stiffened. Little electric spasms fired in her clit, and her cunt clenched down on his length.

"Fuck, fuck!" Rob wrapped his arms around her waist and drilled into her until his own climax hit and he slammed deep, holding her tight to him. His shaft jerked inside her, rapid little spasms as he spurted his release, filling her cunt. Heather swallowed, still trying to catch her breath. Covering his arms with hers, she held onto him as much as he held onto her. She didn't want to let go.

Breathing heavy, Rob pressed his forehead to her upper back. "I love you."
I love you?

Heather closed her eyes and tried to tell herself that she hadn't heard him say those words. But the truth was, she had.

He'd said them.

And she couldn't un-hear them.

* * * *

Heather lay awake in Rob's bed, beside him. The deep pain in her abdomen was back. Coming more and more after sex now. She was still pain-free during intercourse, so she'd deal with it.

Heather glanced at the clock, nearly three a.m. and she knew there would be no sleep for her. After they'd made love—and make no mistake, what they'd done earlier in his bed could only be considered making love—Rob had gotten out of bed and gone to get a wet cloth to clean her up.

It was something he'd always done, his form of after-care even. Or maybe it was just care… He loved her, he told her so for the first time tonight, but he'd been showing for a while now. Rob always managed to make her feel like some sort of cherished treasure. Heather swallowed and glanced over at him, his face obscured in the darkness of his bedroom. He was facing her, curled on his side, one hand resting low on her tummy.

Below her navel. Right where a baby would be if she were capable of carrying one.

Drawing in a shaky breath, she placed her hand on top of his and gently, slowly, carefully slid it several inches higher so instead it rested just below her breasts. Refocusing on the ceiling, Heather blinked and listened to Rob breathe.

Aside from her pain, there was only one single, very big reason why she couldn't sleep. And it wasn't the three-word declaration he'd made.

Instead, the winner of the most fucked-up thing in the world slot was the honest fact that she'd felt the same too. Maybe she had for a while now, she wasn't sure. At the very least, it was a definite that what she felt for him tonight was love. Bright. Clean. And real.

Fuck, how was she going to handle this?

Unfortunately, there was no way on God's green earth she would let those words slip from her lips to him. If she went there, there'd be no coming back from it; she'd never be able to walk away from him.

And as tempting as it was to give him all that she felt, especially tonight, Heather couldn't allow herself to go there. It would mean letting go of too much of her past that she still wasn't ready to let go of.

As some might assume it would be, it wasn't Charles she was holding on to. Charles was gone from her heart. No, it was the baby. The baby she never got to have. Worse, it was the baby Charles got to have with someone else….

Her fertility issues were like an iceberg…the most obvious piece visible above the waterline, seemingly manageable. Something she should be able to navigate around. Yet lurking below the surface hid a mammoth glacier, one hundred times bigger than what society ever deemed acceptable or could even fathom.

She was simply not right emotionally, in the most complicated of ways. And Heather was certain she couldn't effectively articulate them all. Point was, she was fucked up. And had no business pulling Rob toward her heart, only to tear chunks out of him with something he didn't know existed, and she couldn't control.

She was greedy though, that was for sure. And selfish. Selfish to the core.

Letting herself love him, at least openly, wasn't an option. But letting him go felt utterly impossible. Heather closed her eyes and swallowed past the lump in her throat. No, sleeping wasn't going to happen. Not until she figured out how to handle this—how to do what was right and walk away from Rob.

Before he hated her as much as she hated herself.

Chapter 23

Rob sat out on his back patio, hot mug of coffee in his hand, and threw a tennis ball deep into the yard. Tricks retrieved it and brought it back to Rob. Rinse and repeat and so on…

"*Sitz.*" Rob sipped his coffee then threw the ball. This wasn't training, this was just for fun. After all, his canine got to have days off just like Rob did. With ears up at attention, Tricks watched the ball in the air but did not move…and he wouldn't, not until Rob told him to fetch using the German command.

Okay, so maybe this was still a little bit of training, but really, using the commands with him even when off duty was good practice. Plus, Rob didn't use commands for everything, and Tricks got to play regardless. So, win-win.

"*Bring.*" As the dog took off, Rob took another sip of his coffee and glanced at the clock on his phone.

Nine a.m. and Heather was still dead asleep in his bed. Not that it bothered him she was sleeping in. He rather liked her in his bed, sleeping or awake. However, his shift started at noon, so it meant he wouldn't get as much time with her as he'd hoped.

All good, he'd just have to deal because obviously she needed the sleep. Except, there was a conversation that needed to happen too. The one about the fact that he'd told her he loved her.

Yes, he'd said it upon climax while making incredible love to her, but that was beside the point. He still meant it, had been feeling it in his bones for the past couple of weeks, and Rob wanted to make sure she *knew* he meant it. That it wasn't just something to say because he was all caught up in his orgasm head rush, although yes, truth be told, that'd been the catalyst.

"Leave it." Tricks dropped the ball in Rob's hand. "Good boy." Rob scrubbed his palm over Tricks's big head before scratching behind his ears. "You want to go again?"

Tricks sneezed and then let out a little whine.

"I'll take that as a yes." Rob sat back, ball in hand.

The only reason he hadn't told Heather before last night was because he wasn't sure she was ready to take all that on from him. Hell, Rob hadn't planned on telling her last night, except, of course, he was lacking a whole lot of blood to his brain, thoroughly caught up in her, her body and her scent and how she felt and—

Rob blew out a breath at the memory, feeling it right in his dick. He shook his head. God, he'd been so caught up in her, before he could stop himself, the words had come out of his mouth.

"Get ready, Tricks." Rob raised his hand to toss the ball and—

"May I join you?"

At the sound of her voice, Rob's throw suffered a sad sort of fumble and the ball landed only about ten feet away. A quick glance told him Tricks was no longer interested in fetch because the dog was already sitting at her feet, ears at attention. Panting. Tongue hanging out.

Rob shook his head and chuckled before smiling at her. "Morning, baby. Of course you can join me. I've been hoping you were going to get up soon but didn't want to wake you."

She padded over, barefoot, cradling a mug of coffee in her hands and clad in only his T-shirt, which landed mid-thigh on her. Another positive to the list—he for sure loved seeing her wrapped in his shirt. It never failed to have the possessive part of his soul shouting a declaration the likes of "I'm the luckiest man in the world, fuckers!"

Internally, of course.

Stifling a laugh at how caveman his thoughts could be, he sipped his coffee and refocused on her. She'd pulled her hair up on top of her head in a messy little bun, and the skin on her face glowed with a soft shine. All traces of makeup were gone, as if she'd just washed it.

As she passed him on her way to the open chair beside him, Rob caressed the side of her bare thigh with the back of his knuckles. So soft. So sexy. Stopping, she glanced back at him and, showing no hesitation, turned fully, bent forward, and gave him a gentle kiss.

The soft brush of her lips pulled a moan from deep in Rob's chest. Not wanting her to step away yet, Rob cupped the side of her face, and stroked her chin with his thumb.

Drawing back, but not getting very far because of his hold, she caught and held his gaze—her green eyes seeing straight into his soul. A soft smile arched her lips. "Morning."

Did she even know she could do that? Rob drew in a breath, and exhaled. God, he so fucking loved her. "Morning, beautiful."

Letting his hand fall to his lap, Rob sat back and watched as she came around his chair and sat in the one to his right. Tricks followed her, as if she was his long-lost mommy, and sat his ass down on the concrete right beside her chair.

Heather smiled at the animal, smoothed the fur on his head. "Good morning to you too, baby boy."

"That dog is totally in love with you." Rob sipped his coffee.

She shrugged. "I'm good with that."

Okay, open door…he just needed to walk through it. Rob nodded and focused his attention on the yard.

Holding back wasn't going to get him anywhere. He drew in another deep breath and spoke after the exhale. "What about the fact that I'm in love with you? You good with that too?"

Rob couldn't bring himself to look over at her. Seconds ticked by, staring out into the yard. Felt like hours though. He raised his mug to his lips, tipped it back and swallowed a mouthful of coffee.

Fuck…her silence was going to be the death of him.

* * * *

Heather stared into her creamy mocha-colored coffee a little longer than she'd anticipated she would. She had no clue how to answer Rob, how to give him what she knew he needed and most certainly deserved.

Christ, she was tired. She'd barely gotten any sleep last night, and the small amount she did get was disturbed by a more severe pain kicking in, followed by an early appearance by her period.

Her cycle was completely unpredictable now. Thank God she'd brought some pads over to Rob's or things would've been a mess. A heating pad would've helped, too, but she couldn't find it and didn't want to wake him and ask.

The silence stretched, her mind raced and the words poised on the tip of her tongue—

I'm completely fucked up and because of it, I think we should take a break, take a step back…things are moving too fast. I don't want to hurt you.

That's what she needed to say. That's what she should say. But fuck all, she wasn't ready to let him go.

"It's okay. I don't want to rus—"

"No, please? Just...I need some time." She chanced a glance at him, and as she feared, pain had fused itself into his features.

The tightness in his jaw, his brow drawn down low over his eyes. He looked like she'd just punched him in the gut. Or maybe the heart was more appropriate. She swallowed past the tightness in her throat. He wasn't looking at her, not that she could blame him. She wouldn't want to see her either. Hell, she'd rather be anyone else but herself right now. Heather pressed her lips together.

He rubbed his chin with his thumb. "It's okay, babe. I get it. It's too soon."

"I feel so much for you. I care about you, I do. But please understand, it's just, I'm not—" He flinched, and she had to look away. It was too hard to see the cuts she was already making in his heart. Like the coward she was, she focused on the coffee in her mug instead. "It's not too soon, or rather, it wouldn't be for someone else. But for me—" She shrugged. "I have...scars, I guess."

He cleared his throat. "Look, I know you have scars. I just wish you'd let me be there to help you heal or if I can't help, at least to just be there." He leaned forward. "I don't know, I guess help me understand what you're saying here. Do you want to take a break or keep going? Should I cut my losses now?"

Heather jerked her gaze back to him. He still wasn't looking at her. As a result, a dull ache bloomed in her chest. "The right thing for me to do would be to end things, or at least push the pause button. But..."

"But what?" He looked at her, hope and pain mingling in his eyes.

Heather flinched at the rawness in his expression. Goddammit, she was fucking this up. She was fucking him up, and yet she could not stop herself. "But I don't want to let you go."

He blinked. "Then don't. Because I definitely don't want to let you go."

"It's more complicated than that."

"Nothing worth having is simple, Heather." He reached across to her seat and held his palm open. "I don't want simple. But I do want you."

Heather placed her hand in his, her silent agreement to stay with him. Spineless didn't even scratch the surface of what she was, though. Yes, she loved him, but she had no business staying with him. She was doing it anyway.

Rob was silent for a long time, his gaze locked with hers. His expression sad, but still hopeful, or maybe it was caution she was seeing. She wasn't sure what Rob saw in her eyes, but what Heather felt was a world of turmoil swirling inside her heart and mind.

And still, her soul was empty.

Chapter 24

Heather pulled her Mercedes into her parents' driveway and shut off the vehicle. "Here we are." The sunshine in her voice was completely forced, and he probably knew it.

Rob rolled his eyes. "Stop, it's going to be fine."

Yep, he knew. After rolling her eyes back at him, she blew out a breath and opened the driver's door. Two weeks had passed since the "love me or not, here I come" convo had taken place between her and Rob in his backyard. After that, though she still hadn't returned those three terrifying words to him, she'd met his parents and brother over family pizza night, and now the man was bound and determined to meet hers.

"You keep telling yourself that, gorgeous, but don't say I didn't warn you." With both brows raised, Heather pointed her finger at him and got out of the car. Poor guy had no idea what he was he was signing himself up for.

It was a bad idea, but what the hell did she know? They were just her parents, after all.

Rob emerged and rested both arms on the roof of her car and stared at her. "Hey, relax, please? They're just parents. Next week we can go have pizza with mine."

She came around the front of the car, tugging her purse straps up onto her shoulder. "Again. You mean have pizza with them again. Which would be great. I'd love to." She shifted her weight to the other foot and placed a hand on her hip. "But PS, honey, that doesn't count because your parents are normal. And nice. And sweet. And totally cute together. Your brother is cool too."

Rob closed the car door and moved to her. "My brother is cool. This is true. But I'm sure your parents are more normal than you think."

"Right." Staring up into his pretty blue eyes, Heather blew out a resigned breath, took his hand, and walked to the front door. Dread curled in her gut. He was going to *hate* her mom and dad. They were the epitome of privilege, and so was their house. All the best things, that's how it had always been.

She rang the bell to give them warning, but shifted to get her keys out to let them in.

Rob bent to her ear. "You think I'm gorgeous?"

A smile formed on her lips, and she looked at him. "You know good and well—"

The front door opened. "Well now, would you look at that...."

Heather jerked her gaze back, and her smile fell. "Hi, Mom. Look at what?"

Her mother dipped her chin, as if staring at Heather over a set of invisible glasses. "That playful, pretty smile you *had* on your face a moment ago. *Had* being the key word there."

Heather tipped her head to the side and frowned, purposely furrowing her brow. "Hmm."

"Oh, forget it." Her mother waved a hand at her and then looked at Rob and extended it. "You must be Robert."

Rob smiled and shook her mother's hand. "Yes, ma'am. It's nice to finally meet you, Mrs. Winters."

"So polite. Please, call me Michelle." She smiled as she slid her palm free. "It's a pleasure to meet you as well, Robert. Come in, both of you." Her mother took a step back.

Heather chuckled as they moved inside the foyer and her mom closed the door behind them. "As opposed to me staying outside and Rob going in alone?"

"Oh, honey, don't be silly. You know what I meant." After tucking a lock of her light brown hair behind her ear, her mom moved down the hall toward the kitchen. She glanced back but kept moving as she did. "How about we have a drink, sit out on the back patio?"

"Sounds great." Rob smiled and placed his hand on Heather's lower back.

Tension had every inch of her skin tight, and not expecting his touch, she flinched.

Glancing down at her, he mouthed, "You okay?"

Heather nodded and kept them moving. Jesus, she needed to just get through this.

Once in the kitchen, Mom pulled three stemless wineglasses down from a cabinet. "I've got a brand-new batch of white sangria. Heather *loves* my sangria. Don't you, honey?"

It wasn't a question she really expected Heather to answer, nor would the woman pause to see if anyone was listening to her, or still in the room even. As Mom filled each glass with ice and proceeded to add the homemade wine to each, she babbled on.

Mom just assumed they were all giving her their undivided attention. Sadly, in many cases, they all were. Hating that fact, Heather tuned her out and glanced at Rob.

He was frowning.

And looking right at Heather.

Shit. Now it was her turn to mouth the question, "Are *you* okay?" Except he didn't answer, he just stared.

And frowned.

Heather frowned back.

Jesus, she'd tried to warn him, but of course, he had to see for himself. Didn't make it any less mortifying for her though. What was it that had him so freaked out exactly? The house? Her mother's perfectly coiffed hair? Her matching outfit and coordinating loafers?

A mix of sadness and frustration topped with a healthy helping of embarrassment filled Heather's gut. Thank God there was a drink coming, because she was going to fucking need a few to get through the rest of the night.

"I must apologize, Robert. Pierson, Heather's father, is caught at work."

The sound of her mother's voice yanked Heather from her dive into humiliation land. She blinked at Rob. With their less-than-happy gaze into each other's eyes broken, they both turned and focused on her mother.

Who still was not looking at them.

Heather swallowed and watched as Mom arranged full glasses of sangria onto a square silver serving platter, finishing off the display by adding three napkins. "There's a big case. It's very exciting for him. Hopefully he won't be much longer." Pausing, her mother pressed a finger to her lips, then looked in the direction of the refrigerator. "Should I add some cheeses, crackers? I have some, but I was hoping your father would be here to enjoy them too."

Heather sighed. "There's always a big case."

Mom jerked to a stop and looked at Heather. Disappointment at Heather's snarky comment was evident in her expression. And pity there, too. *Oh, even better.* Heather drew in a breath and looked away. Shame curled in her gut like a cold snake.

If Rob didn't know already, he would for sure know now that Heather had way more baggage than the average head case carried around. And none of this shit with her parents came close to the cargo ship of emotional crap she had over not being able to have children.

For fuck's sake...tonight was going to be absolutely fabulous.

Just fucking fabulous.

* * * *

Heather's mother was looking at Heather with an expression Rob was afraid to read into. Afraid mostly because he didn't want to dislike her mother in the first fifteen minutes he'd spent in her presence. But damn, he already might.

Was it always like this? This weird sort of surface exchange between mother and daughter? He glanced at Heather.

Already looking up at him as if she knew what he was asking without him having to say a thing, she shrugged one shoulder, and Rob pulled her closer to his side.

Yeah, it was always like this. Damn. No wonder...

"I wish you wouldn't say things like that. Your father enjoys his work, it makes him happy. I like that he's happy. None of that is a bad thing, Heather." Then, as if the subject was no longer up for discussion, she turned her focus to Rob and her lips curled into a smile. "I understand you're a police officer, Robert? It's because of all of your hard work that my husband gets to be so successful at his career. A bit of the circle of life, I suppose. Thank you for that." Her smile turned genuine, the corners of her eyes crinkling.

Heather snorted and crossed her arms. "Yeah, except Rob puts the bad guys in jail and Dad defends them so they can be back on the street."

Hello, smart-ass comment. The tension he'd felt earlier radiating from Heather's body spilled over in the form of verbal diarrhea. How nice. His woman was definitely picking a fight. But worse, doing it when he was there. What the hell was she trying to prove?

Michelle jerked her eyes back to Heather; this time the annoyance was visible in her expression. Rob took a deep breath as sadness filled his heart. Heather had said her parents weren't normal, but what did normal mean anyway? No one was normal.

She'd also said that although at one time she was close with her mom, now things were difficult between them, but she hadn't exactly been super clear on *how* difficult. Maybe he should've asked for examples? Regardless,

Rob needed to do something to get them back on the light and polite train, or they may as well leave right then.

After drawing in a deep breath, he clapped his hands and rubbed his palms together. "Okay, yep. Circle of life complete for sure. Hey—" He pointed at the tray. "May I carry that tray for you, Michelle?"

Several seconds passed before Heather's mother shifted her gaze back to Rob, and once more that polite smile she'd worn since they walked into the house arched her lips. "Very sweet of you, Robert. Thank you, but I've got it."

Jesus, that was an abrupt shift of emotions. But then—holy wow. All at once he saw it. Stamped all over Michelle's face was the pretty but superficial mean girl Heather used to be. That smile on her mother's face showed Rob so much more than any example Heather could've given him.

Yet he also felt sorry for the woman. As if she simply didn't know any better. Michelle was nice, sweet even, but only on the surface and obviously only if everyone went along with her plan or every desire.

It was a common thing with people who had money. Not *all* who had money, of course, but a lot of them. Rob had seen his fair share over the years.

Worse, children learned what they saw, learned what they were taught, and Michelle was obviously an excellent teacher. The good news was, Heather was no longer her mother's student. For that, Rob was eternally grateful. Aside from that, Heather had gone through some shit in her marriage, and likely her divorce had been extremely hard on her too.

Heather had warned him that she had scars. She wanted him to heed that warning, but he couldn't. If it were up to Rob, she never would've suffered any of it, nor had to live with the scars all the damage left in its wake. But he couldn't fix any of it.

At least what she'd gone through had made her the person she was now. As far as Rob was concerned, the person she was now was everything he ever wanted.

A vivid silver lining in his eyes.

* * * *

"Sorry I'm late." Heather's father came out the back door onto the patio, his suit jacket gone, but his dress shirt still crisp and his tie in perfect place.

Mom immediately got to her feet and rushed over to him. "You've got perfect timing." She kissed his cheek. "We just sat down for some of my white sangria. Have a seat with the kids, and I'll get you one."

The kids...

As if she and Rob were a couple of teenagers. Heather drew in a breath. At least her father was finally home. Now they could eat and get the hell out of there.

Rob got to his feet and extended his palm. "Mr. Winters, I'm Rob. Pleasure to meet you, sir."

Her father turned toward him. "Pleasure's all mine." Letting go of Rob's hand, her father moved to her. He bent and pressed a kiss to the top of her head. "You're looking well."

"Thanks, Daddy. You too." Powerless to stop it, Heather smiled. It never failed to make her feel good when her father gave her attention.

He took a seat in the lounger to her right. "Not too bad for an old man, huh?" He unbuttoned one shirt sleeve and rolled the cuff up, then did the same with the other. "Rob, feel free to call me Pierson. In spite of Michelle calling you both 'kids,' you two are a little old for the 'Mr. and Mrs.' pleasantries, don't you think?"

Rob laughed. "Whatever works."

Mom came rushing out, nearly out of breath, and handed Dad his sangria. "Here you go, honey."

"Thank you." He took a sip. "Mmm. Best batch yet."

Her mother's face lit up like a Fourth of July firework display. "You think so?"

"Absolutely." He took another sip.

Heather's mom smiled, gazing at her husband, all the love in the world shining in her expression. Heather sighed and took a sip of her sangria. Her parents' relationship had always been so "Jim Dear and Darling." Like something out of a fairytale. An authentic, romantic dream of sorts. Heather had no cause to ever think that what her parents shared wasn't real.

That was until Heather's fairytale of a marriage faltered, becoming nothing more than a pretty front hiding the ugly deterioration behind the white picket fence. It made Heather question the validity of what she'd always felt was true between her parents.

"I'm going to go make sure dinner is moving along." Her mother bent and pressed a kiss to Dad's cheek, then wandered back into the house.

Watching them together, Heather still wasn't sure if what her parents had was real or make-believe. Hell, she could barely tell if what she was experiencing with Rob was authentic or not.

She cared about him, yes, but knowing she couldn't give him the life he likely wanted and deserved, she was also holding back a part of herself, a considerable part of her heart. Why go there? Why risk—

A sharp pain radiated from her lower abdomen, as if she'd been speared with a hot poker. A gasp escaped, and Heather closed her eyes.

"You okay?" The tone in Rob's voice was laced with concern.

Dammit, she really wished she'd been able to control her reaction. Heather pressed her lips together and nodded. "Mmhmm."

Her mother approached, reaching for her. "Sweetheart?"

Fuck, she did not need this. Pressing her hand to her tummy, she focused on catching her breath. "I'm fine, Mom. Just a cramp."

"That looks like more than a cramp." Her mother rested her hand on Heather's shoulder. "Do you want me to get you a pain pill?"

Heather shook her head and got to her feet, though she faltered a little. "No, it's fine. Just going to go to the bathroom."

"You sure, babe?" Rob stood. "How about I—"

"No. Stay, please? I'm good. Just girl stuff." Stepping away, she forced herself to walk, slow and easy, as if there wasn't an ice pick tearing up her insides.

Goddamn endometriosis! She wasn't expecting her period tonight, seeing as though she'd just finished a week ago, but that no longer meant anything. At this point, the average twenty-eight-day cycle was a pipe dream.

Just before she made it to the bathroom, her mother spoke up again. "Honey, are you sure you don't want something? Your face has gone white as a ghost. I can tell you're in pain."

"Just get me some ibuprofen, okay? I don't want anything stronger." She flipped the bathroom light on. "Just in case, do you have pads or tampons in here?"

"Under the sink in the basket, where they've always been." Mom smiled, though it was that pity-filled one that made Heather want to throw up everywhere. "I'll get you the ibuprofen. Holler if you need anything else."

"Yep, thanks." Heather closed the door, relieved to be alone.

It sucked being in that much pain with everyone focusing on her. It was too hard to maintain her composure. Sure enough, after getting her pants down, Heather had started her period again. And sadly, ruined her panties completely. Fucking hell, this was getting ridiculous.

Could've been worse though. Thanks to the stabbing pain letting her know something was up, she hadn't soaked completely through to her jeans. After cleaning up as best she could, she opted for a pad rather than a tampon and headed out to the kitchen.

"Everything okay?" Her mother held out her hand, four small brick-red pills in her palm.

Heather grabbed the ibu's from her, tossed them into her mouth, and washed them down with the water her mom handed her. "Yes. Fine. Just started my period like I thought."

Her mother nodded. "Have you been to the doctor lately? Have things progressed?"

"No. And probably." She stared at her mom. This was not a conversation Heather wanted to have, especially with Rob there. "Don't worry about it, Mom. It's fine. I'm going to go back outside, unless you need me to help you in here?"

Her mother pressed her lips together, her eyes like sharp points. She drew in a deep breath, her chest rising and falling with the inhale and exhale. "No, I don't need your help in here, though I appreciate the offer. I know you don't want me to say anything but—"

"Then don't. Don't say anything. I've been dealing with this for a long time, and I am perfectly capable of dealing with it tonight. If it makes you feel better, I'll call my GYN when I get a minute and make an appointment."

Her mother blew out another breath. "Okay. Yes, that would make me feel better."

Heather nodded. "Great."

With that, she turned and headed for the patio. It wasn't that she didn't want to make her mother feel better. She did, but really, Heather planned to schedule the appointment because the waves of gut-shredding pain she was weathering right then were fucking horrendous.

She swallowed as she stepped outside, praying she'd make it to her seat without puking.

"Shame, really, when she couldn't get pregnant, that's when things really changed for her. They'd tried for years but...nothing." Her father sipped his sangria, shaking his head as he swallowed. "I don't think Charles knew how to help her."

Did he just... Heather stopped dead in her tracks before either of them noticed her. She looked at Rob, concern etched in his expression, as he focused on her father and what he was revealing to Rob.

Rob rubbed the back of his neck. "That must've been devastating... for all of you."

Oh, God.

God!

Ignoring the pain in her lower abdomen, she got her feet moving and walked to the seating area.

"Hey, babe. You good?" Rob stood, obviously intent on helping her, but she waved him away.

Without saying a word, she sat, taking as much care as she could not to let any discomfort show in her face.

"You doing okay, sweetheart?" Her father stared at her over the top of his glass.

Heather gritted her teeth and swallowed, trying for all it was worth to rein in her fury. "Fine, Dad. Please, finish what you were saying."

"I was just telling Rob that it's been hard for you."

"So I heard." Picking up her wineglass, she downed a healthy sip. "Anything else you want to share about my life? Would you like to tell him about my divorce, or when I moved back into your house?"

Her father's eyes went wide. "I beg your pardon. First of all, watch your tone. Second, I'm not sure what the big deal is. It's not like I shared something Rob didn't already know."

Rob cleared his throat. "Actually, sir, I didn't know."

Her father cut his gaze back to Rob, before refocusing on her. "Even so, there's no reason to react this way. But regardless, I apologize. I didn't—"

"You're right. My fault. I should know better." She got to her feet, pressing her palm to her abdomen. "Anyway, I realize Mom made dinner, but considering my 'condition' tonight, I think it's best I go home."

"Heather, you're overrea—"

"Please don't." God, she needed to get the hell out of there. "We'll try for dinner another night."

How could her father have just done this to her? Did the man know no boundaries? Two questions she already knew the answer to. She was the fool who kept forgetting. Heather glanced at Rob—fuck, just kill her now. The look of pity in his eyes was downright unbearable.

The good news was, she wouldn't have to look at that pity for much longer, she was sure. Why would he stay with her after finally knowing all of this? A young, virile, healthy man like Rob didn't need to tie himself down with an emotionally and physically broken woman with baggage for days.

She was the trifecta of fuckery.

Chapter 25

"How about I drive?" Rob held his palm out to Heather for the car keys.

"No. It's fine. I can drive." She moved to round the front of the car.

Rob caught her by the arm before she passed him. "Heather, you can tell me that it's fine and you're fine the whole drive home if you want, but you'll do it while *I* drive us there. Do you understand?"

As she stared up at him, fire blazed in her eyes. Clearly her submissive side was at war with her anger, and she was likely debating whether or not she was going to do as he ordered.

He understood the matter, why she was furious at her father, but damn… she was also hurting physically and, at the moment, that was more of a concern for him than her hurt or angry feelings.

"Fine." Her answer was clipped and said through clenched teeth.

He didn't care for her tone, but he'd tolerate it for now because there were more important things to deal with. None of them comfortable, he was quite certain.

They were quiet the first ten minutes or so of the drive. It wasn't until he'd gotten them on the I-17 that she finally broke the silence.

"I'm just going to level set so we're clear. It's not something I am willing to discuss, so please don't ask me about it. If you can't handle that, then it's probably best we don't continue seeing each other."

Rob pursed his lips and exhaled through his nose. What in the fuck did she think she was doing? He shook his head and drew in a deep breath, exhaling through his mouth this time, giving himself some time to get his emotional reaction to her words in check before responding.

"I knew better than to bring you to my parents' house. I'm sorry I went forward with it. It was a mistake."

And the hits just keep coming.

Rob cleared his throat. "Let me get this straight, Heather. You're sorry you went forward with having your boyfriend meet your parents? Or you're sorry for even having a boyfriend that wanted to meet your parents?"

"No. That's not what I sai—"

"Or wait, maybe you're sorry that your father shared something about you, that is so enormous, such a part of you, that I should've already known about—"

"Rob—"

He kept talking, not interested in any fucked-up excuse she might give him. Fury beat through him, and he gripped the steering wheel. "But obviously I didn't know about it, and I assume you never wanted me to know." He glanced at her, and when she said nothing, he shrugged. "That's okay, babe. I know you're private. I accept that about you. I give you that freedom to not share things with me." He held his palm up. "But for fuck's sake, your guts are turning inside out right now, filling your body with pain, and all I can think is how many times were you hurting and I didn't know about it? How often were you curled in a ball in pain and I wasn't there to take care of you?"

His anger was turning back into hurt feelings, and Rob paused, trying to let his emotions settle. He swallowed past the lump in his throat and glanced over at her. She had her arms wrapped around her middle, staring out the passenger window.

As they passed under overhead lights on the freeway, a shadow fell over her body, highlighting over her legs, and then up her body before disappearing and the next glow from the lights making the same journey.

He was trying so hard to not get emotional, to not take her lack of communication personally. To not let it hurt him. But the truth was, it did hurt him. It killed. "The thought that you walked through not being able to have children and all that could entail breaks my heart for you."

"I don't want your pity."

"Is that what you think this is, Heather?"

"Yes." She bent forward and blew out a breath. "Can we stop talking about this now?"

"You're wrong. Very, very wrong. Yes, we can stop talking about this right now, but this discussion isn't over."

"Oh, yes, it fucking is. There is *nothing* more to discuss. I can't have kids. That's it. Deal with it, or don't. But it's fact and it's not changing. So please, spare me. Spare us."

Fab! Every word of that felt *and* sounded very fucking personal. He glanced over at her, and now she was staring at him, that fire back in her eyes, but this time the fire was directed right at him. So, yes, personal it sure as hell was.

He shook his head and focused on the road. "Heather, hear me when I tell you this: if you can't have kids, then you can't have kids." He shrugged. "But there's options I can only assume you've explored, adoption, etcetera. Even so, it's a nonissue for me. But I wish you'd have told me."

"Those options are not for me, so save them for someone else who cares. And really, why should I have told you? It's not something you needed to know, Rob."

An ache bloomed in his chest, and he frowned as confusion sped through him. "What the hell is that supposed to mean? Why would I have not needed to know?"

"Just drop it."

"Heather, tell me why I didn't need to know?"

"Goddammit, you're relentless!" She bent forward again, wrapped her arms around her stomach, and groaned. "Because *this* wasn't supposed to be anything. There wasn't supposed to be a 'you and me'! And you deserve better than some emotional head case with a defunct reproductive system and enough baggage to fill a football field."

"I love you."

"Stop it! You don't."

"I do. I'm in love with you, and I don't care if you can't have babies. I also don't care if you have baggage. Everyone has baggage."

"No. Not like this. You don't understand this." She shook her head, her voice thick with tears. "You don't understand..." Heather covered her face with her hands.

Screw this. Rob jerked the wheel of the Mercedes to the right and jumped off the exit. Getting to the end of the ramp, he hung a hard right, and then another into the gas station on the corner.

After parking, he shut the car off, turned to look at her, and leaned toward her, bracing one hand on the back of her seat. "Then help me understand. Because *I am* telling you, I am completely and totally *in love* with you, and I am *not fucking going anywhere!*"

She was crying, she was in physical pain, and this was the defining point of their relationship. Rob could *not* let it go. Call him an insensitive asshole; this couldn't wait until she felt better. They needed to settle it now.

"I can't do this." She shook her head and looked away from him and then down at her hands. "I'm sorry. I just...can't."

Something about the low tone in her voice, how calm and quiet those last words were, said just about all he needed to know. Rob leaned back in the driver's seat and felt his breath leave him. She was going to make the biggest mistake of her life—of their lives. She was going to take this away from both of them. "Heather, I—"

"Please—" She raised her hand to stop him. "Just, no."

He exhaled, swallowed down the lump in his throat and nodded. Fuck, this was going to hurt.

"I need some time, Rob. Alone...to get myself together. I just... I don't know how long I need. But I need to try and get myself back to a place of being okay. Or whatever okay looks like now. I don't even know anymore." She shook her head. "Being with you, it's been wonderful. But I wasn't expecting you. Or this. And I don't think I can handle all of what being with you means." She shrugged and shifted in her seat. "Right now, I know I can't."

Rob watched as she fidgeted. Twisting her hands in her lap, wiping tears from her damp cheeks, running her fingers under her eyes, brushing her hair away from her face. Then curling her arms around her waist again.

Barely a foot separated them in the small interior of her Mercedes. Yet, from where he sat, Heather was miles away, completely unreachable.

God help him, he should say something, try to stop her. Try to remind her why she belonged with him and he with her. Reassure her again, and as many times as it took, that it didn't matter if she couldn't have kids. He wanted her no matter what. He loved her, all of the parts of her.

What she needed to do instead of running from him, and throwing this chance they both had away, was to pull him closer, to hold him tighter. But Rob knew there wasn't a goddamn thing he could do or say to change her mind.

But that didn't mean he was going down without a fight. Not a chance. "You're throwing us away."

"No." She shook her head. "No, I'm not."

"Yeah, that's exactly what you're doing. You're scared and your body is kicking your ass right now, and instead of leaning on me—leaning toward me—you're throwing me and us away."

"You're not hearing me. And there's no point in trying to get through to you." She crossed her arms and pressed her lips together.

"Babe, I'm hearing you loud and clear." Frustration and hurt beat through him like a bass drum, pounding in his ears. Rob pointed a finger at his chest. "You want me to just fucking walk away?" He leaned toward her. "You want me to just let you fuck our chance up and just *walk away?*"

She raised her eyes, fury blazing in them. "*I am* not *your chance and you are* not *mine!*"

Rob flinched and shook his head. "You done?"

"Does it really matter? I've tried to explain. You're going to think what you want." She pressed her palm to her forehead. "Look, I'm sorry. I am. I should've broken things off months ago. You're an amazing man. But I wasn't—" She shook her head, closed her eyes and sighed through her nose. "I'm *not* ready. I knew it, but I continued anyway, and as a result, I hurt you." She looked directly in his eyes. "I'm sorry for that. Maybe someday you can forgive me."

Rob gripped the steering wheel, as if he held on tight, this out of control situation would somehow regain its tailspin. "You're hurting us both."

She nodded. "I know, but if I don't do it now, it's only going to get worse." A tear fell from the corner of one of her eyes, and she brushed it away before it made it down her cheek.

Fuck, this was killing him. It was killing her too. "Don't do this, Heather."

She leveled her gaze on him. "I have to."

He clenched his teeth and drew in a shaky breath. "You are the love of my life, and I know I am the love of yours…please do not do this. Don't take this away from us."

Heather closed her eyes. "I. Have. To."

"Babe—" He reached for her and grazed her thigh, but she jerked away from him.

"I need this to be done, Rob. I'm sorry, but I need you to let me go." She opened the passenger door and got out of the car.

With dread creeping down his spine and settling in his gut, Rob watched as she walked around the front of her vehicle and came to the driver's side door.

"Goddammit." He gripped the wheel again before he angled out of the car. He stepped aside, and she slid into the driver's seat.

He could stop her. He could try to make her listen. He could try…but he already had. He knew in his gut the minute the conversation took this abrupt turn there would be no convincing her, no changing her mind, yet he'd had to try anyway.

He did and, sadly, failed.

Heather looked up at him. After he took a step back, she closed the car door. Rob pressed his palm to his chest, and as she backed out of the parking spot and pulled away from the gas station, he recognized his heart was still beating—if only for the sake of pushing blood through his circulatory system. Damn if the thing wasn't shredded so badly there was a physical ache behind his rib cage.

She'd destroyed him. She'd destroyed them...and what could've been.

Chapter 26

Heather turned on the water to fill the tub and then retrieved her bottle of Pinot Grigio along with a stemless wineglass.

It'd been less than five hours since Rob found out she couldn't bear children, and consequently, she'd had a complete and total breakdown and ended their relationship.

As she sipped from her glass, she sprinkled some bath salts into the hot water, and followed those up with some bubble bath too.

Just like old times, except the tub in the new house she owned in Arizona wasn't nearly as big as the one she'd had in Baltimore.

That, and no husband to hide from, of course. Then again, there was no Rob to hide from either.

Disgusted with herself, she turned on one of her favorite love/hate playlists and connected her iPad to her Bluetooth speaker. The strum of the guitar from "Poison & Wine" by The Civil Wars kicked off Heather's little misery party for one.

Perfect song... Except, sadly, the band had broken up. Heather recalled reading about the many rumors swirling around about the duo's "relationship." Pfft, who cared what people did in their private lives as long as they were happy? Why was it anyone's business? And wasn't that the point, anyway? To be happy?

Not her though. She must've been absent the day they were giving that lesson. With a sigh, Heather removed her robe and dropped it on the floor beside the tub. With wineglass in hand, she stepped into the bath and submerged herself in the steaming water.

The heat warmed her right to her bones but never seemed to penetrate that frigid space in her heart. She'd been cold and empty for so long there, she couldn't remember what it was like to not feel that way.

The worse it had ever been was the day her ex announced he wanted a divorce. The bastard had done it over dinner. Apparently, he felt their classically decorated formal dining room was the perfect setting to drop the bomb.

Heather took a long gulp of her wine and closed her eyes, the memory of that night so clear, so vivid. It was as if it'd just happened yesterday. He'd been so nasty about it too, tossing insults her way, throwing jabs about her drinking and how she should run off and hide in her bathtub again.

"Well, here's to you, Charles. You coldhearted son of a bitch." She raised her glass and took another long drink. "I'm right where you said I'd be. Still."

Heather closed her eyes and sank deeper in the bubbles. She'd never forget his last words to her that night. Never forget how he sliced right through her mind, heart and soul, as if she'd never meant anything at all, ever, to him.

"Dignified or not, you're a ghost, dead inside, and I'm sorry, I truly am, but I don't want to be dead alongside you. I want to live, Heather... I want to live with her. *And the child* she's *giving me."*

His statement was a punch in the gut so hard all the air had left Heather's lungs.

Once upon a time, Charles had pushed her to get an egg donor. Heather had never been interested in having someone else's baby for her husband though. And no one could convince her otherwise to this day. That baby would not have been hers and Charles's, it would have been Charles's and whoever they bought healthy *viable* eggs from.

And how ironic that Charles got to have a child with another woman anyway. A child Heather would never get to have.

Besides, even if she had chosen that option, who was to say she could've even carried the baby to term? Her uterus was a lost cause.

It'd killed, all of it. And honestly, it was still killing. Like a cancer, slowly eating away at Heather, slowly taking over everything. It had been the worst moment of her life.

And now, walking away from Rob was running a close second.

Robert Caldwell was the love of her life...he wasn't wrong when he'd called her out on that. And yet she'd told him to go anyway. He'd done nothing to her except love her, unconditionally, right where she was, flaws and all. Broken body and baggage galore, he'd loved her anyway.

It was everything she could've ever dreamed of and yet…it wasn't enough. It wasn't what she wanted.

Her goal now was to drink enough wine that she couldn't remember the look in his eyes as she'd slashed into him with her words before finishing him off by ending things. Heather swallowed more wine. Although she knew, truly, there wasn't enough alcohol in the world that would ever make her forget the sound of his voice when he'd pleaded with her to not do what she was so intent on doing.

Or worse, forget the softness and sincerity in his face when he tried to reassure her, to let her know that he loved her anyway. That look had shredded her from the inside out. God, how could he still love her anyway?

Heather had tried so hard with him. Tried to be normal. Tried to *let* herself be happy. With her new life, with Rob, and honestly, she'd succeeded for a little while, but in the end, what it really came down to, what sent her over the edge, was that she absolutely could not reconcile the fact that he was okay with *not* having kids.

It was obvious he really had no idea what he was saying or committing himself to. Regardless, even if he did realize, and even if she could somehow go on "trying" to be happy, that also meant, in some fucked-up way, that she'd somehow given up and accepted her fate.

Not that she could ever admit this to herself or anyone else, but the truth was, Heather hadn't accepted a goddamn thing. And she was sure she never would. How could she?

Regardless of the countless failed in vitro attempts, and the second and third opinions from doctors, Heather could not let it go. She could not accept that there was no medical or natural way she'd ever conceive and carry a child within her.

The fact that Rob was okay with not having kids did not work for her. And it never would.

How the hell could he be okay with it, when she wasn't?

Chapter 27

Rob shined the beam from his Maglite into the dim car. "Let me ask you something. Did you see me back there when you pulled into traffic?"

The young male driver in the car he'd pulled over frowned. "When?"

"Yeah, that's what I thought. You pulled right out in front of me, cutting me off. Lucky for you, I didn't hit you."

"Ah, shit—I mean shoot. Sorry, Officer." The kid shrugged.

The back of Rob's neck tickled, as if the little hairs were standing on end. Not a good sign. Something wasn't right about the driver, or the passenger. "License, registration, and proof of insurance."

"Right, right. Gotta get my wallet out of my back pocket."

"Go ahead." Rob kept the flashlight trained inside the car.

As the driver shifted his weight to retrieve his wallet, Rob focused on his movements, making sure he didn't do anything stupid. It was nearing the end of his shift, plus it was his last night, aka his Friday, and Rob wasn't looking for any kind of action.

Frankly, he just wanted to finish off the workweek with as little paperwork as possible. Two weeks had passed since Heather had ended their relationship, and every single day since had beyond sucked.

Rob rested his hand on the butt of his service weapon as the kid fumbled in his wallet to get out his ID. The passenger just sat there, like some sort of mannequin, his gaze trained out the front window.

Okay, people who were just an average citizen, not trying to hide something, didn't act so stiff. Sure, some could be nervous and afraid they were going to do something wrong, so they overcompensated, but this kid had taken that to a whole different level.

"Gotta get the registration from the glove box. Okay?" The driver handed his license to Rob.

Rob nodded.

The mannequin, aka passenger, opened the glove box, retrieved the vehicle registration, and handed it to the driver.

"Shit. Well..." The driver extended his hand out of the car window and gave Rob the rectangular paper. "Sorry, Officer, I can't find my insurance card."

Based on the warning bells going off in Rob's gut and the way things were playing out, something was definitely up with these two. Rob nodded again. "Been doing any illegal substances tonight?"

The driver shook his head. "No, no sir."

Standard answer, of course. Rob almost rolled his eyes. "What about alcohol? You guys drinking at all tonight?"

"Nope. No sir." The driver stared up at him, barely squinting from the flashlight.

Both of his pupils were hugely dilated despite the glaring bright light of the flashlight—which was an automatic indicator that the driver, at least, was for sure high on any number or combination of things.

Rob aimed his flashlight at the passenger. Still staring out the front window, but now the guy's right leg was bouncing on the seat, as if the thing was running on its own battery. Being nervous could do that to a person too. Or being high on speed or meth was a valid reason. But really, there were lots of reasons to choose from. "You got ID on you?"

The kid ran his fingers through his greasy hair and then scratched his chin—right leg still bouncing. "Nope."

Yeah, this was definitely going to be a longer night than expected. The two appearing to be loaded on God knows what, neither one communicating consistently, were reason enough to let Tricks take a lap around the car.

"You need anything else, Officer?" The driver leaned toward the door.

Lots of things, none of which can you provide me. Rob leveled his stare on the kid. "Hands on the wheel, where I can see them."

"Oh, sorry." The driver did as he was told.

Rob glanced down at the ID in his hand for the driver's name. Blake M. Swenson. Age twenty-four. Mesa. *Jesus*, just a baby, one with a name like Blake...a rich kid's name. Probably riding high on Mommy and Daddy's money.

"Stay in the car. I'll be right back." Training and years of conditioning kicked in, and Rob walked backward away from the car, back to his patrol truck.

Opening his door, Rob slid behind the wheel and immediately made the call for backup. While waiting, he ran the DL number for Mr. Swenson. Lo and behold, it came back clear.

Rob shook his head and exhaled. He really couldn't shake the knot that'd formed in his gut and the tickle raising the hairs on the back of his neck. He knew something was up, and although he really wanted to end the night easy, his work ethic wasn't going to let that play out. "Tricks, you ready to work?"

The dog barked, ears up at attention.

Rob smiled. "Good boy. Why not, right? Easy is overrated anyway."

As luck would have it, another patrol car was only a few miles away. Once that officer got on site, they could get both young men out of the car and then Tricks would get to have some fun. God knows the dog was just as depressed as Rob had been. He deserved a little fun.

After all, they both missed Heather.

* * * *

"Not under arrest, but I do need to run a check on the car." Rob helped the driver sit on the curb in front of the Honda. "Chill and hang tight for a few."

"Not like I got anywhere to go." With his hands cuffed behind his back, the kid rolled his eyes.

The other officer stepped over with the passenger, also in cuffs, and sat the kid on the sidewalk beside the driver. When Rob had patted the driver down, he'd found a substantial roll of cash. According to the other officer, the passenger had nothing on him, not even an ID.

Now it was time to get Tricks out and work the car. Rob approached his patrol SUV, opened Tricks's door and hooked his leash on him. "Let's go to work."

The dog jumped down, obvious excitement radiating through his body.

Rob moved in a wide arc, behind the passenger sitting on the curb with the other officer, in order to come around to the front of the car and work his way backward.

Both suspects' eyes got wide as soon as they saw Tricks.

Rob chuckled and so did the other officer. When Rob got where he wanted to be, positioned at the grill on the car, he gave his partner the command for search. "*Such!*"

With a tight hold on his leash, Rob followed Tricks as he walked beside the Honda, sniffing at the driver's headlight, and onward to the fender.

Tricks continued to sniff, whining on occasion, but moved forward. "Good boy!" Rob rubbed Tricks's head and patted his side. Following his gut instinct that something was in this car, Rob urged Tricks farther down, toward the rear quarter panel and trunk. "Let's go. *Such!*"

When they reached the back of the car and Tricks got to the trunk, he went full-on aggressive find mode. Completely amped up, scratching, yelping, jumping up and pushing at the trunk of the car.

Rob moved to his side. "You find it, Tricks? Is it in there?"

Tricks barked and jumped at the trunk lid again.

"Let's see. Come on, *fuss!*"

Tricks sat, coming to heel as the German command said to do. Rob popped the trunk, and beneath a dirty blanket, in a ratty backpack, was about twenty-plus grams of crystal meth. The haul was divided up into little baggies, obviously ready for sale.

Rob bent over to Tricks, petting his head, ruffling his fur, and then patting his side. "Good boy! Good find!"

Well, damn, talk about a good haul. Not huge, but solid, for sure. Even though Rob hadn't wanted the complication of a stop like this tonight, in the end, he was grateful for the distraction and the extra paperwork.

He hadn't realized how much he needed something to take his mind off of Heather. Tricks barked and spun around, and Rob gave him more praise. Apparently, Tricks needed the distraction too.

Chapter 28

"I hate to ask, but do you think you can get me some more Coke?" Heather shifted on the couch. "My stomach is still off."

Kim got to her feet and came over. "Say no more. I got you."

"Thank you. I really appreciate it." Heather handed her friend the empty glass.

"You want anything else while I'm in the kitchen? Crackers? Pregnancy test?"

Heather blurted a laugh. "That's not funny. And it's also not possible."

"My friend, I'm trying to tell you. I wish you'd take a test."

"Give me a break, will you?" Heather shook her head. "It's just food poisoning. I hope anyway, otherwise you're gonna get sick too."

Kim laughed. "Okay, okay. You win. But, just know, I won't get sick. I got kids, remember? I'm immune to everything."

"Yep." Heather watched as Kim made her way through the open area to her kitchen.

She was grateful Kim had stopped by, bringing her crackers and Gatorade and Coca-Cola—she'd forgotten that was good for an upset stomach. But, good grief, harping on this "maybe you're pregnant" thing needed to stop.

The woman had no idea that every time she brought it up it was like a knife in the heart. Besides that, since she'd been sick on and off all week, her guard was down. In no way was she able to emotionally cope with the idea of a pregnancy that wasn't physically possible.

Heather had only thrown up a couple of times that day, thank God. Although, that routine had gone on for a few days. And Heather knew it could be so much worse. Still, for a nurse, she made for a terrible patient.

She wasn't doing anything to make sure she was keeping herself hydrated. And she hadn't even considered calling the doctor. At least the pain she'd been dealing with had lessened. Last week, she'd been on the verge of giving in and calling the doctor to ask for some real painkillers, and then oddly, things settled down.

Regardless, Heather did need to get into a GYN, but she didn't want to know how bad things had gotten. Ignoring it was never the solution, but it sure felt like the easier path.

Needless to say, Heather's denial ability was at peak performance, and that included how badly she was hurting over breaking things off with Rob three weeks ago. Heather swallowed as a wave of nausea came over her, and just to keep things exciting, her heart ached at the same time.

Did they make pain pills for a self-inflicted broken heart? Likely not. That's what wine was for… She'd have to get into that after she got over her stomach issue.

Kim came back in. "Here you go, my dear. One almost-cold glass of the wonder drug Coke."

"Thank you." Heather put the glass to her lips and sipped. God, that was good.

"Welcome. Be right back, I'm grabbing some crackers for you and coffee for me."

Heather lay back down on the couch and stared blankly at the TV. They were watching on-demand episodes of *Fixer Upper* and had gone through about four so far. Chip and Joanna, the picture-perfect couple.

He was a huge goofball, but also a total romantic and an awesome dad. She was always so poised and elegant. Even when he managed to get her to goof off with him. They reminded Heather of herself with Rob, except not really.

Kim came back in just as a wave of emotion rolled through her. A lump filled Heather's throat, and she looked up at Kim.

Kim frowned, a small pout forming on her lips. "Honey, why do you look like someone just kicked your dog. You okay? Are you going to be sick again?"

Everything felt awful. "I think…"

Kim knelt down in front of the couch. "You think what, honey?"

Oh, God. How was she going to— "I miss him."

Kim's expression turned soft, and she took Heather's hand in hers. "Of course, you do. Have you thought about calling him?"

"I ca—" Tears welled up, clogging her throat. Heather swallowed and covered her mouth with her free hand. As if that was going to hold all the emotion she was experiencing at bay. She shook her head. "I can't," she whispered.

"Honey, I don't understand. You and Rob are perfect together. Why would you give him up?"

Heather shook her head. "I can't."

With a heavy sigh, Kim got to her feet and took a seat in the large chair beside the sofa. She picked up her coffee. "When you're ready, honey."

Heather nodded. She couldn't bring herself to share all the many reasons it was better for her to end it with Rob, than to stay with him. Plain and simple: the pain of staying would've been far worse than the pain she was dealing with from leaving him.

Most people wouldn't be able to understand her rationale, or they'd think she was crazy. Likely they were right, she was batshit crazy. And that was exactly the point, wasn't it?

As wrong as it felt to walk away from Rob, because he was amazing, it felt even more wrong to stay because she was unable to move forward emotionally. He deserved better than what she could bring to the table. He deserved everything.

Heather closed her eyes as another wave of nausea came over her, and with it, another ache filled her chest. She closed her eyes and tried to breathe deep, keep herself from throwing up again.

God, would this ever end?

Chapter 29

Heather woke to a stabbing pain in her lower abdomen. Rolling over to her left side, she curled herself around a pillow and tried to focus on her breathing. Fuck, this was horrid.

Glancing at her phone, she caught the time. Four forty-five a.m. She'd gone to bed a little after eleven the night before, and she'd been fine. Nothing more than the typical, cramping dull ache that seemed to be there always now, and especially since that food poisoning hit with a vengeance last week.

She'd mostly recovered from that, only to boomerang right back into debilitating pelvic pain. "*God!*" Another sharp pain pierced her resolve, and she managed to shift herself to the edge of the bed. A trip to the bathroom to see if she'd started her period was probably a good idea.

Using what felt like all of her strength and a whole lot of determination, she managed to sit up. Immediately, she felt the wetness between her legs. Shit, clearly she was bleeding. Since the sun hadn't started its rise yet, it was still dark in her bedroom. Heather reached for the light on her bedside table and managed to turn it on.

Oh, fuck! Fuck! Heather's eyes went wide, and it took her a moment to comprehend what she was seeing. The amount of blood staining her sleep shorts, bed sheets and pillow she'd been holding could be comparable to a crime scene, if not a fatality.

Heather stood, and before she took a step forward, the room spun. Immediately, she sat again, the soft mattress exactly what her weak body needed. "Shit."

Clearly, she had lost more blood than what she was still trying to come to terms with. She pressed her hand to her forehead. Should she call an ambulance? God, she didn't want to do that. Gut-shredding pain tore through her, and she wrapped her arms around her middle and doubled over.

Slow breaths, in and out, in and out. She needed to do something before she passed out. With shaky hands, Heather grabbed her cell phone from her nightstand, pulled up her contacts and called the only person close enough to help.

With the cell on speaker she listened as it rang and rang and went to voicemail. "Fuck, please answer." Heather hit "end call" and then "call contact" again.

Ring, ring, ring...

"Mmmyou okay, honey?" Kim's scratchy, sleep-ridden voice was music to Heather's ears.

"No. Kim, please—" Heather groaned as another wave of pain swamped her. "Fuck. God...can you take me to the hospital?"

"Holy shit! Yes." Kim coughed. "I'll be right there. Can you unlock the door?"

"Garage code is 1984. I think I can make it to the laundry room to let you in."

"You think? Okay, Heather just be careful. I'm coming, honey. I'll be right there."

"'Kay." Heather disconnected the call.

Walking was probably not a good idea. After drawing in another deep breath, trying to get as much oxygen in her system as possible, she slid off the bed to the floor and, once on her hands and knees, crawled, slowly but as fast as she could, out of her bedroom to the laundry room where the garage entry was.

It took forever, at least it felt like it did, and she had to stop a few times to catch her breath. When she reached the laundry room, her head was spinning as if she'd just gotten off the tilt-a-whirl, spots dotted her vision, and her arms and fingers tingled like she was being poked with a thousand needles.

Not good. Heather lay down, the cool floor a balm to her heated skin. Jesus, her lower back was killing her too. What the hell was going on?

"Honey, it's Kim. Open the door, sweetie. Are you there? Can you hear me?"

Was that Kim she heard? Heather blinked, unable to focus on anything specific. But Kim sounded so far away. Heather just needed to lie there a little while longer. Just rest a little, and then she'd try again to get to the door.

Wait, wasn't she at the laundry room do— Another stabbing pain hit. Heather cried out and curled in a ball, and then her vision went dark....

* * * *

Rob slapped blindly at the top of his nightstand, trying to find his cell phone, desperately trying to silence the fucker. Wasn't it always the case that he couldn't reach the stupid thing? He tried again and—oh, yes. Silence. Finally. He still hadn't found the phone, but now he could sleep, so it didn't matter.

RIIIIINGGGGG!

Fucking hell! Rob sat up, found the charging cord, and followed it to his phone. "How the hell did it fall behind the nightstand?"

With one eye still shut, Rob frowned and glared at the screen. Why the fuck was Jeff calling him at dawn?

He swiped the screen. "Why the fuck are you calling me at dawn?"

"Rise and shine, Rhonda. We got a situation."

"What is it?"

"Heather's in the hospital. I'm heading your way to pick you up and take you over there. Get dressed."

"What?"

"Get dressed, dearest. ETA five minutes."

The phone went dead.

Rob blinked and stared at his phone, trying to process what Jeff had just said. "Fuck. *Fuck!*"

Launching himself off his bed, he headed into his closet. Dressing in the same jeans and T-shirt he wore the night before, he grabbed a baseball cap and sneakers. Before leaving his bedroom, he pocketed his wallet and phone, and made his way to his front door.

Okay yeah, five minutes was too long. He needed to get to her now. Impatience beat through him, and giving in to it, Rob opened the front door.... There was a God because Jeff was just pulling up to the curb.

"Thank fuck." Rob stepped outside, locked up and ran to Jeff's truck. He opened the passenger door, and slid onto the seat. "Let's go, and start talking. What's wrong with her?"

"You're a really heavy sleeper, Rhonda." Jeff flipped a U-turn. "I called you like four times."

"Jeff, come on, man." Irritation crept up the back of Rob's neck, and he squeezed his hands into fists.

"I'm being serious, here. What if someone tries to break into your pad?"

"Jeff..."

"Okay, listen up because I'm only gonna say this once. And side note, I don't know all the details yet." Jeff nodded at him. "Cool, glad that's clear. Okay, Kim called Tish, Tish called me and I called you."

"That's it?"

"I told you I don't know all the details."

"Jeff, what you should be saying is you know *no* details. For fuck's sake, just get us there."

"Semantics."

"Not helping."

"Okay, how's this? The way I see it, you need to be calm. Being all frantic, like I can see you are, isn't going to help your woman."

"Then maybe you should stop annoying me?"

"You breathe. I'll drive. And maybe discuss your sleeping habits because, dude, for real, that *is* an issue. Plus, it'll distract you."

"Whatever." Rob shook his head and rolled his eyes. Drumming his fingers on his knee, he exhaled, only then realizing he'd been holding his breath. Damn, Jeff was a pain in the ass, but he was also right. Rob would be no good to Heather if he was a train wreck. "Okay, you're right. I'm breathing."

"Anytime, Rhonda. N.E. Time." Jeff reached in the center console and pulled out a small white container. "Gum? I know your panicked ass didn't brush your teeth." Jeff winked. "All that breathing you're doing clued me in."

Rob started laughing. Mostly because Jeff was right. He was panicking and he hadn't brushed his teeth. Rob shook a piece out into his palm and tossed it into his mouth. "Thanks."

Jeff reached across the seat and clapped Rob on the shoulder. "All good, brother."

The ride to the hospital took a long time. Jeff wasn't exactly following the speed limit, but regardless, it still took forever. Longer than it should've, and Rob was fully aware that was only because he was pretty much terrified and needed to be there now.

Jeff dropped Rob off at the emergency room and went to park. Rob ran inside and right to the intake reception desk. "Hi. Heather Strat—"

"Rob!"

Rob turned in the direction of where his name was being called and found Kim moving toward him from the seating area. "God, I didn't think you were ever going to get here." She hugged him. "She's in surgery."

"Shit." He ran his hand along the back of his neck. "Is it because of her fertility issues?"

"I think so, but I'm not a hundred percent sure. Whatever it is, it's horrible. So much blood, Rob." Kim covered her face with her hands, shaking her head. "When I got there, I thought she was dead."

"Tell me what happened?"

"I don't know for sure. She wasn't conscious when I finally got into the house."

Rob had to swallow past the lump that filled his throat. The thought of losing Heather made him want to vomit and scream at the same time. Losing her was not an option.

Getting himself under as much control as he could, he took Kim's elbow in his hand. "How about we go sit down."

"Can we go upstairs? There's a waiting room for families. I was staying down here until you got here so we could go up together."

"Yeah, yeah. Of course."

"Thanks." Kim nodded and headed toward the elevators.

Stuffing his hands in his pockets, doing his best to keep his frayed nerves under control, Rob followed. Christ, he had a million questions and a feeling not even half of them were going to be answered.

After landing on the third floor, they both walked into a too brightly lit room. All four walls were lined with those vinyl chairs that had a comfort lifespan of about an hour. Plus, thanks to the arms, which were great while sitting, they didn't allow for anyone waiting for hours and hours to stretch out and try to sleep at all while they waited. At least there was a television mounted in the far corner. Not that people who were waiting to find out if their loved one was going to be okay needed entertainment, more that a distraction would be welcome.

"Speaking of family, do you know how we get ahold of her parents?" Kim picked up a magazine from one of the chairs and sat.

Rob shrugged and moved to the seat beside hers. "I do, but I'm not so sure she would want them to know."

"Really? Sheesh, there is so much I don't know about her." Kim frowned. "I'm a shitty friend. Clearly, I need to do less talking and a better job of listening."

"Come on, don't beat yourself up. Heather isn't exactly volunteering information. Hell, we dated for what, a little over four months? I did a lot of listening, and there's a world of things I still don't know about her."

"I'm sorry to hear that. You two seemed really happy together."

"We were…or I thought we were." Rob blew out a breath and pulled his baseball cap off. "I don't know. I miss her, and I'm still one hundred and fifty percent in love with her. But none of that matters right now. All that matters is that she's okay."

Kim shrugged. "She's going to be. I refuse to accept any other option."

"That makes two of us." Rob leaned forward and rested his elbows on his knees.

"Well, to answer your question, I kicked the door in. Or tried to."

Rob looked over his shoulder at her. "You what?"

Kim nodded. "Yeah. She called me, woke me up. Told me she needed help. I told her to unlock the garage door into the house. Unfortunately, she passed out before she could get the door unlocked."

"And you kicked it in? Jesus, Kim." He chuckled. "I should've known you'd have it in you."

She rolled her eyes. "I told you I tried to kick it in. Hey, I'm strong, but I'm not Wonder Woman."

Rob smiled and remembered how Heather had loved that movie. What he wouldn't give to spend that time again, to have her back.

"Ms. Duke?"

Both he and Kim looked up at the woman clad in green hospital scrubs, standing in the doorway. Kim stood. "Yes, I'm Kim Duke."

Rob moved next to her. Kim turned to him and put her hand on his shoulder. "This is Officer Rob Caldwell. He's Heather's boyfriend."

Rob almost corrected her but figured now was not the time. Plus he didn't want them to not give him any information. He'd be surprised if they disclosed anything as it was.

"Hi, I'm Dr. Neesa. I operated on your girlfriend." The woman held her hand out.

Rob shook her hand. "Hi. Nice to meet you. Is that weird? I mean, honestly, under the circumstances, it's not really nice." He stopped himself and blew out a harsh breath. "Sorry, I'm rambling like an idiot. I'm just really worried, and I need to let you talk."

The doctor gave him a soft, pleasant smile. "It's completely understandable." She motioned toward the chairs behind them. "How about we sit down?"

Rob nodded, and he, Kim, and the very calm doctor moved to the vinyl chairs.

She still had that soft smile on her face, but as it faded, Dr. Neesa began. "Her condition was quite extensive, and she'd lost a lot of blood. I'm so sorry but—"

Although Rob could see that the doctor was talking, he could not hear anything she was saying. Her lips were moving, but things had gone all Charlie Brown teacher on him.

He blinked.

Swallowed.

Cleared his throat.

Kim nodded, shook her head. Her face a grim mask.

A few words made it, coming in clear through the static.

"Hemorrhaging—"

"—uterine."

"Blood transfusion."

"Unable to save—"

God help them, this was going to destroy every part of her.

* * * *

God Almighty, Heather felt like she was swimming in sludge. She drew in a shallow breath, and as the ache in her body radiated to her brain, she fought to open her eyes.

What the hell had happened? Why did it feel like her lids were glued shut? And why did everything hurt, like she'd been run over by a bus?

How strange. She couldn't really remember anything. Heather tried again to open her eyes, and—yay, success! The small accomplishment kicked her adrenaline up a notch. Which, clearly she needed more of except, damn...now that her eyes were open, she focused on the telltale cream-colored ceiling tiles, then without moving her head, as far as her gaze could go. Which wasn't far, but yep, she was definitely in the hospital.

Shit, *had* she been run over by a bus?

Bending her left arm at the elbow, she inspected the IV tube stuck in her hand, nicely covered by that fashionable clear surgical tape. At least they'd nailed the vein on the first hit, no sign of bruises from a miss, anyway.

Eventually someone would come in and tell her what had happened, but maybe if she just relaxed and tried to focus, think of the last thing she remembered. At least that's what she used to tell her patients back in the day.

Heather cleared her throat. God, some water would be goo—

"Hey, you're awake."

Rob...

She turned her head to the right, just as he came to the side of the bed. She sighed at the sight of him. God, he was so beautiful. Inside and out. By far, the most beautiful man she'd ever known.

Heather let her eyes roam over his face and down his chest. He had been hers once, but she let him go. She'd had to because the truth was he was one hundred percent perfect and she was…not. "Hi."

He took her hand in his. "How're you feeling, babe?"

Babe…

God, that killed. Hurt more than her body did, really. "I'm thirsty and sore."

"Let me get you some water." Rob brushed her hair away from her face, caressing her cheek.

Yep, he was trying to kill her. Death by the broken heart she stupidly caused herself, or something ridiculous like that. One good hurt deserved another right?

He stepped away, and before she could even blink twice, he was back in her line of sight, and by the sounds of the squeaking, was bringing the bed table closer. Then the sound of water pouring into a cup.

"Gonna sit you up, just a little." The head of the bed started rising, the whirring sound a welcome distraction from the silence stretching between them. Rob smiled. "There we go."

Heather watched him as he brought the standard-issue plastic hospital cup toward her, the white straw bent and sticking out of the top. She sucked the cool liquid into her mouth.

As she drank, he said nothing, just watched her. His gaze soft, his expression filled with concern…and fucking hell, she wanted to burst into tears. She'd hurt this man. She'd hurt them both.

But that's what people did when they were all fucked up. Hurt people, hurt people. She was damaged, and that made her a lethal weapon. Okay, she was losing it, and like it or not, the tears were going to fall.

And wouldn't that be pretty? Clearly something serious had happened, so likely, she wasn't looking her best. And he was looking at her like she was the most beautiful thing he'd ever seen.

"Enough for now?" Rob pulled the cup away and set it on the table.

Heather nodded. Drawing in a breath, she swallowed and gathered what little courage she had left. "What happened?"

He sighed and rubbed the back of his neck. "Do you want me to call your parents?"

"No. Or wait, how long have I been out of it? Have they not been here?"

"You came out of surgery about three hours ago. You were admitted around five a.m. this morning. No, they haven't been here, because I wasn't sure if you'd want them here."

"I had surgery?" A knot formed in Heather's stomach, making her feel like she couldn't breathe.

Rob stepped away and pulled the chair in the room over. "Do you want me to call them now?"

"No, Rob." She stared at him a beat before continuing. "I want you to tell me what I had surgery for."

Rob nodded and clasped her hand in his. She didn't take her eyes off him, but he was no longer looking at her. He was staring down at their linked hands. Dread filled her lungs, clogging her airway.

Part of her knew what he was going to say, but another part of her was still holding on to hope. The same part of her that *always* held out hope. The very part that had her ending a perfectly awesome relationship because he was okay with not having kids, and she was not.

The truth was, the big secret Heather had kept, even from herself, was that she would *never* be okay with it. No matter what the doctors said, no matter how bad her endometriosis issues were.

She just couldn't accept that as her fate….

"Babe…" He shook his head, breathed in and let it out through his nose. "This isn't going to be easy to hear. Hell, it's hard for me to even say it out loud."

God. Just say it.

Say it!

She wanted to scream the words at him. Wanted to shake him until he told her.

"You were pregnant but—"

"What?" Heather's eyes went wide, and she laughed a little. "Did you just say I'm pregnant?"

"—it was ectopic, and your tube ruptured."

"Wait…how…" Her head fell back on the pillow.

You were *pregnant…*

How could this be happening? Was this some sort of sick joke God was playing on her? How could she have been preg—but she wasn't now. Not anymore. Fuck, how did she *not* know she was pregnant?

And holy shit, she'd had food poisoning, at least that's what she thought she had. It must've been morning sickness. Kim had joked, urging her to take a pregnancy test.

Her one shot and she didn't know? She should've known. If she'd taken a test, she would have.

"I'm sorry, baby. I'm so, so sorry." His voice sounded choked up, as if he was about to cry. Instead, he swallowed, his Adam's apple bobbing with the action. "You were hemorrhaging, and you'd lost a ton of blood. When they went in to take care of the tube, your endometriosis was beyond excessive...."

He wasn't done, she could see it in his eyes, but she just wasn't sure she could listen anymore. Her cheeks were wet, tears flowing of their own volition, but she wasn't making a sound.

"The doctors said your endometriosis was stage four. Your uterus had attached to a big portion of your intestine and bladder, and apparently there were fibroids present too—" Rob looked up at her. "Fuck." He bent forward to her and pressed his forehead to hers. "It's okay. I've got you."

He closed his eyes and cupped the side of her head in his big palm. "So sorry."

She sniffled and tried to pull away, but he wasn't letting her go. Dammit. "Please, I don't want to hear any more."

"Okay, babe."

She closed her eyes, and a cry escaped. Steeling herself, she gripped his wrist. "Just tell me this last thing: they took it, didn't they? My baby, my uterus, my everything—they took it all, didn't they?"

Rob nodded, and still, he didn't let her go. "Yes."

Heather drew in a ragged breath. And then another. The pain in her chest, her heart, far greater than any physical pain she felt in her body. She drew in another breath. How in the hell was she going to process this?

Oh, God!

How was she going to survive this? How was she goi—

Panic rose up her chest, choking her, and a bone-curdling wail emerged from deep within Heather, bringing with it everything she'd held dear for the past five years.

Every hope, every dream, every fantasy and lie.

Everything that had defined her...and ruined her.

Bringing forth her very soul.

And now it was all gone.

* * * *

Rob held her to his chest as she cried.

He was still reeling from hearing everything from the surgeon several hours ago, and then now, relaying it back to Heather. Having to deliver that devastation had gutted him as he unintentionally gutted her.

For her, it was worse. So much worse.

Rob cried too, but for her, not for himself. He was not what was important here. He was not the one who'd lost so much. Yes, technically he'd lost a child too, but Rob couldn't allow himself to think about that loss.

Due to her many issues, the embryo had likely not been viable, but that didn't mean Heather wasn't feeling the loss in her soul as if she'd held that baby—their baby, in her arms.

As a result, his woman was drowning in a sea of agony. It was pulling her under, tossing her around, and all Rob wanted was to rescue her from it. He knew he couldn't, but also, he shouldn't even try.

If she was going to come out the other side of anything from her past and now present, and heal, she needed to walk through it. Every horrid and painful step of it. But she wasn't going to have to do it alone. No way he was leaving her side.

They stayed like that for a long time, her crying as he held her in his arms, doing whatever he could to physically and emotionally hold her together as best he could. Her pain was palpable, flowing out of her in each cry that came from her mouth and every tear that ran from her eyes.

The weight of the emotion was unlike anything he'd ever experienced or felt before. It hung in the air of the room and cocooned them both. It was thick and dreadful and overflowing with loss.

At that moment, Rob would've done anything to take this away from her. But the fact was, there was nothing he could do to make this better. There was nothing he could say. All he could do was hold her, as he was doing, and love her. That was it. That was all.

Rob had his own journey of acceptance to travel down. Sadly, there was no saving someone from this kind of devastation, and there was no making it better. Nothing he could do would ever be enough to fill the void of what she'd lost.

Heather was going to have to do that. God, he hoped she could.

Chapter 30

After a week in the hospital, not feeling as steady as she'd hoped to be, Heather walked into her house. Tricks was right beside her, nearly herding her or making sure she stayed on her feet, which of course if she was going to go down, the dog would likely dive beneath her to break her fall.

Actually, from the minute Rob appeared in the doorway of her hospital room to take her home, the animal hadn't left her side. She'd loved Tricks, so there were no complaints coming from her.

Stopping at the entrance of her living room, she looked around the tidy space, taking in the furniture, the decor. The throw pillows were arranged perfectly on the couch, as well as on the chair in the corner.

The room had great feng shui, giving off an energy she'd always been able to feel. Except right now, she felt nothing. Tricks nosed her palm. Okay, so she *felt* that at least. Heather glanced down at him and stroked her hand over his head. "It's okay, baby boy. I'm okay."

His dark eyes were trained on her, and she swore he furrowed his brow in concern. Was that even possible? Dogs didn't have eyebrows of course, but they sure as hell had a brow, and no doubt, the dog's brow furrowed, or something close to it anyway.

Rob moved past her, setting her bag down at the mouth of the hallway. "He senses that you're not oka—"

"But, *I am* okay." She frowned at her clipped response and tone. "Sorry."

Rob shrugged. "All right, fine. Maybe he senses that *I* know you're not okay."

Heather sighed and rubbed her forehead with the tips of her fingers. "I get it, I had surgery, but it's not a big deal, Rob. And I know you're worried, but I'm good now. Truly."

Rob regarded her, one brow raised, and as if he'd just decided his next move, he crossed his arms over his chest. "Yeah? All things considered, the surgery you had was pretty normal. But for real, you're good now? Sure. Then let's get your parents on the phone. I know your mother has ready-made meals for us. Packed all nice and neat in individual microwaveable or oven-safe containers. May as well let her bring them over, right?"

Direct hit. Boy, she'd called that.

"Ha ha, very funny. We do not need them or the perfectly prepared meals here." Heather shook her head, moved toward him and then bent to pick up her bag.

Rob got to it before she did, grabbing the small suitcase before she had a chance to. "What the hell are you doing?"

Heather propped her hands on her hips. Jesus, he was already being a pain in the ass. "Come on, really? I'm not an invalid. Regardless, I wasn't going to pick it up, I was merely going to wheel it down the hallway to my bedroom."

"Sorry, but that's a no go. You're not supposed to be lifting anything, and I might be going out on a limb here, but I'm assuming that also includes pulling things, too. Go sit your ass down on the couch, and I'll get this down the hall, then make you something to eat."

"I'm not hungry."

"Then something to drink. But either way, you need to get off your feet, now."

Heather gritted her teeth. The need to do exactly what she was told was always present with him. And that was annoying as hell. "Fine."

Yes, she'd lost a ton of blood. Had to have transfusions and everything. Technically she almost died. And yes, she'd also lost a ba… *God.* Heather swallowed the lump that was instantly in her throat. She couldn't even say the word.

After the wave of emotion passed, she got herself back on the train track of thought. Yes, she'd had a major surgery for many reasons and her body was still healing, but she didn't need to be nursed or babied. She just needed some time alone. But something told her she wasn't going to get that.

Blowing out a sigh, she moved over to her couch and sat in the spot she normally sat in, curling her legs to the side. Out of habit, and not because she felt cold, she pulled the throw blanket over her legs. Okay, maybe she was a little cold. And tired.

Heather yawned, and Tricks groaned before he sat, his back to her, his side pressed against her bent knee. The dog was far enough away from her that she couldn't pet his head, but she did trail her fingertip along the back of his neck, tickling his fur.

Tricks looked over his shoulder at her and licked his chops. Shifting, he laid his head on the sofa beside her knee, which allowed her to reach him and smooth the soft fur along the side of his sweet doggie face.

"I wonder if it was a boy or a girl, Tricks," she whispered.

The dog sighed, and his warm eyes stayed locked on her.

Heather kept her voice hushed. "She or he would've been beautiful, huh? We would have loved a baby. You would've protected it, huh? Like I would've. And like Rob would've." A tear fell down her cheek, and she cursed herself, wiping it away.

Rob didn't need to see her crying. But dammit, she wasn't sure she could help it. The ordeal of being discharged from the hospital and the journey home, which really wasn't that far, thirty minutes tops, had exhausted her. That was why she was crying, just overtired. At least she could use that as an excuse if Rob noticed, which he would because that's just how he was.

Heather really needed him to leave. Go to work, or just go home. She needed to be alone, to face her demons per se…examine what she'd failed to focus on while in the hospital.

And it wasn't like they were back together. Although she was pretty sure he had thought they were, he hadn't left the hospital the whole time she was there, save for a few hours here and there.

But she wasn't his problem and neither was the baby they'd lost.

She might do as she was told, when he gave an order, but that had its limits too. He wouldn't get this out of her. Heather couldn't share any of it with him, she wouldn't. It was far too ugly for anyone else to see.

Hell, even she didn't want to see it.

* * * *

Rob looked through her pantry and was shocked to find she didn't have much in there. She had tea though, so that was a start. Grabbing the small box off the shelf, he closed the door and moved to the counter.

Next, he assessed the contents of the fridge. No juice. Barely any milk in the carton—which was near expired. No eggs. No bacon. No cold cuts… clearly a trip to the grocery was needed. He should've asked Kim to pick stuff up, but she'd already done enough.

He peeked his head around the corner. She was sitting on the couch, blanket over her lap, Tricks plastered to her. Yep, his canine was fucking awesome. "Hey, I'm going to run to Fry's. Any special requests?"

It took her a moment, but then Heather looked up. "Sorry, what was that?"

Rob moved into the room. "I'm going to head to Fry's and pick up a few things. Any requests?"

"You don't have to do that."

"I know."

"Really, it's okay. You can go home." She smoothed her palm over Tricks's floppy ear.

Rob eyed his partner. "You ready for Tricks to go home too?"

She frowned and looked down. "No."

"Fair enough." Rob walked over and pressed a soft kiss to her forehead. "I'll be back in a little while."

"Mm'kay."

He glanced over his shoulder before he opened the front door to leave. "Text if you have any special requests."

She nodded and went back to focusing on Tricks.

Rob's chest tightened, and he drew in a slow breath and left the house. God, he'd almost lost her. Even thinking about it had fear boiling over like a pot left neglected on the stove.

Once she'd come out of surgery and was safely in recovery, Rob had gone to her house. Her bed...fuck, it'd looked like a crime scene. He'd stripped the bed and thrown the sheets and mattress cover away.

Unfortunately, the bleeding had been so heavy it'd soaked through all of that and ruined the mattress anyway. Rob had taken care of buying a new one, but Kim had taken up post at Heather's house for delivery of the new one and removal of the old.

Then there was a matter of scrubbing the small trail of blood that Heather had left when crawling from her bedroom to the laundry room and the more than small amount she'd left on the floor in front of the garage door.

Like he said, it'd looked like a crime scene.

But Kim had handled it all. Heather had that tile that looked like wood, so thankfully, it cleaned up with bleach. Kim had even gotten it out of the grout. Rob had no idea how, he just knew the woman was a miracle worker.

Hell, she'd saved Heather's life as far as he was concerned so yeah, he could handle getting the groceries.

This was the easy stuff, really. The hardest part for him was going to be weathering the cold front Heather was sending his way. Continuing to weather it was more like it.

After she'd come out of surgery and he'd told her what happened, she'd broken down in a way that he felt beyond the bounds of his soul. It'd broken him, feeling her pain, and he'd done all he could to carry her through it.

She'd let him. She leaned on him and cried to him, and with him.

But afterward, once the tears had settled, she'd pulled away from him. She locked him out and hadn't let him back in since. Rob knew she just needed time, probably needed space, too. He could give her that, but he had no intention of leaving her house.

She was dealing with years-old hurt from not being able to conceive a child and then the brand-new devastation of conceiving, and not only losing that baby, but losing any future hope for another. Few things came close to that level of emotional destruction.

From what he understood, the fact that he'd gotten her pregnant to begin with had been a miracle. Rob would've rejoiced in having a child with her. He'd never cared one way or the other, and was okay if he never had kids.

But the idea of giving her that gift, or being part of her getting to have it? Yeah, it would've meant the world, it would've meant everything.

But that wasn't what happened. In truth, that gift had been a curse. If he'd known the risk, or what a pregnancy could do to her, what it would cause? He would have taken precautions.

He would've protected her.

He *should* have protected her.

Chapter 31

Later that night, Heather lay in her bed, staring at the ceiling, unable to sleep. Finally, she was alone. Thank God. Well, Tricks was with her, lying in his dog bed, right at the side of her bed, but that didn't count. She *wanted* him there.

Call her crazy, but she was pretty sure the animal didn't care if she talked about how she was feeling. He sure wasn't asking her how she was doing every five minutes. No, Tricks was happy to just quietly lie beside her. And Heather was happy to have him do just that.

Though obviously that also meant he was a package deal. Where Tricks was, Rob was. But wait, didn't Rob need to go to work soon? Maybe Tricks could stay with her while he was on patrol.

Oh, crap…Heather rolled her eyes at her forgetfulness. Tricks was a K9 dog after all. When Rob went to work, so did Tricks. Damn.

Heather rolled to her side, easing her sore body into a different position so she was facing the bedroom door. When Rob came back from the store, he'd been pretty low-key, and honestly, hadn't said much at all.

He cooked dinner. Served them both. He did the dishes. And then he sat quietly, drinking a coffee while watching TV with her. She wasn't really watching though, maybe he was.

She more or less just stared at the television and thought about what it would've been like…to have his baby. What would it have looked like? Would it have had her eyes, or his? Blonde hair or brown? Would they have gotten married? Heather sighed. Would she have wanted to get married?

Jesus, the fantasy was endless and scary and beautiful and—

The sound of Tricks getting to his feet, shaking his fur and trotting out of her bedroom, filled her ears. She wanted to call him back, but maybe he needed water or to go out, or just to be with his owner.

Heather closed her eyes, placed her palm on her stomach and drew in a breath. Fantasy was the key word, really. Especially now. What a cruel joke life had played on her. Or was it God? Not that she prayed to any such God anymore.

And maybe that was why? Maybe she was being punished.

Or maybe it was just how life went sometimes. After all, she'd never been a very religious person, as far as church was concerned anyway. But she did believe in God—or something greater than herself anyway. It was just easier to call that greater thing God. Years ago, a patient once told her God stood for: Good Orderly Direction. That had made sense to her.

As a nurse, Heather had put her faith in medicine and science, as well as an underlying energy that was responsible for creation. But being in the medical field, she saw a lot of loss over the years. Young and old, people died. People lost loved ones. People got well. People got sick.

Some people had babies, lots of them. Some people didn't deserve to have them and got to have them anyway. And some people never got to have any, ever, no matter how much they deserved them.

Life took and it gave, and it didn't discriminate. That was how life worked.

Yet when she was going through all those years of hormone treatments and surgeries and rounds of in vitro, she had forgotten all about those lessons, and the fact that sometimes life was just life and not everything worked out the way a person wanted it to.

The kids in the pediatrics unit, usually the ones with terminal cancer, used to say: You get what you get and you don't throw a fit. Well, she'd thrown a shit ton of fits, hadn't she? She was still throwing them. And frankly, it was time to stop.

No, God wasn't punishing her. It was just the cards that she had been dealt. It was life. And sometimes life fucking sucked in the most horrible ways. But it always went on even if a person wasn't ready for it to.

She'd lost so much over this thing she couldn't let go of. This need. This obsession. Having a baby had become her life, her everything. It was all she could see. As a result, she'd lost a husband, a home, a career…a life.

The only good thing that came from the devastation she felt those years ago was that the not-so-nice person she was had been changed forever. A reality check like that had a way of carving out the ego of a person and bringing them to their knees.

That part had been the only silver thread in all of it. But outside of that, because Heather was unable to let go and see past her body's limitations, to move forward, Heather had lost everything.

But really, was that why she'd lost it all? She no longer thought so. Looking back, and looking at where she was now, the truth was she hadn't lost a thing, she'd turned her back on everything. She was the one responsible.

And then life, because it went on whether a person noticed or not, gave her Rob, and what did Heather do? She'd gone and thrown that away too, turned her back on him.

Heather rolled to her back and covered her face with her hands. God, she wanted to scream. She'd been given a chance to rebuild her life, to move forward, to accept, and she'd squandered it. She'd tossed it out as if there'd be another and then another.

And now, now she really had lost everything, hadn't she? Now, any fantasy or obsession, or thick denial she had that maybe, *maybe* she'd somehow, someday, by some miracle bear her own children, life had taken that away from her too.

Heather had been unable, for over five years, to accept that she could not have children, at least not bear them in her own womb, or conceive them with her own eggs.

Fuck, who was to say she didn't *need* to lose her uterus? God knew nothing else had brought her to a place of utter surrender. Logic and knowledge had nothing to do with the heart and what it could or could not accept.

Losing the very thing that had served as the last thread to hold on to, so she could maybe someday have what she wanted, begged and had pleaded for? Yeah, that was a healthy serving of *openyoureyesandseewhatyoualreadyhave!*

Well, now she had no choice in that matter, did she?

God, or the universe, or life—sometimes did for some what they could not do for themselves.

* * * *

Rob shifted on the couch in Heather's living room. All those times she'd mentioned wanting to furnish her guest room, he never thought he'd be the one who needed her to have done it.

It wasn't that the couch was uncomfortable, it was just…that it was the freaking couch and not her bed. As it was, he hadn't had a good night's sleep, in a real bed, the entire time she was in the hospital. He'd slept in the vinyl recliner. Stiff and very squeaky.

But this was what Heather needed from him right now. No matter what, he was determined to do whatever it took to help her, even if it meant sleeping on her damn couch, away from her.

Tricks trotted out from the hallway, his nails clicking on the tile.

When things got quiet again, Rob picked up his head to see his partner sitting near the entry. "What's up, Tricks? You need to go out?"

Tricks sneezed and stood, shaking his fur coat.

"I'll take that as an affirmative." Rob peeled the sheet back and got to his feet. Striding over to the dog, he moved past him toward the back door in the kitchen. "Come on. You know where to go."

Tricks trotted behind Rob, and when Rob opened the back door, the dog lunged outside into the night air and onto the lawn.

"Guess you really had to go." Rob chuckled and stepped out onto the concrete patio, wandering a few feet away from the house. He stared out in the darkness of her backyard feeling absolutely fucking helpless.

Thank God for Tricks though. His canine partner had been at Heather's side from word go. Literally. Rob had the animal with him at the hospital most nights, and Tricks slept on the floor beside her hospital bed. Since he was a service dog, technically a police officer, the nurses had no issue with it—though he couldn't say if hospital administration would've been so forgiving without formal approval.

Rob glanced over his shoulder toward where her bedroom was and wondered how she was doing. Was she sleeping? Was she lying there in tears? Did she need any pain meds?

Christ, he wished he could curl up behind her and just hold her. At least in the hospital he'd been in the same room, able to get her something if she needed it, take care of her. But here? No go.

Tricks came prancing back to him.

"All done?"

Tricks trotted past him and sat in front of the door.

"I'll take that as a yes." Rob stepped beside the animal and opened the way back into the house.

Tricks moved to his water dish and started lapping. As he did, Rob locked the back door. He walked to the edge of the kitchen, where it merged with the living room and the hallway.

He stood for a moment, wishing he had x-ray vision and could see through walls, as well as darkness, absolutely tortured by the fact that he couldn't go to her. She needed space. Not that she'd said so, he could just tell by her mannerisms and her insistence that he go home.

Rob ran his fingers through his hair and resumed his prone position on the couch. Tricks came trotting in, and instead of going down the hall to Heather, he came over to Rob.

Rob got up on one elbow and stroked the dog's head. "What're you doing, partner? Come on now, you need to go down the hall and take care of our girl. You know I can't be in there. She's not ready for that right now, so you gotta be my eyes and ears."

Tricks sneezed and gave Rob his usual grumble/whine.

"Yeah, okay. Thanks for that. Don't be sneezing on her like you just did me because that shit is gross." Rob chuckled. "Go on now, get down there."

The dog headed off, his nails clicking on the tile floor as he trotted his way down the hall into her bedroom.

Rob closed his eyes and let out a sigh…not one of relief, more one from exhaustion and stress.

Tomorrow was another day. He hoped she'd be willing to talk…even if just a little.

Chapter 32

Heather stood in the shadows of the hallway, listening as Rob instructed Tricks to come back to her room, to go take care of her, and her heart melted into a puddle of goo.

Tricks approached her, and she patted his head and pointed in the direction of her bedroom. Thankfully, the dog kept moving, heading to where his doggie bed was in her room.

Rob didn't know she was standing there, and she wasn't sure what to do now. The things she'd heard him tell the dog, they were no big deal, but for some reason they were. His concern for her was like another slap in the face, another realization she'd been missing. Though she hadn't known she was missing it.

She knew Rob was amazing. There were so many wonderful things about him, and all of them the reason why she fell in love with him. This incredible, beautiful man had given her his trust, his acceptance and his love in spades, and she had had no idea how to accept any of it.

Too self-absorbed in her brokenness. But no matter how tall her walls were, he'd managed to break through them, and low and behold, Heather had fallen hard for him. Completely and totally.

Until he found out she couldn't have kids, and true to form, accepted that and told her he wanted her anyway. Well, that had been the snag in her pantyhose, hadn't it? No way could she stay with him. He was totally fine not having kids, and the very thought of her letting go of her obsession, her life focus, was too much to handle.

So, like a coward, she ran. Heather ended things, breaking both of their hearts, and ran back to her bottle of wine and bathtub. Well, no more of that. She was done running. Done obsessing and done missing her life.

God had given her a second chance, and technically now, a third. No way in hell she was going to waste it.

Heather peered out into the darkness of the hallway, to the living room. She could barely make out Rob's form on her couch beneath the sheet.

Drawing in a breath, she turned and went back to her room. After giving Tricks a pat on the head, she climbed into her bed and pulled the sheet and blanket over her.

It was amazing how differently she saw things now, how different she felt deep within. Acceptance was a miraculous thing, when it actually took root. And that was all that was needed too, just a simple, small root.

* * * *

On the end table behind his head, Rob's phone beeped with a text message. He tipped his head back and grabbed the phone. The notification preview showed it was from Heather. *Shit.* Without bothering to open the message to read it, he dropped the phone and was up and moving down the hallway to her in less than thirty seconds. Maybe even fifteen.

Skidding to a stop in her doorway, he grabbed the jamb to steady himself. "Babe, you okay?"

"Yes. I'm okay."

Rob stepped into the room. "You texted. Do you need something? Help to the bathroom?"

"Did you read it?"

A few more steps and he was next to the bed. "No. I just jumped up and ran to you."

"You ran to me?" She let out a little laugh.

She was laughing? How was she...Rob wasn't sure what was going on, but he wasn't about to question it. Yet. "Of course I ran to you, bombshell. When you need something, I take care of it, I take care of you. That's the deal. That will *always* be the deal."

"You mean it, don't you?"

Her voice was so low he almost couldn't hear her. Careful not to crowd her, he sat on the edge of her bed. "I have always meant it."

He had a feeling she wanted to say something to him, so he figured he'd give her the time to do that. Rob stayed there for what felt like forever, gazing down at the shadows of her face, the moonlight through her sheer drapes the only light illuminating her.

When the silence became too much to bear, he cleared his throat and broke it. "Do you want to tell me what you texted, or should I go get my phone?"

"No. It's fine." Her warm hand landed on his forearm. "Can you just…"

"What is it, babe?" He brushed his thumb over her hairline at her forehead.

"Do you think you can get in bed with me?"

Holy wow! Really? Rob drew in a breath, pulling on every ounce of calm he had in his body. How he managed to keep his excitement to himself, he had no idea. But he had, and that was all that mattered.

Playing it cool was definitely the better way to go, no need to freak her out. "Of course I can."

"Thank you."

After getting to his feet, Rob walked around to the other side of the bed, drew the covers back and crawled in beside her. Turning on his side, he slid one arm under his pillow, and as she scooted her back to his chest, he curled his other arm around her and pulled her closer.

Rob closed his eyes and pressed his nose to her hair. Taking a moment to just breathe her in, he thanked God one more time that she was still walking the earth. He'd almost lost her.

"Rob?" she whispered.

Keeping his tone to a whisper as well, he answered. "Yeah, baby?"

"I need to say some things to you, but I need you to just let me say them, okay? I don't want you to reply, at least not until I'm done. Can you do that for me? Is that okay?"

She was still whispering, and Rob figured this was how she needed it to be. Fine with him. Sometimes whispering was the only way to say the things out loud that a person had never said before. He sighed and then breathed her in again. "Yes, I can, and that's perfectly okay."

"Thank you." Heather shifted, rolling to her back but staying snugged against him.

He still had his arm around her, and she took his palm and slid it to her lower abdomen, where her uterus had been, where their baby had been, too. The gravity of where she'd placed his hand did not escape him. But he stayed quiet, even when he wanted to tell her it was okay….

"For over five years now, I've been drowning myself. Swallowing gallons and gallons of guilt and regret and loss and anger. And whenever I managed to surface, I would grab ahold of the only life raft I could see. My obsession, my need. My want, my desire, my, my, my…me, me, me. It was always about me." She let out a bitter laugh. "My whole damn life I was like that, you know? Just pathetic. And then it wasn't about me anymore, it was about me having a baby. Different but not really, because at the end of the day, it was still… All. About. Me.

"But the further that dream of having a baby got away from me, the further I got away from myself. The old me anyway, I had yet to figure out who I was beneath all of that. I was selfish though, that was for sure."

She drew in a deep breath, and blew it out, slowly. "When you met me, I was a shell. Empty. Dead inside. My heart beat, yes, but I was a walking corpse. And then I met you. God…you were such a bright light for me. Like a beacon or a lighthouse in the storm, you know? And you didn't even know it."

Rob smiled, remembering those early days between them, only a few short months ago though it felt like so much longer. He pressed a soft kiss to her shoulder.

"I wasn't looking for you, but there you were. God, so beautiful and fun and clean…and for the first time in so long, I felt like I was alive. And I wanted that, I needed it. Selfish or not, I wasn't ready to let you go. Damage be damned. But then you found out my secret, my shame, and I couldn't face you. And I couldn't face what you knowing meant."

Rob frowned, not completely understanding what she meant, but remained silent regardless, hoping he'd be able to see what she was trying to show him.

"You see, you were fine without having kids, but what I am trying to admit out loud, and for the first time, is that I was *not* fine with it. None of it. I wasn't okay with the fact that you were fine with it, and more importantly, I was not fine with the fact that I couldn't have them. Bottom line, I had not accepted my fate, and the fact that you had meant I had to let you go.

"I couldn't keep my fantasy, my sick obsession, and keep you too. That wasn't going to work. So I chose my obsession. I broke the heart of the man I love, and I broke my own heart, just so I could stay sick in my madness."

Rob had to bite his tongue to keep quiet. Fuck, it was hard to hear her blame herself like this, to heap all this on herself. He really wanted to stop her, but she'd asked him to remain silent, so yeah. Bleeding tongue would have to do.

"But life took over, and you knocked me up. How the hell did you do that? I mean really? Talk about super sperm." She laughed.

Rob laughed too. In part because he could not believe she was joking about something so serious, and also because it was kind of funny. How the hell *did* he get her pregnant? For all intents and purposes, it wasn't medically feasible, yet it'd happened.

After her laughter faded, she wiped her eyes and turned her head toward him. "I know it's not funny, not really, but it kind of is."

"It's okay."

She nodded. "Point I'm getting to is, life had its way, and it kicked my ass, and now I get it. So simple, right? You'd think after all this time I would've figured out why I was so fucked up, but I couldn't see it. Kind of like a fish doesn't know it's in water." She cleared her throat. "But I see now. I know now. I get it." She turned fully to face him and snuggled closer.

Rob held her tighter.

"I can't have babies, at least not any from my own making or from my own body. And that's just life. Tough shit. Get over it. It happens every day to people. Why me? Well, why not me? What makes me so goddamn special? Nothing. I'm just me." She wrapped an arm around his waist. "My point is, I *get* to still have a life. With or without babies. I'm still supposed to live my life. I see that now. I know it deep in my heart and soul like I've never known it before. And if you still want me, I get to live a life with you."

Rob pulled her tighter against him. God, he loved this woman. He so fucking loved Heather Winters.

"Can I talk now?"

She giggle-snorted "Yes."

"Good, because I think my tongue is bleeding from biting it so hard. You're gonna have to take care of me. I might need first aid."

She tipped her head back. "Stick it out, let me see?"

"See?" Rob stuck his tongue out, and Heather kissed the tip of it.

"Better?"

"Much!" He pressed his forehead to hers and then shifted so his lips were close to her ear. Whispering, he said, "I love you, Heather Winters. A part of me has always loved you. I want nothing more than to have a life with you. I want the rest of my life with you."

Heather exhaled, and with it, he felt her body sag against him.

"I'd be honored, Robert Caldwell."

Rob smoothed his palm up to the back of her neck. Cupping it, he tilted her head back and took her lips in a soft kiss.

A communion between them. A promise filled with hope and a future. A gift.

Meet the Author

Dorothy F. Shaw lives in Arizona where the weather is hot and the sunsets are always beautiful. She spends her days in the corporate world and her nights with her Mac on her lap. Between her ever-open heart, her bright red hair, and her many colorful tattoos, she truly lives and loves in Technicolor! Dorothy welcomes emails at: dorothyfshaw@gmail.com. Or find her online at Facebook.com/AuthorDorothyFShaw and twitter.com/DorothyFShaw Newsletter sign up: http://bit.ly/DFSeNews.

Acknowledgments

A big shout-out and thank-you to the following awesome men in law enforcement for their dedication and service to the community, as well as their help with this book. Officer Matthew Warbington. And always, my wonderful adopted Dad, retired Connecticut State Trooper, Sergeant Robert Gawe.

A special thanks to my friend, and very talented Nurse Practitioner, Amy Connolly for her medical consultation.

Author Sidda Lee Rain...as always, love you to the moon and back. I hope I always know you.

Last but not least, to my Facebook Night Writers group. To those that wrote with me (talking to you, authors Khloe Wren and Brooklyn Anne) night after night, thank you. I could not have finished this book without you.

Avoiding the Badge

JUST WHAT THE DOCTOR ORDERED

Rayna Michaels may be a veterinarian, but she knows a little something about the human heart—especially when it comes to worried pet owners. Law enforcement's bonds with their K9 partners are legendary, and Derek Hansen is a perfect example—he's had his dog Axle in more times than she can count in the last few months. And Derek's sculpted muscles and heart-stopping smile would be truly irresistible, if only he wasn't an officer of the law . . .

Derek can't get Rayna's stunning face and no-nonsense smarts out of his mind. Any excuse to see her will do, until he works up the nerve to ask her out. He's not sure where her resistance to cops comes from, though he's more than willing to prove he's one of the good ones. But when casual dating turns into explosive lovemaking, Derek knows he has to come clean about his past before the woman he loves finds out what he's been hiding and turns tail to run . . .

Chapter 1

"Ahem... Heeeee's heeeere."

At her head vet tech's declaration, Doctor Rayna Michaels looked up from the lab report she was reading in the back of the main treatment area and furrowed her brow. "I'm sorry. Who is 'he'?"

Andrea leaned her hip against the counter and dipped her chin. "Seriously?"

"Always." Careful to keep her expression blank, Rayna stared at the woman.

Andrea sighed and rolled her eyes. "*He* as in the hottest pet owner we have." Even as Rayna returned her focus to the lab report in her hands, Andrea continued. "Come on, really? *He* as in 'the cop' who's so freaking hot we could fry an egg on his unbelievable abs. We haven't seen the abs, but we all know he's got them. In spades. The same *he* who's so totally into you—so into you that the rest of us are green with envy."

He was not and they were not. Rayna sighed and set the report back on the counter. Yes, she knew *exactly* who Andrea was talking about, but no way was Rayna going to let her vet tech know that.

And yes, Officer Derek Hansen was handsome—very handsome in fact. The kind of handsome every hot-blooded woman, self-assured man, or more specifically a gay man—her receptionist Billy had pointed out last time Officer Hansen had been in—on the planet took notice of. If they didn't, they were likely dead, because *very* handsome was not only accurate, it was also an incredible understatement.

Dark, close-cropped hair, just a little longer on top. Dark, straight brows. Green eyes. Full lips. Always clean-shaven, but Rayna bet he looked good with a five o'clock shadow, too. His nose wasn't perfect, but it fit his face perfectly. And then there was his body...

Rayna sighed. Great. The mere thought of how good-looking Hansen was had heat spilling through her system like warm syrup. If she hadn't put the report down, she could've used it as a fan—though that would've been way too obvious. "I'm sorry, but you're going to have to be a bit more specific."

"I swear, Doctor Michaels. Sometimes I don't even know what to do with you." She threw her hands up in the air with a harsh sigh, then let them flop back down at her sides. "Fine. Officer Derek Hansen is here with Axle for yet *another* 'checkup.' Specific enough?" Andrea smirked.

"Well then, let's hope Axle is okay. I know Officer Hansen has been a tad...cautious, possibly overly so, since his canine partner was injured. But honestly, as you know, there is *nothing* wrong with taking good care of your animal. Especially one as important as Axle." She smiled, knowing her statement was only going to annoy Andrea further. Which served as a fantastic distraction from the heat rising in her body. Rayna cleared her throat. "What room is he in?"

Andrea let out an exasperated groan and grabbed a file off the counter. "Exam room four. And not for anything, but he's been in twice already this month. This makes visit number three. I think it's a sign." Andrea grinned and started to turn away, but then stopped. "All professionalism aside, enjoy the view for the rest of us, please? You know we're all going to want a full report when you're done in there." After a wink, she headed for the short hallway leading to the front of the office.

Rayna watched her go before picking up the lab report and reading it over once more. Deep breaths, in and out. In and out. In and—

It wasn't working. Desperate for some relief, she fanned herself with the lab report.

Around six months ago, Officer Derek Hansen's canine partner, Axle, had been injured in the line of duty. Apparently, her clinic had been the closest place to where the injury happened, and when he'd burst in the front door, of course she'd immediately treated the animal.

The injury hadn't been anything too serious, thank goodness. Axle had needed a small laceration stitched up, but the animal had also popped his kneecap out of joint on his left hind leg. Leg injuries could lead to hip issues with many big dogs, but shepherds especially. Ensuring Axle was healed properly was essential for his career as a police dog, but more importantly, the animal's overall well-being and quality of life.

However, after the dog had healed, Officer Hansen continued to bring Axle into the clinic—to the tune of every three weeks, give or take, for what he called "regular checkups." It didn't mean anything more than that the man was caring for his animal. Rather typical for an officer and their canine partner. Those teams never left each other's side.

Besides, who was she to turn away a patient?

Hansen wasn't a man of many words, but he was always polite, respectful. And, of course, considering Rayna was counted as a red-blooded woman, she'd also noticed he was gorgeous. How could she not? She had a pulse, after all.

Still, checking out her patients' owners wasn't something she made a habit of, or ever did, so she made sure to keep their dealings strictly business. It would be unprofessional and highly inappropriate for her to act in any other way.

Every time he'd been in the office, Rayna tried for all she was worth to *not* focus on how beautiful he was or how incredibly well built his body was, but with each visit, she failed. Plus, whenever she was in one of the exam rooms alone with him, her skin got warm all over, and without a doubt her face was the shade of a fire truck, her spray of freckles becoming little red spotlights.

Worse, each visit, she emerged with the effects he had on her nervous system on display for all to see. As if she were having some sort of allergic reaction, the skin covering her sternum and neck was completely flushed and blotchy. Her entire office staff would not let her forget it.

Frankly, not noticing the officer wasn't possible. After all, how could anyone with a set of functioning eyes *not* notice a well over six-foot-tall, hard-muscled, incredibly gorgeous cop?

The answer was plain and simple: they couldn't.

Rayna grabbed her mini medical bag filled with doggie treats and moved to exam room four's entrance. With another deep breath to cleanse her mind and hopefully cool down her body, she pressed her palm to the metal panel of the door.

As she was about to push it open, Andrea sauntered back into view, a stack of files in her arms. "Good luck! He looks really, *really* good today," she whispered.

Rayna's eyes went wide. She was going to kill Andrea if Officer Hansen heard the woman's comment. "Are you done yet?"

Andrea grinned from ear to ear. "Nope. I have to get these files updated in the system."

Reining in the nervous tension crawling up her spine, Rayna switched topics. "How many more appointments are on the schedule for today?"

"Lucky you, none. He's your last one. You get to take *all* the time you need." Andrea placed the files on the counter and sat in front of the computer.

"Great." What on earth did luck have to do with it? And wait, he looked good *today*? How was that different from any other day? The man *always* looked good. Like when he crossed his thickly muscled arms over his very broad chest, the veins in his forearms stood out in harsh relief against his tanned skin.

A flash fantasy of running her tongue along all those perfect veins made—oh dear, she hoped like hell the heat rising from her stomach to her chest like a wildfire would settle enough for her to do her job.

And do it without her face glowing bright as the Arizona sun.

* * * *

"Oh yeah, that's right, Axle. I heard her, too. She's coming." With nervous energy pumping through his system, Officer Derek Hansen took a seat on the small bench in the vet clinic exam room and did his best to appear calm, cool, and collected.

His five-year-old black- and rust-colored shepherd glanced over at him and licked his chops before going back to pacing around the tiny room.

Doc Michaels was right on the other side of the door. Derek would know her voice anywhere. Not that he'd been paying attention or anything. It was merely one of those things a person picked up in his line of work.

At least that was the story he was going to keep telling himself. Derek extended his legs, crossing them at the ankle, and focused on Axle again. "You should probably sit down, too. Seriously, try not to look so eager, dude."

Axle gave a small huff, followed by a whine, before resting on his haunches and facing the entry door to the exam room.

Derek let out his own whine, not audibly of course—at least he thought so until Axle jerked his big head Derek's way. Okay, fine. His partner heard it, thanks to his keen canine hearing. Whatever, as long as the doc didn't hear him, Derek was good.

The door shifted open a crack. "Andrea, would you call the Bensons and let them know the tests were all negative for Caspian, please?"

Derek straightened, ready to hop to his feet, then stopped himself, remembering he was supposed to be going for calm and cool. Oh yeah, and collected, too. Damn.

The door opened the rest of the way, and after she walked in, she set her little baby-blue medical bag down on the counter as she smiled down at Axle. "Hello there, big boy!"

Axle's ears dropped, flopping all puppy-dog style. Derek rolled his eyes and smothered a grin. His partner was such a ham.

She squatted down in front of the dog, scratching his ears. "Aren't you so handsome in your uniform?" She moved her hands over his head, and Axle's ass started wiggling. "You certainly are."

"You keep talking to my partner like that, Doc, and you're gonna give him an ego." Unable to sustain his calm presentation any longer, Derek got to his feet.

Doc Rayna smoothed her palm down Axle's back and glanced up at Derek. "I think he's far too humble to fall into such a trap." She grinned, stood and held out her hand. "Officer Hansen. How've you been?"

He took her soft palm in his own and tried like hell not to revel in how petite it was in his larger one. "Please, call me Derek."

She ducked her head before sliding her hand free. "Sorry, I know you've said that before. I tend to forget when you're in uniform."

"Understandable." Derek watched as she moved her small medical bag to the side and pulled the stethoscope from around her neck. "Yeah, so I know we were just here, but he's had a couple chases and takedowns this week, so I figured, best bring him in."

"He's a busy boy." She gave Derek a small smile and knelt in front of Axle again. With ease of movement, she pressed the round disk to the dog's chest. "Is he eating, drinking okay?"

"His appetite seems fine. Plus, he's drinking water whenever I do during shifts."

She glanced up and nodded as she slid the stethoscope disk to the other side of Axle's rib cage. Derek's breath caught in his throat. Jesus, her blue eyes were brighter than an Arizona summer sky. From the first time he saw her, Doc's eyes captivated him. He'd never seen eyes as beautiful in all his life.

Her eyes were nothing compared to her smile though. Doctor Rayna Michaels had a smile that made Derek's insides melt. Those precious lips, the bottom fuller than the top, did things to him that were not normal— maybe normal for other guys—but in no way normal for him.

The crazy part was she also had a banging body. Like, seriously fucking hot. All petite but with curves in all the right places, and a head full of long, obviously natural red hair he was dying to run his fingers through. Plus, she had a whole "pretty without any makeup" thing going on, with freckles for days, too. Amazing.

But the smile...

God help him, her smile got him in the gut and made him want to get on his knees and worship at the Altar of Doc Rayna. True story.

What made the urge crazy was Derek was not the kind of man who got on his knees for any woman. It was always the opposite. He was a dominant guy; he preferred to be the one in charge. Call the shots, give directions, and control the situation. In addition, he enjoyed a bit more of the rougher play, too. A little bondage, a little pain play, but only with the right partner.

The doc didn't strike him as a woman who'd head down the BDSM trail. Derek was okay with that. Though he'd be a bald-faced liar if he said he hadn't thought about how unbelievably hot she'd look on her knees before him. Hands cuffed or bound behind her back, while he played with her nipples until she squirmed... Derek stifled a groan.

Still, if rougher play wasn't her thing, he'd handle it. He'd respect it and accept it, because the woman aroused a whole other side of Derek he hadn't even realized existed. One which had nothing to do with sex. The physical attraction was there for sure, but it went far above and beyond carnal desires.

She rose and swung the stethoscope around her neck. "Everything looks good to me."

Derek shoved his hands in his pockets. "That's great. Yeah, he earned his pay this week for sure. Chased down the bad guys. But the suspect last night struggled more than usual when Axle got hold of him. I figured, after this week, plus the tussle last night, it's always best to have him checked over, you know? Make sure the knee is still good." In combination with a shrug, Derek nodded to the side once, hoping he didn't sound like a complete moron. Or worse, like he was full of shit.

The story was true...for the most part. Axle *had* taken down a perp the night before and a few others earlier in the week, but the dog was fine. Regardless, it was a "plausible" reason to see the gorgeous doctor. Far be it from him to not take advantage of the opportunity.

Sadly, Derek knew he was running out of excuses to see her. What he wanted to do was ask the woman out, though from what he could tell, she didn't appear to know he even existed.

"Oh?" With her brow furrowed, she glanced at Axle again, watching him sniff around the floor in the exam room. "He doesn't appear to be favoring it. I think... Hmm...let me have another look." She bent again and palpated Axle's back haunches, then moved down to the knee the dog had injured originally. "Have you noticed any signs that he's having pain?"

Doc was the consummate professional. Polite, of course. She smiled, she made chitchat between professional conversation regarding Axle, but that was it. No more, no less. Derek definitely wanted to take her out on a date, get her out of her natural environment and see if she'd drop the professional persona. But whenever he thought to ask, mustered up enough nerve, he couldn't seem to get the damn question out of his mouth.

Lack of balls, anyone? Please...that was not a label that had ever been attached to Derek. However, with the doc, he turned into a tongue-tied, pimply-faced, sweaty-palmed teenage boy with not a damn bit of game whatsoever.

Because what if she wasn't interested in him?

Though some women from his past might disagree, Derek didn't consider himself to be an egotistical asshole. Not *all* women were attracted to him, obviously. But man, if he got turned down by this particular woman, he wasn't sure his ego could take that kind of hit.

Realizing he hadn't answered her question, he got his mind back on track. "No, you're right. He doesn't seem to be favoring it at all, but you know, I just wanted to be sure."

"Honestly, I think he's fine." She stood again and retrieved a small dog biscuit from her medical bag. "But if you're really concerned, we can do some X-rays. Or just keep an eye on him for now. Whichever you prefer."

Axle, knowing what was coming, sat, ears at attention, eyes locked on his doctor. Not begging, but definitely ready for the treat. Doc Rayna smiled down at the animal, tenderness clear in her expression. Bending at the waist, she smoothed her small palm over the dog's head before feeding him the biscuit. "Here you go, good boy."

Once again, everything inside Derek went soft as things south of his belt attempted to go rock-hard. He tamped the urge down quick. The last thing he needed was to be waving that flag at her. "I think I'll just keep an eye, for now."

Jesus, the expression in her eyes when she looked at his partner made Derek want to pull her against his body and never let her go. Her heart was pure sweetness, and he could see it in everything she did.

He wanted to know if everything else about her was pure sweetness, too.

* * * *

"Sounds good!" Rayna turned away from Officer Hanse—Derek's—gaze and closed up her little treat carrier.

He'd started calling her "Doc" sometime after the first month he'd been visiting her practice. Now, it'd become a sort of nickname for her. Regardless, something about the way he said it, the tone in his voice, always had hot lava pulsing through her veins.

As a result, every inch of her skin was prickling with heat. And she was quite positive her neck was flushed red to the point it looked like she'd been lying out in the sun for way too long.

"Thanks so much for taking the time with him, Doc. He really likes you."

Swallowing hard, then silently blowing out a breath, she grabbed the blue medical treat bag and turned partially toward him, making sure to avoid his gaze.

With a small smile she couldn't keep from arching her lips, she directed her attention to the dog. "Well, he's a likable boy." Rayna bent and smoothed her palm over Axle's head again. "How can you not love that sweet face and those big dark eyes?"

The dog sat, ears flopped down, tongue hanging out and tail wagging side to side so fast he was giving the tile a buff job. Considering the animal was a force to be reckoned with when he was on patrol with his handler, capable of taking down criminals of any size, Axle definitely turned into a big softie when he was near her.

Rayna glanced up at Officer H—she pressed her lips together—Derek. *Okay, that's just...* She couldn't bring herself to call him by his first name. It felt like doing so would wipe away some imaginary line she'd drawn between them.

Even so, curiosity tickled the back of her mind. Was the man as big of a softie as his canine partner? Judging by the expression he wore in that moment, he likely was. Officer Derek—*okay, a compromise*—was looking at her as if she was some sort of superhero or...good grief, she wasn't even sure what, but whatever it was, it was definitely in a way she'd never have expected from a hardened, good-looking man like him.

Clearing her throat, she straightened and extended her hand. "Be safe out there, okay?"

His lips split into a shy smile. "Always, Doc. Axle has my back, and I have his." He grasped Rayna's palm, his big hand dwarfing hers as he wrapped his fingers around in a firm though not painful grip.

Tingles spread from Rayna's hand, zipping up her arm. Heat flared like a fire blast through her body, and her stomach got tight. She almost fanned herself, but since he was still holding onto her, essentially, he saved her from embarrassing herself. Oh dear. *Wrap it up, Rayna!*

Any minute now she was going to spontaneously combust. Especially if he didn't let go of her hand. Rayna forced a smile. "You make a great team."

"Definitely." Eyes going soft, his smile relaxed into a far too sexy smirk. He nodded. "A perfect match."

Was the room getting smaller? Another moment passed and he'd yet to let go of her, which was awkward, but in a sweet sort of way. A nervous giggle she was trying to contain escaped, and she glanced down at their still-linked hands.

He pulled his palm away like he'd been burned. "Oh, wow! I'm sorry. That was weird. Sorry."

"It's okay." She laughed as relief blasted through her, and she moved to the door. "Have a good day."

"You, too. Thanks again, Doc."

She glanced back as she opened her way into the back area. He'd shoved his hands in his pockets and was still watching her. His expression carried a small hint of embarrassment, but he was still smiling, so maybe he didn't care. Her cheeks, however, burned hot as fire, and Rayna couldn't help but smile back.

When the door closed behind her, she pressed her back against it and blew out a breath. "Good grief."

Andrea strolled by, either the same or a new stack of patient files in her arms. "You need a cold shower?"

Rayna groaned and held out her hand. "Pass me one of those files."

Andrea furrowed her brow as if confused, but then did as Rayna asked.

Rayna took the file and fanned herself with it as she stepped away from the door and past the woman. "Not a word, Andrea. Telling you right now, not a word."

"Yes, Doctor." Andrea laughed.

Rayna continued into her small office and closed herself in. The space was about half the size of her twelve-by-twelve exam rooms, and yet there was way more oxygen to breathe in there than in the room with Officer Derek. Hansen. Derek. Ugh...whatever.

Rayna took a seat in her small desk chair and crossed her legs. Whoa! The rub of her wet panties sent a shockwave of lust ricocheting through her. With a hard swallow, she closed her eyes, willing the ache to settle.

She didn't spend much of her time, if any, fantasizing about men, much less dampening her panties over them. Yet here she was, drowning in a puddle of arousal. Literally.

Ugh...with her eyes still closed, she fanned herself with the file. Immediately, an image of him appeared in her mind. His dark, close-cropped hair. His tanned skin. Eventually he'd go back to his PD's contracted vet, right? He had to. Didn't he?

Good grief, what if he didn't?

Printed in the United States
by Baker & Taylor Publisher Services